# AND TIME STOPPED

## DIMENSION 9 – BOOK 3

### KEEPER OF THE WATCH SERIES

# KRISTEN L. JACKSON

Black Rose Writing | Texas

ISBN: 978-1-68433-958-7
PUBLISHED BY BLACK ROSE WRITING
www.blackrosewriting.com

Printed in the United States of America
Suggested Retail Price (SRP) $19.95

And Time Stopped is printed in Garamond Premier Pro

*As a planet-friendly publisher, Black Rose Writing does its best to eliminate unnecessary waste to reduce paper usage and energy costs, while never compromising the reading experience. As a result, the final word count vs. page count may not meet common expectations.

This book is dedicated to anyone struggling with thoughts of suicide, or anyone who is now, or has ever been, a victim of bullying. Don't lose hope.

Visit stopbullying.gov or suicidepreventionlifeline.org (1-800-273-8255) to find out more, seek help, or donate funds to these important programs.

# AND TIME STOPPED

Journal Entry, Present Day

*Dear Future Keepers,*

*We've written this down in the hopes that we will survive our year of jumping and pass this information, as well as our watches, on to you—our future ancestors. We pray that you will read this journal and find solace in the knowledge that others have been on the same path you are now only just beginning. Take heart. You are not alone. If you're reading this, it means the hunters have failed in their quest to destroy the remaining watches...at least on the last jump. Be on guard, they may be searchin for you even as you read this.*

*Once you've coupled with your watch, it will become a part of you. Your very lifeblood will power the watch as it pumps through the timepiece just as it pumps through your own heart, and in fact, your heart will beat in time with the watch while it is a part of you. Embrace it. You will have the unique ability to commune with ancestors who have come before you as your blood mingles with theirs. Your stamina will increase, and your body will not tire due to your heart's steady beat.*

*Be prepared to jump to each new world consecutively on the following dates only. You will remain in each new dimension until the next date on this list. I'm sure you've noticed that your birthday is listed. That's because all keepers were born on one of these chosen dates. Your destiny has been set since the moment of your conception.*

*All jumps are automatic—you won't be able to control your departure in any way, so don't even try. You'll find most jumps are...uncomfortable. Be strong, the pain won't last.*

*When you've completed your eighteenth year, your journey will end and you will return home with the option of living out the rest of your years in the dimension of your choice. Your status as a keeper of the watch ends the moment you turn nineteen, along with your ability to traverse the twelve dimensions. Your watch will go dormant as it waits for the next keeper in your bloodline. Tuck it away along with this journal until the day comes for you to pass it on.*

*But you're just beginning. Take care of yourself. Take care of your watch. Add any information you deem important to this journal to continue the legacy. Our family heritage lives on through only you. Protect the watch with your life, and remember: things aren't always what they seem. May God bless you on your eighteenth birthday and the year that follows.*

*Signed,*

*Alyx Eris & Chase Walker*

# PROLOGUE
## ALYX

*Jump Time: September 9th, 9:09 am*

Floating.

She was drifting on air, hurtling through a suspended tunnel. Her stomach performed an internal backflip, ripping an involuntary giggle from deep inside her.

Bright lights and sunbeams interspersed with the occasional gentle lightning flash caused Alyx to scrunch her eyelids and shy away from the light, but for the first time, there was no pain. Only a vague, peaceful giddiness.

She squeezed Chase's hand and felt his answering pressure, and with the other arm hugged Bo closer to her chest, his soft fur tickling her neck. A slight smile turned up the corners of her mouth.

Even with her deep, violet-blue eyes closed, she knew the three of them had survived the jump together, just as she knew where she was. The voices of children at play reached her ears from a distance, the squawk of seagulls calling interspersed with their youthful banter. More sounds filtered through: ocean waves lapping at the shore, the soft hum of a small plane.

When the wind and light faded, she felt the give of the sand underneath her and pushed herself up. If only every inter-dimensional entry could be this tranquil—but she knew from first-hand experience it was not, and relished the reprieve a simple magical spell had wrought. Each dimension differed in ways both big and small. The parallel world they had only recently vacated had been full of magical wonders that didn't exist where she came from.

Becoming a keeper of her family's ancestral watch—not by choice but by fate, blood, and the right birth-date—had opened up her world in so many ways; the biggest of which was the ability to jump to a new world each month of her eighteenth year. Twelve realms in all, including her home-world. Each consecutive jump-time locked into a date predetermined by the watch's inventor Elias Walker, giving keepers no control over their travels. When it was time to go, their bodies

I

were launched to the next dimensional plane, ready or not. Alyx was honored to be one in a long line of the chosen keepers that began in the last century, though the responsibility was not without its perils.

She and Chase had less than a year to defeat the hunters who resided in each place they visited and were working toward the extinction of all the watches, their keepers along with them. The hunters had succeeded in eradicating nine of the mystical watches, along with their keepers. There were only three left. Hers. Chase's. And one more. This time around, the keepers were being forced to go on the offensive to protect their own.

Part of their mission during this year of traveling the twelve dimensions was to find and protect the last watch and keeper. A nearly impossible feat since they had no idea in which realm they would find her—or him. The other part was to rid all the worlds of the hunters before they destroyed every last watch—along with the unique ability to travel and explore new worlds. Not a simple task, especially since in Dimension 8, the dimension they'd just left, one of the two hunters—Ursa, the woman—had actually tried to help them.

Forcing her eyelids open, she pushed back her chocolate brown-with-purple-tipped-hair and squinted into the sunlight, then forced herself to focus on Bo. He lurched up, licking her chin with his tiny sandpaper tongue, his tail a blur as it whipped back and forth.

"Oh, Bo. What are we going to do with you?" She looked up, meeting Chase's eyes. "How will we explain a chimera hybrid pup in a non-magical world?" She glanced around at the people enjoying a beach day, thankful no one was paying attention to them, hidden as they were by the dunes that separated the beach from the town. "We have to hide him." Her worried eyes landed on Chase, those cerulean blue eyes smiling into her own. His dimples were showing, and his blonde hair was tousled, curling up at the tips willy-nilly. The excitement in his voice had her answering his smile with one of her own. "I don't know, but that was lit! Welcome to Dimension 9." He tilted his head. "Think we can use that spell every time we jump?"

"I doubt it. Unless there's magic here too, but the chances of that are..."

"Yeah. Pretty much non-existent." He caught Bo in mid-flight as the animal leaped from her lap to his. "Wait. Where are his wings?"

"What do you mean, where are...?" Her eyes widened. "He looks different here."

"Yes, he just looks like a puppy. A regular, mixed-breed mutt. I guess you need magic to see him as he really is." He ran his hands down the creature's soft flank. "There's our answer. It seems this is not a magical world, after all."

"No." She tilted her head. "Except for our watches." Just then the light reflected off the purple glow of the petite, octagonal-shaped brushed chrome watch face, and she squinted. For a moment, she was lost in the crimson red liquid that pulsed through the hour and minute hands and the numbers of the clock. Blood. Her blood, to be exact—the power source of the watch itself. Alyx's heart kept rhythm with the ticking of the clock. Her family's magical timepiece had remained dormant for years as it waited for her to reach legal adulthood.

"Do you think we can still use any of it? The magic from Dimension 8, I mean?" She glanced at Chase's watch, the cobalt blue lines that connected the blood red numbers from twelve to six and intersected from three to nine on his hexagon-shaped timepiece, the blocky rim as shiny as mercury in a thermometer.

"Not sure. I mean, our bloodlines are enchanted, wouldn't you say? It's how we became keepers." He shrugged. "There's only one way to know." A barely audible chant fell from his lips, and he met her eyes. "Unless I'm invisible right now, I don't think so." Chase had mastered a cloaking spell in the last dimension, making him invisible to those around him, while Alyx's magical strength had been creating portals.

"I can see you." She sighed. "Let me try." Familiar words fell from her tongue, but no portal manifested in the air above them as it would have just one hour ago, in another place. Another version of reality. A frown darkened her features. "I think I'm going to miss the magic."

"Me, too," he agreed with a nod.

Alyx pointed at the bag. "Check the journal," she said.

Chase removed the old box from his backpack, grasping the shoe-polish brown, bound journal between his fingers. Her nostrils flared as the scent of worn leather reached her. Luckily, Chase's uncle and other ancestors had hidden some helpful clues in this box back in his home- world—along with this journal written by previous keepers—and it had been very useful in the world they'd just left behind. He flipped through the yellowed pages, and stopped at the page that had only minutes ago read 'Dimension 8.' Now, the page was deceptively blank, as it had been at the start of their journey in that world.

"What about the next page? Dimension 9?" she asked.

Chase turned the page, and she watched his eyes widen. "This page has lots of notes. The Young family seems to be mentioned a lot here. That's where we need to start our search. I went to school with a Jared Young. A common name, though." He stood, extending a hand to Alyx. "After I check on Mason. I need to make sure he's okay in this world." Pain flashed across Chase's face, and she knew he was recalling the events leading up to his best friend Mason's death in the world they'd just vacated. He needed reassurance that Mason's 'other-self', the version of him that lived in *this* world, was okay. She nodded, a far-off look in her eyes as she, too, relived that moment.

Brushing sand off her pants, she surveyed the ocean waves rolling in and out on the horizon. "Sounds like as good a place as any. To start, I mean."

"Let's head to his house first this time." He reached for her hand, and they walked toward the residential section of town. Bo struggled in her one-armed grasp until she lowered him to the ground. "We need to buy him a leash."

He nodded. "On the list." Chase surveyed the area as they strolled. "Seems like home. I don't see anything weird, do you?"

"No. You're right. Seems like everything is normal."

He winked. "We could use a bit of normal." A slow heat traveled up her neck, and her eyes darted away.

Suddenly, Bo took off running. "Bo!"

Chase yelled, "Bo! Come back here!"

They ran after him, glad for their status as keepers and the stamina that came along with it. After ten minutes of sprinting, their hearts maintained the steady beat of the clock—which meant their bodies did not tire in the usual sense, though they still couldn't catch the pup. "Why isn't he listening?" she asked.

"This is all new to him, too." Their sneakers slapped on the street, waves of heat rising from the blacktop, and Alyx recognized where they were headed. The Gull Street Bridge. They continued to follow the ramp onto the bridge itself, mostly deserted, and she briefly wondered how far they'd have to go in their pursuit of the pup. They ran along the pedestrian lane off to the side of the bridge, designed for runners or people lacking wheeled transportation. She couldn't think of any good reason for Bo to be running across the bridge, but kept trailing behind the animal, who remained just ahead but always still in sight.

"I wonder if he knows where he's going?" Chase said, his voice tinged with exasperation that mirrored her own.

"Seems like maybe he's just getting some exercise."

"Wait. Is someone up there?" Chase picked up speed, and Alyx's feet quickened to match his stride.

"Where?" she asked.

"On the railing." He pointed, then took off as fast as he could to reach the person who was even now climbing up onto the bridge's edge, his intent clear. "Wait! Don't jump!" Chase screamed, Alyx keeping pace right behind him.

"Oh no. No! Don't jump!" she shouted.

.    .    .

# CHASE

The person let go just as they reached the railing and Chase grabbed for the boy's arm wrapping both his hands around the jumper, hanging over the side with his body bent in half, his precarious hold the only thing keeping this boy from falling to his death onto the freeway below. Wind from the cars zooming by underneath blew into his face making him squint. He flinched when one stopped to honk the horn before continuing. The overpowering odor of exhaust stung his nostrils, but he held the answering cough inside for fear of moving even that much. A burning tore up his arms as he held the dead weight, clasping the boy's arm with one hand and a fistful of shirt in the other.

He looked down at a patch of red hair just before the jumper looked up. He could feel the wetness on his palms and his grip began to loosen.

Recognition dawned and mixed with despair as Chase redoubled his efforts, his shock almost causing him to let go.

His own voice was raspy, the words torn from his throat, "Mason? Oh, Mason. Why? Why would you do this?"

# CHASE

# CHAPTER 1
## *CHASE*

"He's slipping! Help me." Chase's breath came out in shallow pants, the sun-baked metal bar of the bridge's railing burning into his gut as he fought to keep his grip on his best friend's hand. Sweat trickled down the side of his face, and he could feel the slick skin of his hand slipping...

And then Alyx was there, grabbing onto Mason's arm below Chase's hand, reaching as she hung precariously over the railing.

Chase took a deep breath. "Hold on, Mason."

"Let me go!" Mason twisted in his grasp, and if Chase hadn't grabbed his friend's shirt, he surely would have wiggled out of his grip. "Why can't you just let me go?" Sobs wracked the boy's body as he hung from the wrong side of the bridge. Mason whimpered one barely audible word, voice cracking, before falling eerily silent. "Why?"

Cars zipped by below, and still they held on. Chase's arm cramped, a steady burn rising slowly up his arm. He ground his teeth against it. Another car horn blared through his concentration, and he dared to take his eyes off his friend for just a second.

A man leaped from the car below. Recognition clicked like a light switch. *Bray.* Chase slowly let out the breath he hadn't known he was holding, though he didn't answer when Bray shouted, so intent was he on maintaining his hold. "Hold on! I called 9-1-1!"

Chase gasped as the burning reached his shoulder, but through sheer willpower, he retained his grip. Muscles bulged and veins protruded. More sweat dripped down his forehead and into his eyes, and he blinked the sting away.

*There's no way I'm letting go.*

Heat permeated off Alyx's bicep, pressed up against his own, her sweat intermingling with his as she, too, strained to keep her hold. Chase's eyebrows slanted in deep concentration. The only thing that existed at this moment was his grip on Mason and his determination not to let go.

Seconds crawled into minutes, and finally the sound of blessed sirens registered as if through a tunnel, though no relief came through the numbness now settling into his hands.

*Hurry! I can't feel my fingers.*

Though he'd been oblivious to Bray's arrival, he heard a familiar steady voice from behind his back, and then a gentle touch. "Help is on the way. What can I do?" asked Bray.

Through clenched teeth, Chase hissed, "He's slipping!" His arms trembled and shook, and he fought to hold on just a little longer.

Alyx remained silent, though he could feel her arms vibrating beside his own.

Raising his voice, he called out, "How long?"

"I see them. They're almost here." Bray leaned over the rail next to him, looking down at Mason's head. He'd stopped struggling and hung like dead weight. Bray leaned over the edge, his frustration evident in his voice. "I can't reach him without compromising your hold on him. Just hold on!"

A cacophony of sirens and running footsteps interspersed with slamming car doors and other voices caused relief to flood his entire body, though he remained set in his goal.

"Dune Harbor police. I'm Officer Murphy. Hang on, we're here to help."

The crackle of static came across a walkie-talkie. "It's the Moore boy."

In a matter of minutes, a rope was tied to the railing, and an officer was lowered down alongside Mason, who continued to hang complacently. The officer wrapped the other end of the rope underneath Mason's arms, gave a tug, and called up, "Ready!"

A hand on Chase's back startled him, and he turned toward a voice in his ear. Another familiar face—though the recognition would again be one-sided. *Carson.* Carson Murphy. In both worlds where they had previously met Carson, he had run the souvenir shop on Main Street. Apparently, in this world, he was a cop. "You can let go now, son. We've got him," Carson whispered.

Next to him, Chase saw Alyx do just that, stumbling backward into Bray's arms.

He tried to let go, really tried, but his fingers would not listen to his brain's command. His grip remained firm until his friend was up and over the railing. Chase sank down onto the cement, his back against the railing, and dropped his head down to his bent knees. Now that Mason was safe, Chase couldn't seem to control his own erratic breathing. Two EMTs lifted him by the arms, leading him to the back of one of two ambulances.

"Take it easy, you're okay. Your friend's okay. Concentrate on your breathing." An oxygen mask appeared out of nowhere, and he breathed the wave of freshly pumped air into his lungs. "That's it. In and out."

Alyx wrapped her arm through his. "Mason's okay. You saved him."

"We. We saved him. This time."

Carson—known as Officer Murphy in this dimension—cleared his throat. "This time? Has Mason attempted suicide before?"

Chase jerked. "Um. No. Not that I know of."

"I'm assuming you two are friends?" Carson tilted his head, eyes narrowing.

Chase made fleeting eye contact with Alyx before staring at the ground. "No. Not really."

"So, you know him, or you don't?" Carson's eyes sharpened, boring into his.

Chase shook his head. "No. I don't know him. We just moved here."

The officer crossed his arms. "So, how did you get involved in this, then?"

"We just saw this guy." Chase pointed to the other ambulance. "We were walking with our dog, and he ran up here, and we grabbed Mason."

"How did you know his name if you don't know him?" questioned Carson.

Chase let out a slow breath. "Well. He must have, you know, told us his name before he jumped."

"So, you're sayin' he just stopped to introduce himself, and then jumped off the bridge?" Officer Murphy tilted his head, a frown deepening the lines in his forehead.

"Well, when you say it like that, it sounds..."

"Ridiculous? I agree. Once you're cleared medically, I'd like you and your girlfriend here to come in and make a statement."

"Officer, we really don't know anything more than what we've already told you..."

Carson crossed his arms. "Fine. Then you'll come down to the station, put it in writing, and we'll all be on our way. If what you say is true."

"What do you mean, if what we say is true?" Chase asked. "Why would we lie?"

The officer leaned in, his nose only inches from Chase's. "I mean, you have to admit something doesn't add up. You weren't harassing the boy, were you? 'Cause if you were, it's a simple thing to find out. All I have to do is talk to Mason..."

Chase sighed. "Go ahead. He'll tell you all we did was stop him from committing suicide."

"Well then, like I said, if that's true, I'll pat you on the back and you'll be on your way. After we file a report."

Just then David and Jean Moore, Mason's parents who Chase knew so well in his home-world but didn't know at all here, lunged out of a silver Ford Explorer, tires screeching. Their tear-streaked faces looked frantically around until they were led to the second ambulance. Though they seemed to be in deep conversation, Chase couldn't make out the words. As he strained to listen, both Mr. and Mrs. Moore turned their heads in unison, squinting in his direction with stern faces.

Chase inhaled quickly, rounding his shoulders.

*Why are they looking at me that way? Didn't I just save their son's life?*

He didn't have to wait long to find out. Mrs. Moore marched over to stand directly in front of them. "Well, what are you waiting for, Officer? Aren't you going to arrest these criminals?"

"Criminals, ma'am?" Carson asked.

"Yes. Mason says they were harassing him and tried to throw him off the bridge. That's attempted murder," Mrs. Moore spat.

Mr. Moore joined her, hands slammed onto his hips, his eyes boring holes into Chase. "Or maybe I should push *them* off the bridge." He took a menacing step toward Alyx, and the officer placed himself between them.

"Whoa, David. Calm down. Think of the election. Take care of your son and let me do my job. I was just about to take them in to get their statements. According to them, Mason was trying to jump off the bridge and they stopped him."

"Mason wouldn't..." David Moore shouted.

"That's a lie!" Jean Moore's hand fluttered to her chest.

"As I said, let us do our jobs. We'll sort this out, but I'm gonna need Mason to come in and give a statement too." Carson tipped his head in Mason's direction.

Mrs. Moore glanced at her son, who was having trouble meeting her eyes. "He's not feeling up to it right now. He's been through an ordeal. We'll bring him in tomorrow."

"I'd really rather he come today, if possible, Jean."

David Moore placed a gentle hand on his wife's arm. "Fine. Let's just put this behind us."

# CHAPTER 2
## *ALYX*

The police department was a one-story, yellow-brick structure, paint on the shiny black shutters appearing barely dry, with vibrant flowering pots perfectly lining the walkway. An American flag, crisp red, white, and blue, flapped with the sound of newly washed bedsheets snapping in the September breeze. The seashell embedded concrete sidewalk added to the allure of the building. It was the epitome of small town charm.

Once inside; however, the misleading cheeriness of the entrance evanesced into cold, sterile grayness. A middle-aged secretary squinted through red-framed bifocals at a computer screen which illuminated her pale face with an eerie glow in the poorly lit front room. Though she'd tried to brighten her cold, metal industrial desk with pictures of loved ones, she'd only managed to highlight the lack of homeyness in the place once you walked through the gleaming glass double front doors. She nodded distractedly and continued tapping keys, her long, manicured fingernails clicking with each letter.

A few more taps, and she glanced up, eyes looking over the rim of her glasses, her one look taking in Alyx's entire appearance in a beat of time. "Let me guess, parking meter expired? Drinking underage? Driving the wrong way on a one-way? Cat stuck in a tree?"

Carson interrupted, "They're with me, Sadie." He ushered Chase and Alyx past the desk, through a room packed with wall-to-wall barren desks, some occupied, others vacant. No one spared them a glance as they plodded to the corner cubicle. An ancient, rusting vending machine sat in the opposite corner, and the smell of burned coffee wrinkled Alyx's nose.

Glancing at Chase as he crossed his arms and sat back, Alyx rounded her shoulders, asking, "Why are we here? We told you everything we know."

Officer Murphy barely looked up as he powered up the computer. "It's procedure. And your story doesn't mesh with Mason's."

"We told you..."

Carson interrupted, "Enough. Let's get this done, and if you're as innocent as you say, you'll be on your way." He squinted at the computer screen, tapping some keys. A sigh escaped. "This thing is so slow. Think the current mayor will approve new technology for the police department?" He shook his head. "Looks like we're doing this the old-fashioned way," he mumbled, yanking open his desk drawer, the squeak of metal against metal like tiny daggers piercing Alyx's brain. Flipping to an empty page on the yellow tablet, Carson cocked his head, pencil hovering above the pad. Alyx raised a brow in response.

The silence boomed in their tiny corner. Cut off from the rest of the room as they were.

Chase cleared his throat. "What do you want to know?" Alyx frowned in his direction.

The officer sighed. "What were you doing on the bridge?"

Sitting back to cross her arms, Alyx's lips formed a thin line.

*Let Chase handle this. He's better at 'peopling' than I am.*

Chase answered, chin thrust forward. "We told you. Our dog ran away from us, and we chased him there and saw someone getting ready to jump off the bridge."

"How did you know he was gonna jump?" Carson asked.

"Well, he was climbing up on the railing, and when he saw us coming, he leaped. Good thing I was there to grab onto him, or he'd have succeeded," Chase answered.

"Why would Mason say you were hassling him if all you did was help?"

"I don't know. Why does someone who's suicidal do anything?" Chase shrugged. "Maybe since it was a botched attempt, he's embarrassed or something."

"Maybe." Carson scribbled something on the page. "Where do you live? I'm sure your parents are worried about you by now. You want to give them a call?"

Alyx's eyes shot to Chase's face, which had suddenly turned three different shades of crimson. "We live..."

A familiar voice interrupted from the other side of the room, "Carson? Hey, Carson? I'm here to give my statement," Bray called, voice gaining volume as he approached.

Carson Murphy stood, clasping Bray's hand in a quick shake. "Bray. Thanks for coming in. You could have stopped by later this afternoon. No rush. Hope this doesn't throw off your sales for the day."

"No, I wanted to come in. I heard the Moores were telling tales about these two," he gestured toward Chase and Alyx, "and I wanted to set the record straight."

"Okay." Carson plopped back into his chair with a squeak. "What do you know?"

"I was on my way to work, and Mason was teetering on the railing, and as I watched he stepped off the bridge. Then he," he pointed in Chase's direction, "caught him by the shirt and held onto the Moore boy with all he had. I pulled over and called 9-1-1, and while I was on the phone, the girl," he indicated Alyx, "added her support to help keep Mason from falling. They saved him. If not for them, you'd have been scraping a body off the road this morning instead of talking to us right now."

"You sure they weren't bullying the kid before he jumped?"

Bray considered, then decisively shook his head. "Well, no. I wasn't there before he jumped. But that's not the impression I got."

Carson scribbled a few more notes, then tossed pen and pad onto the desk and leaned back, stretching his arms over his head. "Good enough for me."

"Besides, you know Mason has had some trouble this past year," Bray added.

Carson held up his hand, palm out. "That has nothing to do with this."

Bray stammered, "What do you mean, it has nothing to do with this? It has everything to do with this, if you ask me. Jared is somehow involved, I just know it. I witnessed him harassing Mason just last week. Dawn and I had to have a talk with our boy, Ty, about how to treat others. He's at an impressionable age and I don't want him thinking it's okay to disrespect a friend just because he saw Jared do it."

"It's not Jared's fault if Mason had to repeat his senior year. Mason should have studied more. And keep your voice down, you don't want to upset Sadie Young..." Carson lowered his voice and looked pointedly toward the lobby and receptionist's desk, where Jared's mother was speaking animatedly on the phone, manicured hands flying as she gestured.

Bray shook his head. "No. No, it isn't. But it gives you a motive for suicide, though. And I don't care if it upsets Jared's mom." He jerked his head toward the lobby. "She and Jim need to keep their boy in line. I know he isn't Jim's real kid, but he took on all the responsibilities of being a parent the day he put his name on the kid's birth certificate."

"Jim raised Jared, adopted him even though he knew the boy wasn't his when he married Sadie." Carson stood, a long sigh deflating his shoulders. He reached up, rubbing a slow circle on his temple. "That has to count for something. And

Jared isn't the one who tried to jump off a bridge. You ask most people, he seems like a well-rounded, polite teenaged boy. He's never had any trouble here at the station. You can't pin Mason's suicide attempt on him. Innocent until proven guilty, right?"

"I'm telling you; I know what I saw when Jared thought no one else was watching. Mason walked by on the street, minding his own business, and Jared purposely tripped him and pushed him down in the gutter, then bent down and whispered something in his ear. Mason stayed in the gutter until I went over to offer him a hand, almost as if he was afraid to get up until Jared was out of sight. I got the impression that it wasn't the first time." Bray didn't back down. "And, with Mason dealing with the added pressure of his dad, David Moore, running for mayor, Mason doesn't have a father figure who's there for him right now. All David seems to care about is getting elected. Can't be easy for a troubled teen to deal with all that."

Alyx stood, and for the first time, spoke, "Excuse me? Can we leave now?"

Carson jerked, as if he'd forgotten all about the two of them. With one brisk head shake, he answered: "Yes. You have an eyewitness. You're free to go, even though I still think there's something fishy about this whole situation." He nodded to emphasize his words. "And if I find out you two are causing trouble 'round here, well. Let's just say I'll be watching you. Both of you. And get your dog a leash. We have strict leash laws in this town."

Alyx turned to go, but Chase didn't move. She backtracked, taking his hand. "Let's go."

"But I..." Chase stammered.

She tugged while Chase continued to drag his feet. Alyx leaned in close to whisper in his ear, "Let's get out of here. We need to find Bo."

Chase's head whipped up, eyes going wide. "Yeah. Yeah, okay. But I wanted to hear more about..."

As they reached the lobby, the door swung inward with a whoosh of air. Jean Moore stomped into the building, sucking in her breath when her wild eyes found Chase.

"You. You're leaving?" she screeched, her head bobbing. "Officer Murphy? Why aren't these two bullies locked up?"

# CHAPTER 3
## *CHASE*

Chase was propelled along by Alyx's hand tugging at his. He hesitated as they passed Mason, taking in every detail, desperately trying to establish eye-contact. *This* Mason was bordering on obese, eyes underlined with deep purple half-circles, oily red hair hanging over his pimple-marked forehead and eyebrows. His shoulders slumped forward, making him appear much smaller in stature. Mason did not look up, just shuffled past with no indication he knew they were even there.

"Mason..." Chase whispered as he passed. No response. Alyx gave another tug, pulling Chase forward.

He stumbled out the door, squinting through the sudden burst of sunshine. Alyx's words hit him like a linebacker.

"What are you doing?" she demanded.

"What?" his eyes went wide.

She huffed. "We need to stay out of this, Chase, or you'll end up in jail. The Moores think you tried to kill their son. And Mason doesn't want our help."

"Sometimes, when a person says they don't *want* help? That's when they need it the most." He reached for her hand. "Did you see his eyes? I've never seen Mason look that empty. It's like his eyes are screaming for help but no one can hear him. It's deafening, if only someone would listen to the signs in the silence." Chase glanced back over his shoulder. "I can't stay away from him, Alyx. I'm sorry if you can't understand that."

"Understand? No, I don't. This is *not your Mason*. Why can't you differentiate between the Mason who was your friend and his other-selves? We go through this every time we jump, and you..."

"Alyx." Chase slid his hand up her arm, giving it a gentle squeeze. "Alyx. I'm sorry. But if I can help..."

"That's the problem. You want to help everyone." She looked away.

"Is that such a bad thing?" he asked.

"Yes." She blew the hair out of her eyes, slowly shaking her head. "No. I don't know."

"They said he's been having trouble. He didn't even graduate last year as he should have. He's still in high school. I can't think of anything worse than having to repeat your senior year."

"Oh, I can think of a lot of worse things." She crossed her arms.

"They also said something about Jared. That secretary, Sadie? That's his mom. She has a picture of Jared on her desk."

Alyx shrugged, hands splayed in front of her. "What does any of this have to do with us?"

"It has everything to do with us because their last name is Young. As in Dimension 9—the Young family? They come from a keeper bloodline. We'd already decided we needed to search him out in this world, remember?"

She sighed, the wind whistling through her teeth. "Okay. Maybe this is part of our mission, after all. But we still don't want to end up locked in jail. What good are we there?"

His shoulders drooped. "You're right. Let's find Bo, and maybe we can come up with some kind of plan." He twined his fingers with hers.

She looked at him sideways. "Do you think this Jared is a keeper?"

"No. Not a keeper of an enchanted watch. I knew him in D-6 which means if he's here, he can't be since we keepers only exist in one world. Plus, they said Young was his adopted name, not his biological father's name, so it would be impossible for him to be a keeper of the watch. But maybe someone else in his family is. Or was."

"Were you friends? Back in your home-world?" she asked.

"Depends on your definition of 'friend.'" Chase shook his head. "Not really. He played on the football team with me. But he liked to pick on Mason at home. There, I kept him at bay, but..."

"But you weren't here to do that in this world." Her shoulders slumped.

"Right." Chase stared off down the street with unseeing eyes.

• • •

Alyx clutched the bag containing a leash, a bag of dog food, and some other newly purchased items, eyes frantically searching. The Gull Street Bridge was deserted except for an occasional car leaving town.

"Bo!" Chase and Alyx yelled, over and over. After several minutes passed, Chase frowned.

"Where do you think he would go?" he asked. "The forest? That's where he lived in his world."

"I don't know." She looked around, brow furrowed. "I was hoping he'd wait for us..."

"Me too." He took a few more steps. "Bo!"

Scrutinizing both sides of the street, they continued their search throughout the afternoon.

Alyx sighed. "I'm worried about him. He could get hit by a car, or taken in by someone who thinks he's a stray." Her worried eyes found his. "I can't believe we just left him here. We have to find him."

"There was a lot going on. We didn't have a choice." Chase reached for her hand, giving it a squeeze. "We'll find him. He's a smart little guy. Or, he'll find us when he's ready." His smile didn't reach his eyes.

Alyx scanned the area, mumbling, "I hope so."

"Let's get something to eat, find a place to stay. Then we'll search some more."

She nodded her head absently, her eyes on continuous alert for some sign of the hybrid pup.

Chase, too, continued looking for the small creature. It was a miracle it even existed at all. Fathered by a mystical beast called an Enfield, Bo was one-of-a-kind—though in *this* world his appearance had drastically changed.

Not to mention that he and Alyx had bonded with the little guy in Dimension 7, and then its mother died, leaving the pup with no one else. Precisely the reason Bo had jumped into their transport when they were transitioning from one world to the next. He'd chosen them. It was now their responsibility to keep him safe.

Alyx interrupted his thoughts. "Where are we going to stay? Should we buy a tent and camp out in the woods?"

"Maybe. But I'd rather stay closer to town, you know." Chase stared off into the distance.

"We could go to the hotel. The one we stayed at in D-7."

"If it exists in this world." Chase nodded absently. "I don't know..."

Chase halted in front of a familiar house. Without thinking, his subconscious mind must have taken him in this direction. He'd walked this route thousands of times back in Dimension 6—his home-world. It had been like a second home. But in D-8, he'd fought hard to destroy this very house because black magic had consumed it.

A chill raced down his spine, his body shivering despite the heat radiating off the blacktop. He felt Alyx's answering tremble through their clasped hands.

"Mason's house."

"Chase, you can't..."

He tugged his hand free and took a step toward the house.

# CHAPTER 4
## *MASON*

Mason stared at his clasped hands. His fingernails had grown too long, the ends jagged, he noted absently.

*Who cares? I'm supposed to be dead. Who looks at a corpse's nails, anyway?*

Muffled voices reached him as if through a long tunnel, the words echoing in his brain, but not really reaching him. It was all gibberish. His mom's 'This Is the Last Straw' voice clashed with his dad's firm 'I Want Answers' tone. Officer Murphy's 'Now, Now, Let's All Settle Down' monotone underlying everything.

*None of it matters. I even suck at killing myself.*

He sighed, his shoulders shrinking in on his already rounded posture.

*Shouldn't be surprised. I can't do anything right. Never could.*

Mason squeezed his eyes shut against the burning. His head pounded an erratic beat, and he thought his cranium might explode so great was the mocking force of each heartbeat that seemed to scream: *Hello! I'm still pumping, Loser.*

*Jared will love this. A botched suicide attempt. I shoulda just swallowed pills like he told me to. He even offered to give me the bottle. Is it so wrong that I didn't want Jared to dictate the very last thing I did in this life? I wanted to do it from the bridge, where it all started. Make my death symbolic or something. Send Jared a message in my last act as a human being. Stupid. Everything I do is stupid. That's why I need to disappear, for good—the one thing Jared and I can agree on.*

A humming began in his ears.

*I just want the pain to stop. Why won't it stop? I don't want to play this game anymore. I can't. Can't do it anymore. Can't be what everyone wants me to be: Mom's baby. Dad's perfect politician's son. Jared's plaything. The dumb, fat kid at school that had to repeat his senior year. Loser.*

The wheezing in his chest became audible, and his gasping breath caused a brief silence to descend upon the police station before chaos took over.

"Mason? Mason!" Hands roamed his body, and he wanted to swat them away but was powerless to do anything except breathe.

*Irony at its best.*

*Why is my body fighting so hard for air when all I really want to do is stop breathing?*

Mason's body flopped out of the metal chair and onto the floor with a *thud*, no longer aware of the buzz of activity that surrounded him.

# CHAPTER 5
## *ALYX*

Alyx glanced sideways at Chase, then back at the stained wood front door of the house that had wreaked havoc on them just days ago. Chase had risked his life to destroy it in the last realm they'd visited.

*Days ago, but another world away*, she reminded herself. Dimension travel could mess with the mind. People they knew became strangers again, and places changed in a second's time.

As they stepped onto the front porch, she did not experience the same sense of foreboding she had last time. *A good sign.* This place did not reek of death as it had in D-8, either. *Another plus.*

She sucked in a breath, rounding her shoulders, as Chase rapped on the door.

The door swung inward, and a petite middle-aged woman in yoga pants, dark hair with gray roots peeking out piled atop her head in a messy bun, filled the frame. "Yes?" she said. Alyx did not recognize her, and wondered if Chase did.

"Hi. Do the Moores live here?" Chase asked.

"The Moores? As in, David Moore?" She chuckled. "You're joking, right?"

Chase cocked his head. "No. I guess Mason doesn't live here, then?"

The woman crossed her arms over her chest. "You're in the wrong neighborhood, honey. They live in the gated community on the other side of town, away from the tourists. Haven't lived on this side of town for a long time now. Not since the boy was little."

"Oh. Okay. Sorry to bother you," he replied.

"No problem. Have a nice day." The door started closing.

"Wait," Chase raised his hand. "Do you know anything about Mason? We saw him earlier, and…"

The woman's face went tight. "Who did you say you are…?"

"I'm Chase." He gestured toward Alyx. "And this is Alyx."

"Why do you want to know about the Moores? You look too young to be reporters."

"No. We're not reporters, ma'am. Just friends…"

The woman snorted. "Friends, you say? If you're his friends, why are you knocking on doors asking questions you should already know the answers to? Trying to dig up stories to discredit David Moore in his bid for the mayorship, I bet. He's a good man. Sorry. I can't help you."

"I understand. Thanks."

Alyx sighed as the door closed firmly, the sound of the deadbolt sliding into place making her eyes go round. "What was that about?"

Chase shrugged. "I don't know, but the Moores seem to have done well here."

Alyx snorted. "Sure. Except for the fact that their only son tried to kill himself this morning."

Chase sucked in a breath, the color draining from his face. "Yeah."

"Let's just book a room in a hotel so we have a place to crash, and continue searching for Bo. I don't like him out there all alone."

He nodded. "Okay. Let's go."

•  •  •

"At least we don't have to worry about money here." Alyx counted the rest of the cash, replacing it in the box along with the keeper ancestral journal. When they'd found the ancient box in Chase's home-world, it had included envelopes packed with currency from several dimensions—Dimension 9 among them—along with some other items they'd found helpful on their travels. A vial of blood had been essential in the magical world they had only just left behind.

"Yes, convenient." Chase flopped into a wingback chair with worn upholstery in the corner of the hotel room, leaned his head back, and closed his eyes.

"Okay, what's wrong?" Alyx stood, hands on hips.

"Nothing."

Her bark of laughter echoed off the walls in the tiny space. "Nothing? You're moping like a child."

Chase ran his fingers through his hair, then stood and began pacing. "You want to know what's wrong? I witnessed my best friend's death just days ago, and we come here and he's about to die again. I don't know why he seems to be fated to die in each world, and there's nothing I can do about it."

"Chase, you know..."

"You're going to say it's not him. But it *is*. Well, okay, it's a shadow of him—his other-self—but underneath all that, it's the same person, Alyx. Why can't you understand that?"

"I'm trying to understand it, but I guess I have nothing to compare it to. I didn't have any friends in my world."

His head swung around so his eyes met hers, and he took a step forward, reaching out. "Alyx..."

She held up her hand. "I didn't say that to get your pity, Chase. It's just a fact. I didn't *want* any friends. I had my family. My training."

Chase's hand dropped.

"I wish... I don't know." He shook his head. "I wish that we'd known each other back then."

"Impossible, since we're from different worlds. You know keepers only exist in their home-worlds, Chase." Alyx shrugged, hands splayed in front of her. "And anyway, you wouldn't have liked me. In fact, you wouldn't have even noticed me."

"That's not true..."

"Yes. It is. You were busy with your games, your friends. Sports. Girls. We weren't interested in the same things at all." She looked away. "Truthfully, I wouldn't have noticed you, either."

"It's true, we were raised very differently." He took a slow step forward, and didn't continue until her eyes met his. "But I definitely would have noticed you," he said with a gentle hand squeeze.

*How does he do this to me?* Heat climbed up her cheeks until she thought maybe her hair would go up in flames. "None of that matters, anyway."

"No. Because I know you now. That's all that matters." He winked, then began slowly leaning forward until their lips just barely brushed.

Her breath caught in her throat, and she felt herself leaning forward to accept his kiss...

*Yip-yip-yip.*

They jerked apart; eyes wide. "Is that...?"

Chase strode forward and in one motion, unlatched the door and threw it open.

# CHAPTER 6
## *CHASE*

"Bo!" Chase's relief was instantaneous as Alyx ran out the door, squatting to catch Bo as he leaped into her arms, showering her face with puppy kisses, his little body trembling in excitement.

A laugh shook Chase's shoulders as he bent to scratch Bo behind the ears. "Where have you been, little guy?"

He smiled as Alyx hugged the pup close. "We've been looking for you everywhere. How did you find us?" Her eyes shot up to meet Chase's. "How *did* he find us?"

Chase shrugged. Straightening up, his eyes scanned the street. Cars drove leisurely by, people in swim suits walked clutching boogie boards or glided by on skateboards. An occasional biker whizzed by. No one paid them the slightest bit of attention. "Good question."

"Hey! No pets allowed in the hotel rooms," the proprietor leaned over the rust-speckled white metal railing, calling down from an upper floor.

"No problem, sir." Chase appeased. "Let's take him for a walk."

Alyx fastened the collar around Bo's neck, snapping the leash on. Bo scratched at the collar, his hind leg a blur, then ran in mad circles, trying to catch the leash between his teeth. Once he succeeded, he growled deep in his throat and shook his head wildly back and forth, his little puppy growls forcing a smile to bloom. "I don't think he likes his new things," she chuckled.

"He'll get used to it. We don't want to lose him again," Chase replied.

"No. Or get into trouble with Carson. Officer Murphy, I mean."

Chase nodded.

Bo dramatically threw his body on the ground, paws in the air refusing to stand. "C'mon Bo. Let's go for a walk," Alyx coaxed, tugging on the leash.

The pup snorted, legs flailing in the air. One lone whimper escaped before he turned his back on them.

Chase and Alyx looked at each other. "Maybe we'll just carry him for now." Chase lifted Bo. The pup lay its head on Chase's shoulder, snuggling as close as possible.

"We can't carry him everywhere."

Chase ran his hands over the soft fur, heading toward the sidewalk. "No. He'll get used to the leash. Eventually."

"Where are we going?" Alyx asked.

"I was thinking, maybe we should go by the Young house—if it's the same as where I come from—and just check it out. I overheard Mrs. Young say she was working late when we were at the precinct. I don't know, maybe we introduce ourselves and see if the rest of the family knows anything about their ancestry and the watches in particular. We'll see what their response is and take it from there."

"I don't know if that's a good idea." Alyx was shaking her head.

"Remember how George Apollo helped us in the last parallel world? He knew all about the twelve dimensions because it's his heritage, even though he wasn't destined to be a keeper himself."

In Dimension 8, the Apollo family served as watch keepers of that realm. George, though not born on one of the corresponding birthdates and not in possession of a magical watch, had arrived with his griffin Apollo—named for the family's surname—without a minute to spare. If Apollo hadn't been there at the final battle to fight off the hunter's chimera, an Enfield named Enzo, all would have been lost.

Slowly, Alyx nodded. Maybe the ancestors of Elias Walker's chosen bloodlines in each world could be useful to their cause. "Okay. You may be right. But what will we say if they know nothing about it?"

"We'll just say we got the wrong house or something. Improvise." He winked, his cheeks dimpling with his smile.

"Improvise." She rolled her eyes. "My parents would hate you, you know."

He laughed, unconcerned. "Nah. I'll win them over, just you wait and see."

A snort escaped. "You can try. *If* we live long enough to make it back to my world—the fourth dimension."

•　•　•

The September sun—still blazing with the full heat of summer—beat down on them like a laser. In just a few weeks' time, Chase knew temperatures would begin to lower in preparation for autumn, but there was no evidence of the upcoming seasonal change today. Chase's shirt clung to his back. One lone rivulet of sweat made its way down the side of his face, and he swiped at it.

Bo, now walking on his own, trailed behind them, head drooping as he looked up from under his lashes.

Chase shook his head. "Sorry, buddy, it's too hot to carry you. You have to walk."

Alyx hid her smile behind her hand and coughed. "He looks so forlorn."

"Don't let him trick you. He's perfectly capable of walking. Besides, he needs the exercise."

"I know." She glanced down at the pup, her voice rising in pitch, "What a good boy you are, Bo-Bo. You're doing great."

The animal's ears perked at her change in tone, but almost as if he remembered he was mad at them, Bo purposefully lifted his head and ignored her.

"Wow." Chase chuckled.

Alyx met his eyes, gnawing on her bottom lip. "Maybe he just needs to be carried a bit more. He's just a pup..."

"Nope. He's walking. I'm surprised at you. I thought you were tougher than this. You're letting a *puppy* train *you*." Chase kept moving, observing in his peripheral vision how she felt about his declaration by her stiffening posture. He smiled and began whistling, Alyx stomping along beside him, her mouth in a thin line.

They walked a few more blocks in silence until voices up ahead caught their attention. Muffled at first, but as they approached, the words became clearer. A candy-apple red Jeep Wrangler stood at an angle in the middle of the street, pointing toward the curb, and the passengers—maybe four of them—were talking to some teenagers on the sidewalk.

Chase recognized them as they drew nearer. Colin and Annabelle—Anna—twin siblings they'd met on their last jump. They were Brian's younger brother and sister. Brian had been Chase's friend in high school, as well as in all the dimensions they had visited so far. And Anna, well, she had been lost to dark magic in Dimension 8. Chase took a deep breath, pushing all the memories into the background. *That was then. This is now*, he reminded himself.

Colin was pushing his dirt bike, trying to ignore the raised voices coming from inside the car.

"Yeah, that's right. You push that bike, Loser. You need the exercise, anyway," a voice called from the window, followed by boisterous guffaws from the car. Colin continued walking, his face flaming.

"You leave my brother alone!" shouted Anna, hands on her hips.

"Aww, look at that. He needs a girl to defend him. That so *sweet* Colin."

More laughter.

Colin kept walking forward, and the Jeep followed slowly. He tripped over an uneven crack on the sidewalk, but managed to keep moving through more howling laughter from the Jeep.

Anna stepped forward. "If you don't leave, I'll tell my parents."

Colin hissed, "Anna." The pained expression on his face visible as he glared at his sister over his shoulder before continuing his escape.

The Jeep screeched to a halt, and the driver jumped out and stalked to stand directly in front of Anna, his six-feet-tall frame towering over her. *Jared Young*. Of course.

"Try it, *little girl*, and you'll regret it. We're just having some fun here. If you get your parents involved, or any other adult, it's gonna be a lot worse than this. For you and your brother. Understand?" He flicked Anna on the forehead, and she took a step back, rubbing her hand over the instant red circle where his fingers had made contact.

Chase and Alyx were still half a block away, but Chase picked up his pace.

"Hey!" Chase yelled.

All heads swiveled in his direction.

Jared snorted. "Look, whoever you are, this has nothing to do with you, so just keep walkin' your ugly mutt and don't involve yourself in things you know nothing about."

"It seems like you're harassing these kids here. Is *that* what this is about?" Chase handed the leash to Alyx and stepped up into Jared's space, nose-to-nose. They were approximately the same height and build, lean muscular bodies, both in good shape. By all appearances, an even match. "I think you should be the one to move along."

The sound of car doors drew Chase's attention, and another familiar face momentarily distracted him. Brian. *Why is Brian with them?*

In his distracted state, the shove knocked Chase backward, but he remained upright and stepped forward again. "Look. I don't want to fight, but if you touch me again, you're going to regret it. I'm not the type to back down. I'm warning you now."

The three friends—including Brian—now stood behind Jared. Jared jerked his head backward. "Oh yeah? You gonna fight all of us?"

"I don't want to, but I will if I have to. Just get in your car and drive away. They're just kids. Why do you want to pick on them, anyway? Does it make you feel big to harass people smaller than you?" Chase snorted, sending a warning look over his shoulder to Alyx.

Alyx stood behind him on the left, Anna on the right. Colin cowered on the sidewalk, not meeting anyone's eyes.

"What, you and your little girls are gonna take us down?" Jared's friends laughed, the sound like fingernails on a chalkboard.

Chase chuckled. "You have no idea, bro."

Alyx stepped forward, dropping the leash. "Insult me again. I dare you."

Jared closed the distance. "Oh, I don't want to *insult* you, honey. Someone as smokin' as you? I can think of a lot of things I'd like to do with you. Insulting isn't one of them. Why don't you come over later and I'll show you…?" He ran a finger down the side of her face, then cupped her chin and leaned in as if to kiss her.

Alyx reacted in the only way she knew how. She threw her head forward, her forehead slamming into his nose, then with her foot she swiped his legs out from under him. Jared went down with a *thud,* blood streaming from his nose. "Oops," Alyx said, taking a step backward to look down her nose at him.

Bo barked and snarled, and Chase held him back. One of Jared's friends stepped forward, kicking out at Bo. At the same time, Chase grabbed the leash and yanked back; the attacker's foot never made contact. Chase punched the would-be kicker in the face and the boy stumbled backward, clutching at his cheek. No one else stepped forward.

Chase winked at Alyx, then looked back at the rest of the group. The only one he recognized was Brian. "Why don't you guys help your friend up and leave. We don't want any more trouble."

Jared stumbled to his feet. "You're already in trouble. My mom works at the police station. When I tell her you attacked me…"

"You do what you have to do. Maybe you want everyone in town to know that a *girl* took you down? Just get out of my sight," Chase spit at his feet.

Jared glared at them, walking backward toward the Jeep, blood drying in tracks from his nose to his upper lip. "This isn't over."

"It is for me," Chase answered, turning away. He approached Colin and Anna, dismissing the group in the street. "You guys okay?"

Colin began walking, pulling his bike along, head down. He mumbled, "Thanks a lot. You just made it worse."

Chase glanced up as the Jeep sped away, tires screeching. He watched until it disappeared around a corner.

"Worse? How is standing up to them making it worse?" Chase asked.

"You don't understand. I can't stand up to them. I'm not like you. They'll never leave me alone now." Colin shook his head.

Chase sighed. "How long have they been bullying you?"

A far-off look clouded Colin's eyes. "Forever." He swung his leg around his bike, pedaling jerkily away.

# CHAPTER 7
## *ALYX*

Alyx picked up Bo, and watched as Chase turned to look at Anna. "I didn't mean to make it worse. I was trying to help."

Anna was staring at Alyx with star-struck eyes. She spoke, but didn't turn to look at Chase. "It's okay. Colin says I make it worse, too. I don't see how it could be any worse."

"Who were those guys?" Alyx asked.

"They're jocks. Jared's the leader. He's the starting quarterback of the football team. *And* he's our neighbor."

"Quarterback?" Chase shook his head. Jared hadn't been the quarterback in his world. He'd been the second-string punt receiver. He'd been a bully then, too, though he'd gained confidence here in this dimension. Jared had been a year behind Chase in school; in D-6, Jared was a junior when Chase was a senior, which meant that in this world Jared had just started his senior year.

Alyx cocked her head. "Anyone else?"

"Yes." Anna's eyes dropped, cheeks flaming. "My older brother. Brian."

"Your brother?" Feigning ignorance, Alyx continued her quest for information. "Why is he a part of that group?"

Anna shrugged. "Jared picked on Brian in elementary school. One day Brian realized if he joined them, they didn't pick on him anymore."

"Great. So, he's become one of them, even stooping to harass his own brother and sister instead of taking the heat himself. What a stand-up guy." Alyx shook her head.

"Brian's not so bad, really. He was just trying to survive high school like the rest of us. And anyway, he graduated last year, so he barely ever hangs out with Jared and his clones anymore," Anna said.

"Why isn't he in college?" Chase inquired.

"He decided to work with our dad this year on the fishing boat." She looked away. "Dad asked him to." She turned to Alyx and took a deep breath. "Can you teach me to do that?"

"Do what?" Alyx asked.

"To fight." Her eyes went big. "You were amazing back there."

"Oh. Yes. I guess I could teach you self-defense. If you want." Alyx turned to look at Chase, brows raised.

He shrugged. "We're only going to be here for a month. But we can teach you what we can while we're here."

"Thanks," Anna rushed out, still addressing Alyx, completely dismissing Chase. "I mean, that was lit. You know?" Her hands gestured as she spoke, "You were like, oh-no-don't-touch-me, and then it was head-to-the-nose, *whack*, then legs-gone, and oh-hello-down-there, Jared. Is that blood on your face?" She stopped for a quick breath before continuing, "Does your head hurt?"

"Maybe a little." Alyx absently rubbed her forehead, unsure how to take all this praise. Not to mention it was difficult to keep up with the conversation. The girl talked like she was running a marathon. "But not as much as his nose hurts." Alyx laughed. "I think it's broken. His nose, I mean."

"Haha! That would be sic! Jared's nose broken by a *girl*. And a small one, at that." Anna's cheeks flamed. "I mean, not small in a bad way, just like, you're not big. You know?" Relief washed over her face at Alyx's nod. "Can't think of a better guy for that to happen to."

Alyx frowned. "He said he's going to report us to the police..."

Chase interrupted, "Never gonna happen. He'll never admit a girl brought him down. I know this kind of guy. Trust me."

Anna nodded in agreement.

"I hope you're right. We can't afford to get in more trouble with the law," Alyx murmured.

"More trouble? Wait, you're like, fugitives or something?" Anna's eyes went wide.

"No, nothing like that. We witnessed an attempted suicide this morning and stopped the boy from jumping off the bridge. We had to go into the police station and give a report, that's all," Alyx answered.

"Whoa. You guys are like the superheroes of the town or something." Anna sighed, an expression of awe on her face.

"Yep. That's us." Chase laughed. "I always wanted to be a superhero."

Alyx rolled her eyes. "No."

They stopped in front of a small single-story, white brick house that needed a fresh coat of paint. Anna pointed. "That's me. Looks like Colin's already here." The bike lay abandoned on its side in the middle of the lawn.

"Should we come in and try to talk to him?" Chase hesitated.

Anna shook her head. "Nah. He'll be okay now that he's home. Besides, he wouldn't want to talk to you, anyway."

"Where does Jared live?" Chase asked.

Anna pointed at a two-story brick house three houses down from hers.

"So, when do you want to, you know, get together to teach me your moves?" Anna asked Alyx.

Alyx shrugged, hands splayed. She hesitated, glancing at Chase, then back at Annabelle. "Give me a day or two to get settled in. How about we meet you here on Wednesday night, after school? Is there somewhere we can go?"

"Perfect! I get home around this time every day. There's a park about two blocks away. We'll go there. I'll see you then." She blushed again, then ran up to the empty porch and disappeared into the house.

Alyx turned to Chase, brow furrowed.

"What just happened?" she asked.

"You have a fan club, that's what." Chase laughed at her expression of horror.

# CHAPTER 8
## *CHASE*

Chase approached the Young house. He didn't know if this was the same house the family had lived in his home-world, Dimension 6. In truth, when he'd known Jared back then, they'd never been good friends and Chase had never been invited to Jared's house back home.

Shielding his eyes with his hand, he squinted up at the large brick structure, then marched up the steps to the small porch. A riot of hearty emerald ferns grew in hanging pots, and palm-tree-like potted plants added more shades of green to each corner.

"The lady that lives in the old Moore house gave me an idea. Follow my lead," Chase called over his shoulder as he approached Jared's house, rapping on the white screen door.

Straining forward, Chase couldn't detect any movement from inside the house. He knocked again to be sure, then turned to Alyx.

"Nobody's home. Guess we'll have to…"

A white Ford Escape pulled into the driveway as they were descending the porch, a large man in both height and width unfolded himself from the vehicle. His gray-speckled dark hair was combed over in a failed attempt to hide his balding crown.

"Can I help you?" he inquired briskly.

"I'm Chase." He walked forward; hand extended for a quick shake. "This is Alyx. We're seniors at Dune Harbor High, and we wondered if we could ask you some questions for a paper we're working on? It's a survey. If you're willing."

The man tilted his head. "You know my son, Jared? He's a senior at DHH."

"Yes. We do." They nodded.

"I don't remember seeing you two around," James—Jim—Young stated.

Chase replied, "We just moved here. Haven't been here long."

With a curt nod, Jim Young spoke. "Well, go ahead. Ask your question."

Chase held up his arm. "We're doing a survey about timepieces. We both wear watches." He pointed, indicating Alyx's watch. "And we are trying to get an accurate count of people who still wear watches or timepieces of any kind."

Mr. Young showed his bare wrist. "You can see that I don't. No need, with cell phones displaying the time. Didn't think anyone wore them anymore."

"Okay, thank you, sir. So, you're not a keeper of the watch?"

His eyes widened briefly. The older man tilted his head, a calculating gleam lighting his eyes as he studied their watches more closely. After a brief hesitation, he shook his head. "No, I don't own a watch." He started walking toward the house. "Make sure your dog doesn't leave a mess in my yard." Mr. Young reached for the doorknob and disappeared inside, the door banging behind him.

"He's lying," Chase murmured.

Alyx agreed. "Definitely."

"Why lie? He clearly knows what we are, but he denied it. To what end? He saw our watches, so he must know we're keepers."

Alyx stared at the closed door, eyes narrowed. "We shouldn't have come here."

"Yeah. Yeah, I think you're right." Goosebumps traveled up his arm, and continued tingling up his neck. "Let's go."

• • •

Turning the corner onto Main Street, the heart of Dune Harbor town, Chase stopped in his tracks. He barely recognized the place he had known so well in his world. He sucked in a breath and let it out slowly. The contrast was almost too much to take in at once. He blinked.

In dimensions Six and Eight, this same street had the feel of an old-fashioned hometown, with quaint shops and inviting streetlamps lining the street, restaurants with a welcoming family atmosphere, and a true relax-and-enjoy vacation appeal. On his first jump, Dimension Seven's Main Street had been destroyed in the hunter's quest to locate watches.

But here, lights flashed and blazed, the beat of celebratory music filled the streets, and people in various stages of 'party-mode' hung out up and down the streets. This Vegas-style feel to the town's main tourist attraction left Chase temporarily speechless. He stared, wide eyes reflecting the myriad of colorful blinking lights.

"This place gives me a headache," he said. "Is that a casino?" Taking a few steps, he halted again. "Wait, they're all casinos."

Bo whined, and Alyx stooped to pick him up. "Let's just go back to the hotel. We don't have any business down there." She gestured toward the scene in front of them.

"Oh yes, we do." Chase jerked his head toward a small crowd gathered at the corner. He walked briskly, closing the distance.

"Chase, I don't..." Alyx trailed behind him, stammering. Her words fell away when she recognized Jared. She sighed. "Chase, just let him be. Let's just go."

"Don't worry, I'm not gonna start anything. I just want to see what he's doing here."

Chase hung back, just on the outskirts of the group. He strained to hear over the music pumping into the street through speakers mounted on the building fronts. Only a few words reached him, but the body language was hard to mistake. Two teenage girls backed away from Jared. One had her arms folded protectively over her midsection, the other clutched her small purse in front of her with white knuckles. Both had eyes downcast, and pink coloring their cheeks. Jared leered at them, his posse of 'friends' surrounding him, egging him on. He swatted the taller girl on the backside, and she flinched. Just then, he looked up, staring past them. Jared didn't seem to notice them watching him. Chase smirked, noting Jared's nose swelled to twice its normal size, and dark purple circles lined the underside of both eyes.

Chase made eye contact with Brian, the only one of the bunch who seemed uncomfortable by the exchange with the two girls. Brian's face flamed when he noticed Chase and Alyx, his eyes widening.

Just then, the girls broke free and walked toward them while Jared's group disappeared into the crowd of tourists. Chase reached a hand out, gently touching the taller girl on the upper arm.

"Are you okay? Was that guy harassing you?" he asked.

The girl jerked away from his touch. "We're fine." Her downcast eyes told a different story.

Alyx spoke to the girl in a hushed tone, "Are you sure? Do you know Jared?"

Her eyes flew up to Alyx's. She nodded. "We go to the same school. It's just Jared being... Jared, you know? Do you go to Dune Harbor High, too?"

Before Alyx could answer, Chase interrupted, "Yes. Well, we will. We're new here, and we have to register and all, but once we do that, we will go to Harbor High."

"Oh. What grade are you?" The girl asked.

"Seniors. We're seniors," Chase answered.

"We're juniors. I'm Ellie, and this is my best friend Sophie. See you at school, I guess." The girls turned toward the street, swallowed by a crowd exiting the casino behind them.

Chase turned to look at Alyx, a determined gleam in his eyes. He tilted his head.

Alyx was already shaking her head vehemently. "No. No way."

"We have to. I don't see any other way."

"There has to be another way. I'm not..." her voice rose an octave.

"Yes, you are. We both are." Chase winked. "We're going back to school."

# CHAPTER 9
## *ALYX*

"I'm not going. I didn't go to school back home; I'm definitely not going to high school here." She crossed her arms over her chest.

"All the more reason for you to go. You missed out on high school the first time around. Here's your chance to make up for that."

She huffed, pacing the hotel room. "I didn't *want* to go then, and I don't want to go *now*. You don't get it. My parents let me get my diploma online, and I was happy to do it. You can go back to school if you want, but I'm not. I escaped that torture the first time around. What would we accomplish, anyway?"

"We have to keep an eye on Jared, right? He's the descendant of the keeper family in this world. And maybe we can help end his reign of terror on the school."

Alyx was shaking her head before he finished. "None of that is any of our business."

"You're wrong. Mr. Young, Jared's dad, knows something he's not telling us. And maybe we can find the hunters through them."

She re-crossed her arms, glaring at him.

Chase took advantage of her silence. "And how many girls do you think Jared targets at school? So far, he's gone after you, and those two girls Ellie and Sophie, and that's only the ones we saw. There are bound to be others. Not to mention Mason and Colin. You said it yourself. I was there to stop the bullying in my dimension. It's this bad because I wasn't here to do that in this world. Maybe I can fix that. Like that old movie 'It's a Wonderful Life' or something."

*It's a Wonderful Life?*

She shook her head. "What about the hunters? Remember them?"

"Isn't it possible that the hunters have already been eradicated from this world? By a previous keeper, or natural causes, or I don't know, a change of heart like Liz in D-8? I mean, if they don't come after us, why do we care?"

"It's part of the mission! We find and destroy the hunters, protect the watches, and record what we can for history's sake. It's what we signed up for."

"You know as well as I do that the mission has changed. If the last world taught us anything, it's that people can change, especially world-to-world. The hunters could be good here. They could have a family, and maybe, just maybe, they've forgotten all about us."

"I need air." Alyx shoved out the door, the cheap, lightweight plywood not giving her the satisfying banging sound she needed right now. "Don't follow me," she barked over her shoulder.

Her feet pounded on the cement, picking up speed until she was at a full-out run.

She missed running. Her daily exercise regimen back home had been grueling, and she'd loved every minute of it. They hadn't taken the time to train lately, and she felt the effects of that lack of routine. She could run like this for hours and, thanks to the stamina that came along with being a watch-keeper, she would not tire since her heartbeat kept perfect time with the ticking of the clock. One advantage of being a chosen keeper of her family's ancestral watch.

*He's right. I know he's right. The last dimension changed everything about their mission.*

Picking up her pace, she felt droplets of sweat dripping between her shoulder blades.

*People aren't always what they seem.*

She'd been the first one to trust the female hunter, Ursa O'Ryan—known as Liz in the last world. Liz had helped them on their last jump, even though her 'other-self' had tried to kill them in all previous dimensions they'd visited. So far, Pavo O'Ryan, the male hunter, had remained evil in all worlds they'd visited.

*Nothing about being a keeper is what I thought it would be. And school? Even the idea of going to school scares me more than a thousand hunters.*

She knew nothing of classes, teachers, friends.

*Will I be expected to make friends?*

Stopping, she slammed her hands on her hips and blew air at her long bangs.

*This is ridiculous. I am a keeper of the watch. I've trained for all kinds of situations. I can handle a few weeks in a high school.*

What could go wrong?

• • •

Her hand clutched the computer print-out, and she glared down at the list of classes and times. The words blurred and seemed to leap from the page in a mocking dance, and she took an involuntary step backward.

"See you tomorrow at 8:00 am," the secretary said. "You'll report directly to your homeroom when you arrive. It will take a bit of time to gather all of your transcripts and information, but in the meantime, you can begin classes right away so you don't fall too far behind."

Chase leaned in, scanning her paper. "Hey, we have English and Math together."

Alyx's wild eyes darted back and forth between the paper in her hand and Chase.

*Tomorrow? That's it? How can it be this easy to register for school? Shouldn't there be a lot more involved in this process?*

Cheeks flaming, she shivered when a drop of sweat ran down her back. She flinched at Chase's touch when he led her through the office, pushing through the glass double doors onto the sidewalk entrance to the high school. Feet moving of their own accord, she shuffled along, pictures of textbooks and cafeteria food flashing through her brain.

"Relax, Alyx. It's just school." Chase flashed that cocky grin, and her eyes narrowed.

"Oh? And what happens when they can't find our transcripts, or even our social security numbers?" She retorted.

"Good question. Guess we'll have to figure something out before they discover our deceit." He shrugged.

"What's the point of all this if we're just gonna get kicked out in a few days, anyway?" she asked.

"We'll just have to do as much as we can for as long as we're here. Maybe we can get some false papers made or something."

"And where do you think we'll get those?" she cocked her head.

"I have no idea. Never needed fake identification back home."

Alyx snorted, rolling her eyes. "I can't believe I let you talk me into this."

"Know what?" Chase threw his arms around her and planted a smacking kiss on her cheek. "I can't believe you let me talk you into this, either."

When her eyes flew up to his, he winked, a grin spreading.

She punched him in the side. "You're an idiot."

# CHAPTER 10
## *CHASE*

Chase sauntered up the cement steps leading to the sprawling school building. When he reached the top, he turned, only to discover that he was alone. Spinning, he found Alyx frozen at the bottom of the steps. He jogged back down two steps at a time, a smile lighting his face as he reached for her hand. She pulled away, slamming her hands onto her hips.

"You're gonna be fine. Trust me," Chase soothed.

She snorted, wild eyes meeting his. "Why don't you go, and I'll stay back with Bo. That way, we can watch from both outside the school and inside at once."

He shook his head with an answering grin that negated the need for words. Holding out his hand, he waited. A moment passed before Alyx sighed, placing her hand in his. The breath he hadn't realized he was holding escaped through his teeth, and he brought her hand to his lips for a light kiss before gently tugging her up the steps.

"I'll help you find your homeroom, and then we share second period, so I'll see you then. You're gonna be fine, I promise."

They walked through the double front doors into a world that was so familiar to Chase, it was like a homecoming. Scuffed pewter gray squares of linoleum speckled with white covered the floor lined with steel-gray lockers flanking the hallway. Students scattered, busily working combinations, hustling down the hall and around the corner while others stood in sporadic groups clutching books like a lifeline. The smell of disinfectant mixed with a cacophony of perfumes, deodorants, and sweat enveloped him in a cocoon of nostalgia. His nostrils flared, eyes crinkling as the corners of his mouth tilted slightly upward while memories swirled around him.

"Why do you look so happy to be here?" Alyx accused, wide eyes the only sign that she was uncomfortable. Her rounded shoulders exuded confidence, even though Chase knew she felt anything but. Only someone who really knew her, like he did, could see the fear she hid so valiantly behind her wall of fortitude.

"This reminds me of simpler times. I had control of my life when I was in high school." He glanced down at her, the smile fading from his eyes. "At least, I thought I did." He began walking. "Let's check in at the office to pick up our books and class schedule. Then we'll look for Jared."

Alyx nodded absently, her rounded eyes glowing violet with a thousand questions as she followed behind. Chase glanced repeatedly over his shoulder, offering smiling encouragement as he wound his way through the hall and pushed into the office.

After taking Alyx to her homeroom and placing the books in the new locker that reeked of lemon-scented cleaning detergent, Chase turned and inhaled sharply as someone slammed him backward into his locker, the back of his head banging loudly on the metal. Instant pain throbbed through his skull.

A familiar voice growled through the haze. "What the hell are *you* doing here?"

Chase shook his head to clear the cobwebs and took a step toward Jared. "Didn't you hear? I'm the new kid now. Better get used to it."

Jared, either moving quicker than Chase gave him credit for, or because of his own reflexes being dulled by the head-slam, shoved Chase back a second time into the locker. The agony that exploded in the back of his head only fueled his fury. When his head cleared, Chase noticed Jared's posse flanking him, offering support in numbers as usual.

Despite the pounding in his skull, Chase's eyes blazed as he threw his elbow into Jared's gut, grabbed him by the shirt and whipped him around until Jared was the one up against the cold metal. Bringing him forward, he threw him back again. "Don't ever touch me again, or you'll regret it. I told you, I won't back down to you or your pet dogs here," He said, nodding toward the others.

"No, you listen. If *you* ever touch *me* again..." Jared hissed.

"What? What will you do?" Chase demanded, a hard glint in his eyes. "Your empty threats don't scare me."

Jared sneered. "You have no idea. I own this school. You better stay away from me, or..."

Chase laughed. "You think you own this school? That's all about to change for you."

"Who do you think you are, coming in here and...?"

Jared's incredulous expression brought a calculating smile to Chase's face. He pushed Jared once more, just as Miss Stephens came around the corner. "Hey!" she yelled, quickening her pace. "What's going on here? Are you okay, Jared?"

Jared's face flushed, shoulders slumped, his demeanor undergoing a quick 180-degree turn. "Yeah, Miss S. This new guy was trying to push me around." He purposely dropped his eyes to the floor in a show of supplication, but Chase caught the dark smile just before he lowered his head.

She eyed Chase, cocked her head, and put her hand on his arm to guide him along. "Come with me." Her lips formed a thin line, displeasure apparent in every jerky move she made. "We'll sort this out with the principal. New, you say? This little episode wasn't your best start."

"Jared pushed me first. He came after me," Chase mumbled. She was right, this was not how he had wanted to start the day. *What will Alyx say?* He sighed. *It's a good thing she was safely dropped off in her homeroom, or she definitely would have been involved, too. Then we'd both spend the day in the principal's office.*

Miss Stephen's eyes narrowed as she marched on. "This way."

As they passed a door labeled 'Guidance Counselor', Chase glimpsed a middle-aged blonde-haired man just before the door closed. Recognition tugged at his subconsciousness, though he couldn't place where he'd seen the man before. Shaking his head, he dismissed the tingling at the base of his neck, and marched on toward the school office, though he risked one more furtive glance over his shoulder with a frown.

# CHAPTER II
## *ALYX*

*Where is he?* Alyx thought for the hundredth time.

Chase was supposed to be in English class with her, but though her eyes were drawn to the door every time someone new entered the room, none were familiar.

She'd barely made it through homeroom and first period and was overwhelmed by the sheer number of assignments her first-ever teacher had doled out with a smile, as if she should be thankful for the busywork that would only keep her from her true purpose here. Her eyes rolled involuntarily, so that she peered at the teacher through the slits in her bangs. Probably in his forties, or at least somewhere in that range, wearing a collared shirt that accentuated the gut hanging over his belt, straining to hold up his wrinkled khakis. His gray-speckled brown hair formed a V over his forehead. Mr. Stokes' voice droned on without changing pitch or pace, and a silent sigh lifted Alyx's shoulders. He was talking about an author... Jane something-or-other.

*Who cares?*

Another sigh.

*Why am I sitting here wasting time...?*

She jumped when she heard her name.

"Everyone, please welcome Alyx," the teacher picked up a paper on his desk and squinted down at it, "Eris. Alyx Eris. She's new here. Please make her feel welcome."

A girl sitting next to her reached out and touched her arm. "Hi. We met the other day. I'm Sophie."

"Hey," Alyx answered, barely glancing her way. In that brief contact, she remembered the girl from Main Street. The same girl who had been harassed by Jared. Rounding her shoulders, she leaned toward Sophie. "Are you okay?"

"Okay? Sure, why wouldn't I be?" Sophie tilted her head, her hair falling to hide her face like a curtain.

Alyx shrugged. "Last time I saw you, Jared..."

Sophie interrupted, pushing her hair behind her ear. "Oh, that's nothing. I'm fine." Her eyes darted around the room to check for eavesdroppers. "No harm done."

Alyx was unsure how to proceed, having little experience with socializing. But the girl's words sparked her ire. "It's not 'nothing' if someone touches you when you don't want..."

She jerked at the sound of the teacher's voice. "Miss Eris. I don't know how it was done in your old school, but here it's impolite to talk while the teacher is talking. Have you read *Pride and Prejudice* in your past studies? Is that why you feel you have no great need to participate in our discussion of the book?"

Her cheeks heated. "No. No, I haven't read it."

"Well, then. You have some reading to catch up on." He tossed her a dog-eared paperback that landed with a *smack* on her desk. "I expect you to read the story in its entirety by Friday. That should keep you busy. In the meantime, try to pay attention. You just might learn something."

Alyx nodded, leaning forward to stare down at the book, glad that her hair shielded her suddenly rosy cheeks from the room of curious eyes—every one focused on her. She'd caught the smirk of the boy to her right before turning away, and squelched the urge to throw her fist into his already crooked teeth. Her shoulders rose on a purposeful, deep breath. Tuning out Mr. Stokes and everyone around her, she picked up the book and studied the cover. There was nothing to indicate what the tale might be about, not even a small clue who the characters might be. Just the words on a blank background. Maybe it told of a great war, or some other kind of battle. Her spirits lifted a notch. She could always use new ideas on combat methods that have succeeded and failed...

With one sentence, Mr. Stokes' voice shattered her images of swordplay and canon-fire. "I want you to think about marriage in the time-period of the novel as well as the location the story was written. Compare the importance of marriage to Elizabeth Bennet and her sisters then, and then think about what marriage means now in present day in contrast. I want you to write a 500-word essay on the topic, due tomorrow. I'll give you some time now to get started. Alyx, you can take this time to begin reading this classic tale. I'll give you until Monday to complete the essay." He turned, dismissing them all as he sank into his chair with a squeak, rolled his chair sideways, and began madly scrawling who-knows-what in a yellow-lined notebook.

Alyx leaned back in the chair and opened the book and read the first line: "*It is a truth universally acknowledged, that a single man in possession of a good fortune, must be in want of a wife.*"

Alyx slammed the book closed. Her eye-roll was long and exaggerated, followed by an equally drawn-out sigh.

*Torture. That's what this is.*

Just then, Chase sauntered into the room and right up to Mr. Stokes' desk. He handed the teacher a paper, then scanned the room, eyes landing on her. His smile spread as he winked.

Her eyes narrowed.

*His fault. It was his fault she was sitting here right now.*

She crossed her arms and glared at him.

His smile widened as he turned back to the teacher. Mr. Stokes handed him another well-used copy of Jane Austen's masterpiece. Alyx clenched her fists at Chase's enthusiastic voice. "Oh, great. *Pride and Prejudice.* I love the use of irony Austen uses throughout the tale."

"Oh, so you've read the story?" Mr. Stokes asked, his face aglow.

Chase nodded, turning on the charm. It was one of his many talents. "Yes. Yes, I have. But I'll be happy to read it again to refresh my memory."

The teacher's head was nodding like a bobble-head doll. "Great, great. You can find a seat back there." He waved at the two empty desks toward the back of the room.

"Thanks, Mr. Stokes." Chase smiled and winked again on his way past Alyx. He flopped into a seat at the back of the room, too far away for conversation. She fidgeted with her pencil, glancing back over her shoulder repeatedly to meet his eyes. Grinding her teeth each time he smiled that cocky grin of his. She leaned back, crossed her arms, and tried to focus on the book in front of her.

When the bell rang, Alyx had herself mostly under control.

Mostly.

She marched to the back of the room. "Where were you?" she demanded.

He lowered his voice, "I was talking to the principal."

Her eyes whipped up as her anger dropped away. "What? Why?"

Chase shrugged. "I had a brief confrontation with Jared this morning."

"What?" Her voice rose, and she noticed several people looking their way. With effort, she continued in a whisper. "What do you mean, confrontation?"

"I'll fill you in on the details later, but the principal is leaning toward blaming the new kid. Not the golden-boy. Jared's got all the teachers fooled."

"But that's not fair!" She fumed.

He cocked his head, looking at her sideways. "No one ever said high school was fair."

She huffed. "Then why are we here? It's not too late to…"

Chase interrupted, "We're not leaving. I've drawn Jared's attention. That's exactly what we wanted. Right?"

She blew out a long breath, deflating. "I guess."

"And I saw someone who looked very familiar. I just can't place where I…" Chase looked away, then down at the floor as his voice trailed off.

"Who?" Alyx asked.

"Nevermind. It was nothing." His smile didn't reach his eyes. "Let's go. Next period is this way."

Alyx stared at his departing back, a frown wrinkling her brow as she plodded along behind him.

# CHAPTER 12
## *CHASE*

The dream came on him with the power of a hurricane, sweeping Chase along in its twirling winds, tossing him here and there as if he was light as a dandelion seed with no choice but to go where the storm chose. Each time his dream-self would become aware of his surroundings, of the people around him, he would be thrown once again in the swirl of air that left no mercy, no time to recover from the last scene that played in his subconscious brain. Though deep down Chase knew none of it was real—knew it *couldn't* be real—each act in this subconscious drama seemed more tangible than the scratchy hotel bedsheets under him or the watch that gently pulsed iridescent blue on his left wrist. In fact, all of it was rooted in truth, as dreams tend to be.

His uncle appeared before him, reaching out a hand toward him. Uncle Charlie was talking, but Chase couldn't hear the words. Despite knowing this dream-visit was somehow essential to success in this current world, all he could do was look helplessly at his uncle's lips as they moved in a frantic attempt at silent communication. A growl escaped Chase's slumbering lips, and his body thrashed, bedsheets trapping his legs.

"Uncle Charlie! I can't hear you..." Dream-Chase took a step closer, but the gap between them never lessened. His uncle was now gesturing frantically, muffled words tumbling from his lips as he desperately tried to communicate with his nephew. Chase ran toward his uncle, the man who had raised him from infancy, the only father he had ever known. As his legs pumped up and down, up and down in his sleep, his breathing became labored. In the dream he closed his eyes, and when he opened them again, the scene shifted. His uncle was on the kitchen floor, clutching his chest—just as he had been on the day he'd lost him forever. Only this time, Charlie was still trying to talk, to tell him something important. Chase relived that day—the worst day of his life—and all the pain that came with it. There had been nothing he could do then, and there was nothing he could do now. His heart beat painfully in his chest, as it had the day his uncle's heart had stopped forever. Dream-Charlie whispered one intelligible word before his eyes closed. "Forgive."

Chase's body tossed and turned as he plummeted yet again through the hurricane and was dumped into the ocean. As if it was second nature, his arms and legs began kicking and moving, pulling his body along with the current. Suddenly, fins appeared above the water and he froze, staring at those triangular gray fins. Dolphins? He smiled as he remembered swimming with a pod of dolphins in Dimension 7, and held his hand out toward one of the circling animals. He counted six fins in all. But these creatures seemed to move differently than the dolphins had, gliding in a graceful yet smoothly intentional way instead of the playful dolphin leaps and dives he'd witnessed that long-ago day, and the shape of the fin was not curved but pointed up in a straight and perfect isosceles triangle...

One beast swam close enough to bump into him, rough skin brushing against his own, and he gasped and pulled his hand back at the sudden horrific realization that the circling sharks surrounded him. They swam in lazy rings around him, occasionally coming in for an exploratory swipe or nuzzle. Testing their prey, preparing for attack.

Chase screamed, thrashing around in the water. One shark, he was almost positive it was a bull shark, stopped its lazy trek and darted toward him, its mouth wide, close enough that he could see the serrated edges of those dagger-like teeth coming for him. Chase, entranced by the yawning cavern of white nothingness, stared down the throat of the shark, knowing it was the last thing he would ever see as that mouth closed around him...

His fist came up to fight the creature, just as he was ripped from the water and thrown down at the edge of the magical pit in Dimension 8. He was leaning precariously over the gaping hole, holding onto Mason as his friend dangled over the source of magic that shrouded the town of Dune Harbor in D-8, just as he'd held on to him on the bridge here in D-9. Only this time, he couldn't hold on, and Mason plummeted down into the depths of the Earth, lost to him forever. His friend's scream echoed even after he disappeared from view, tearing the chasm that had formed in his chest even wider while reliving Uncle Charlie's passing. Chase lifted his sorrowful eyes, looked up into the eyes of Liz—the hunter known as Ursa in other dimensions who had turned to the light in that one world—and heard her voice as if she were in the hotel room with him. "You could not save him then, and you cannot save him now." A tear ran down her cheek before she, too, jumped into the glowing pit.

Once again torn away, he realized he was now free falling in the air, so far above the ground that trees looked like dots below him. His hand found nothing as he searched in vain for a parachute string. There was no chute, no safety net, nothing to stop his fall except the ground below. He acknowledged certain death as it stared him in the face. As he plummeted, the wind pushing back his hair and tightening the skin on his face, his arms and legs pushed by force splayed into a star, he became aware of a flailing movement to his left. Turning his head against the force of the wind, he jerked when he saw he was not alone. An old man fell alongside him, his long white hair billowing behind him. Not a stranger, exactly. This was the mysterious man he'd encountered in Dimension 7. The gruff man who had helped him save Alyx from certain death in that place. The very same man who had alerted him to unknown powers within the watch itself when he'd discovered he could use it to turn back time within that dimensional plane. Since then, he'd come to Chase in dreams only. And here he was again. Chase suspected the identity of this man—though if it were true, the man must be impossibly old—but it had never been confirmed. Elias Walker. His very own ancestor, and the creator of the watches themselves. Could it be?

"What should I do?" Chase called through the wind; his teeth so dry his lips stuck to them.

"The watch. Protect the watch." The man's blue eyes—eyes a mirror image of his own—bored into his.

Chase guffawed. "I think nothing can protect the watch now." He looked down at the ground that seemed to rise toward him, though he knew the opposite was true.

He continued staring so intently, Chase couldn't tear his eyes away. "Let him help."

"Him? Who?"

"It's for you to solve."

"You're speaking in riddles. I don't understand…"

A picture of the school counselor's door flashed, a blond man in shadows. Just as quickly, the image ripped away.

On the bed, Chase's eyes jerked open. There was a pressure on his shoulder. He blinked, staring up into wide violet eyes.

Alyx.

She stood next to the bed, gave him another little shake. "Chase, wake up. It's a dream, just a dream," she soothed. He placed a hand on her arm, just to prove she was real.

His shoulders rose on a jagged breath. "Yeah." Running his hands over his face, he slowly pushed himself up. "Sorry. Did I wake you?"

"Yes, you were running a marathon in your sleep, and talking."

He pushed himself up on his elbows. "Talking? Did I say anything interesting?"

She shook her head. "Nothing I could make out. Just gibberish."

He nodded, heading for the bathroom.

She placed a hand on his arm. "Do you want to talk about it?"

"No. It was nothing, just a dream." Chase closed the bathroom door, bolted it, and turned to splash cold water on his face. "Just a dream," he muttered to his reflection.

# CHAPTER 13
## *ALYX*

Annabelle stared up into Alyx's face with wide eyes and a look of pure worship. Alyx shook her head and sighed, baffled by the awe she saw in the girl's expression. *How can I ever live up to this girl's expectations?*

Pushing those alarming thoughts aside, she continued her instruction. Alyx was showing Anna how to break a hold if someone grabbed her from behind, and the girl was a quick learner. She mimicked every move with an intensity that reminded Alyx of herself. A flicker of respect for this girl blossomed. She could understand this want—or more accurately, the *need*—to learn how to be independent and take care of herself.

They'd met several times at the edge of the neighborhood's small playground as planned, and found that it was the perfect space for learning self-defense. The pair stood in a small soccer field, empty now, the soft grass sorely in need of a mower providing a perfect cushion for their training.

"Your elbows and knees are invaluable. They are weapons you always have with you, and you should use them as such."

Anna nodded; eyes wide. "Will you teach me how to use actual weapons?"

Alyx straightened from her crouch. "I can teach you that, too, but you won't always have weapons available. First, you need to learn how to use what you've got."

Heat flamed up Anna's cheeks. "I'm afraid I don't *have* much. I mean, look at me." The girl gestured to her small frame.

"You're wrong." Alyx cocked her head. "That's an advantage. Your opponent will take one look at your size, immediately underestimate you, and in that one second they don't acknowledge you as a true threat, you'll take them down. Trust me."

A tiny smile lifted the corners of Annabelle's mouth. "I think I like the sound of that. And I do. Trust you, I mean. I saw what you can do." She nodded, lifting her hands, elbows bent, legs in a squat. "Okay, I'm ready. Let's go. I mean, if you think you're ready to..." Her voice trailed off into a gasp when Alyx once again grabbed her from behind.

Alyx's voice was sharp. "Let's see what you've learned so far. Break my hold."

The training continued well into dusk. As the sky glowed burnt amber, Anna gasped. "OMG. What time is it? I have to go." She raced to retrieve the backpack she'd flung on the ground, turned to run toward home. Suddenly she stopped, spun around, and ran back to Alyx, flinging her arms around her in a quick bear hug. She whispered, "Thanks, Alyx." Just as quickly, she turned and jogged the other direction. Before she disappeared through the pine trees bordering the park, she called back over her shoulder: "See you tomorrow!"

Alyx stood, wringing her hands as a tidal wave of emotion swept over her. Her heart swelled, and she felt the sting of unshed tears burning behind her eyes. Taking one purposeful, deep breath, she turned to walk back to the hotel, thinking to sort out the well of feelings that swamped her. Movement behind her registered in her peripheral vision, and her body readied out of habit. She turned to take on this new threat, only to realize that it was Chase standing there, his eyes almost glowing with heat as they burned into hers.

Without stopping to think, she marched over to where he stood, grabbed his t-shirt while rising onto tiptoes, and slanted her mouth onto his, effectively swallowing his look of astonishment with her kiss. As their mouths fused and they each sank deeper into the kiss, into each other, her arms lifted to pull him even closer, hearts throbbing in unison. She felt his arms holding her just as tightly, as if they couldn't get close enough, never close enough. Heat burned between them, like the iridescent blue heart of a flame that consumed everything in its path. She slanted her head the other way, gripping his hair to get closer to his heat, closer to his heart. Sinking further and further into the sensations that overwhelmed her, but she didn't care. She embraced the emotions, the heat. She was desperate to stoke the fire, never wanting this moment to end.

And then, just as suddenly as the kiss began, he was gone. His arms gripped her biceps as he gently pushed her away. She gasped, her breath catching as her eyes focused wildly on his. *Why?* Her eyes pleaded, even as she stepped toward him once again. She growled when he took a step back. "I..."

"Alyx." Chase took a jagged breath and gently lay his forehead against hers. "Whoa. I don't think I'm ever going to recover." He leaned slightly back, his eyes flaming into hers, contradicting his actions.

"Then, why...?" Her voice was raspy to her own ears. She cleared her throat.

Chase tilted his head toward the sliding board and swing set at the other side of the park. A family of four; mother, father, and two young children, had entered the park from the south entrance.

Alyx felt her heart stutter as heat climbed up her neck. She hadn't noticed they were no longer alone. "Oh." Her horrified eyes met his. "Oh."

Chase reached for her hand. "And I don't know what that was all about. I mean, don't get me wrong. I liked it. A lot." He caressed her hand and cleared his throat. "But I want to make sure you're ready for what that was leading to. I don't want you to do anything you'll regret. It's always your choice, Alyx."

"I know it is." She laughed, before her eyes took on a serious edge. "I know. It's just one of the things I love about you."

They walked back to the hotel, clasped hands swinging between them as the sun completed its descent and darkness shrouded the small town of Dune Harbor and its inhabitants.

Occasionally, Alyx peeked at Chase's profile through lashes unadorned by cosmetics. Her eyes traveled his jawline, covered in the patchy stubble of new adulthood, his lips full and soft, though they had been firm against her own just minutes ago. Reaching up to touch her own lips still tender from his kiss with her free hand, she continued her perusal. His nose, a slight bump marring its perfection from an enthusiastic tackle during his football years in high school, upward to his rounded cheekbones she thought must surely ache from all that smiling. A small feminine smirk turned her mouth upward, and she sighed, a lightness filling her soul in a way she had never experienced before in her eighteen years on this Earth. Her heart swelled.

As a child, she hadn't dreamed of finding a man, creating a family, finding love. Unlike the book her English teacher was making her read, *Pride and Prejudice*, she did not seek marriage as the Bennet family had in the story. Alyx Eris needed no man to protect and provide for her, she could do that on her own, thank you. No, she'd fantasized about battles fought and strategic war plans. All she'd ever wanted was to survive and succeed on her own; make her family proud. In all her daydreaming, Alyx had never looked beyond her eighteenth year. She'd never considered a true partner in life or the reciprocal love of a man until now...

When he sensed her perusal and turned to meet her stare, his aquamarine eyes immediately crinkled at the corners in an answering smile.

"What are you thinking?" he asked. His fingers tightening around hers.

Her smile widened into a grin. "I was thinking of all the people I could be stuck with in this year of dimension travel. I guess you're not the worst, Walker."

Chase chortled, throwing his arm around her shoulders. "You're not so bad yourself, Eris."

Alyx threw her elbow into his side and took off running. "Race you to the hotel," she called over her shoulder, a giggle escaping as she picked up speed. She saw the competitive gleam amp up the blue in his eyes before he, too, burst into a sprint, the sound of their combined laughter filling the night air.

A retired couple walking by with three chihuahuas on retractable leashes couldn't help but smile at the sight of them running by.

Neither Alyx and Chase, nor the dog-walkers, knew they were being watched from the vehicle parked in the shadows across the street.

# CHAPTER 14
## *CHASE*

Chase jerked at the sound of glass shattering, followed by a deep *thud,* from the bathroom where he stood in front of the sink. He burst through the door ready to defend. Alyx stood next to the bed, staring at the broken window, curtains gently swaying in the sea breeze that now had access to the room.

"What happened?" Chase asked. He ran to the front door, nearly ripping it off its hinges as it flung wide. Twin red taillights disappeared around the corner with a screech of tires too quick to identify the make and model of the car. He turned back to Alyx. "Did you see anything?"

She shook her head. "I was making the bed and the glass shattered." Bending to pick something off the floor, she held it up, saying, "This came through the window."

Chase approached, studying the object. "A brick. Someone threw a brick through the window."

Alyx rolled her eyes. "Had to be Jared. Who else?"

"There's a note." Chase pulled two rubber bands off the ends of the brick, unwrapping a note. "How original."

Alyx stepped forward, reading the note aloud: *"End yourself or someone will help U, LSR."*

"This is low, even for Jared. Makes you think, though." Anger shot out of Chase's eyes and he took a step toward the door.

Alyx clasped his forearm. "You're not going after him. It's what he wants you to do."

"I'm not sure that's true." Chase paced. "The note says: End yourself. So, what, he wants me to kill myself?" He turned, his pacing escalating. "How many people has he urged to commit suicide? And has anyone actually offed themselves because he goaded them into it?"

Alyx sank onto the bed. "Mason," she breathed.

"Exactly. Mason." Chase's body took on a threatening pose. "I can't stand by and..."

"Chase. Think about it. We're only here for three more weeks. What can we do to change the way Jared treats people in that time?"

Chase cursed, running his hands through his hair, making it stand on end. "I'm not sure. But I think I have an idea."

"Are you thinking of taking this to the police? Because remember, Jared's mom works at the police station, so..."

"I think Carson—Officer Murphy—would be willing to help us, but no. We're not going to the police," Chase said.

"Then what's your plan?"

"I wouldn't call it a plan, exactly. But I think we have someone to go talk to in the morning that may help us. Even if he doesn't want to."

•　•　•

The clouds of the overcast sky hung low as they approached the Young house. Rain threatened to fall at any moment as the winds picked up, sweeping the heavy gray clouds across the sky as if someone had a remote control and was pushing the fast-forward button. Chase reached for Alyx's hand, giving it a gentle squeeze when she placed her hand in his as naturally as if they'd been holding hands for years. A small smile tugged at the corners of his mouth.

"This is a waste of our time," Alyx complained.

Expecting the argument to continue even though they were less than a block away from their destination, Chase picked up where they'd left off at the hotel. "I don't think it is. We have unfinished business with Jared's dad, anyway. He seemed to know about the watches but denied it last time we were here. And I don't think any dad wants his only son to be responsible for the deaths of others. So maybe we kill two birds with one stone."

"And maybe we make another enemy," Alyx murmured, though there wasn't much heat in her words as she knew her argument was already lost.

The first drops began falling from the sky, landing on their heads and speckling their shoulders with cool wetness. They picked up their pace, hands still clasped.

As they approached the red-brick house, the door flew open. Jared lurched through the doorway as if in a hurry, halting as he spotted the two of them on his porch steps. His eyes widened.

"What are you doing here?" he demanded. He slammed his hands on his hips in a show of superiority, but also took a step backward, contradicting the severity of his stance.

"We came to talk to your dad. About this." Chase held up the note, cocking his head. "You know anything about this, Jared?"

"Uh…" Jared stuttered, face flushed, visibly gathering his composure. "What's that? Never saw it before. And my dad's busy. He doesn't have time for you losers."

"Jared?" A masculine voice called out just before Jim Young appeared in the doorway, towering over his son. His eyes gave them the once-over, recognition lighting his eyes. "You two. What do you want?"

Movement from inside caught Chase's attention, and his eyes flew to Sadie Young, lurking behind the open door, eyes downcast. Hands wringing, she didn't say a word, but listened while trying to shrink into invisibility. Chase dismissed her, addressing Jim instead.

"Good morning, Mr. Young. We came to talk to you about this." Chase held up the note once again. "Someone threw a brick along with this note at our hotel window last night. We think it was Jared, and thought you'd like to know."

Mr. Young took a menacing step forward, grabbing the note out of Chase's hand, reading it aloud. "End yourself or someone will help you." He smirked. "So, what's the big deal?" he asked, crumbling the note and shoving it into the front pocket of his jeans.

"What's the big deal? He broke the window and someone has to pay for it. One of us could have been hurt if we'd been standing by the window. And do you really think it's okay to try to goad someone into committing suicide?"

The big man turned to his son, a threatening look crossing his features. "You do this?"

"No, sir." Jared hung his head. "I don't know anything about it."

The man turned back to Chase. "See, Jared says he knows nothing about it."

"Okay, fine. If that's the way you want to play this. But we know you know what we are, and we know you lied to us about the watches. And if you can live with yourself if someone actually kills himself because of something your son did or said…"

"You think you're so smart? You don't know anything, kid. Those watches? They're cursed, so I want nothing to do with you and yours, got it? And a person can't make someone off themselves. I mean, you could say to me right now: why don't you go kill yourself? And I'm not gonna do it, right? It's just words. And Jared says he didn't do it, so he didn't do it. Now, get off my property. Next time you come here, I'll call the police."

"Can I have the note back?" Chase held his hand out.

"Get off my property." Jim Young glared at them.

Alyx tugged on his hand, and Chase slowly nodded as they backed off the porch.

A steady, light rain pelted them as they hurried back to the hotel, not saying a word until they closed the door behind them.

"That was... interesting. And now we don't even have the note, so if we wanted to take it to Carson Murphy at the station, we can't." Chase said, a thoughtful tilt to his head. "Mr. Young all but admitted that he knows about the watches. And now we know he'll defend his son's actions, no matter what he does."

Alyx shrugged. "What did you expect? An apology?" She sat in the corner chair, pulling a book out of her backpack. "Now if you'll excuse me, I have to finish reading this boring book before Monday." She held up the tattered copy of *Pride and Prejudice.*

Chase's laugh echoed, Bo jumping on his legs at the sound. He reached down to scratch the pup behind the ear, eliciting an almost purring sound from the animal. "It's a classic. I'm proud of you, Alyx. You're really embracing this whole school thing." His eyes sparkled as hers shot daggers back at him.

Alyx snorted, her lips forming a thin line as she flipped to the page she had marked and began reading.

Chase's laughter filled the room as he, too, prepared to complete his assignments for the week. The rest of the weekend was quiet and uneventful. Boring, even.

Until Monday afternoon, when things got more complicated.

# CHAPTER 15
## *ALYX*

Grumbling as she trudged up the street a block away from the high school building, Alyx scowled sideways at Chase. As usual, he was full of early morning cheer and energy, and it left her irritated. How could anyone wake up as happy as he appeared to be?

Glancing at the brick facade as they approached, the cheerful turquoise of the school colors on the flag seemed to mock her as it snapped in the early morning coastal breeze. Seagulls eager to greet the new day cawed merrily in the distance, the sound causing her frown to deepen.

A growl rumbled in her throat. "Shoulda called off." She stubbed her toe on the bottom step leading to the main entrance, the unforgiving concrete sending a shock wave that radiated from the tip of her toe up her leg. Alyx cursed. "It's not like we're staying here long, anyway. What does it matter if we miss a day of school?" *Mondays suck.*

Chase responded with a grin, which only raised her temper another notch.

Students milled around outside, delaying the inevitable. An air of quiet resignation settled around the building at the start of a new week.

Chase held the door open, gesturing her in first. She glared at him as she swept by, a deep sigh lifting her shoulders. Another day of sitting through mundane classes seemed like torture of the worst kind.

Flinching at the sound of yet another perky voice so early in the morning, she squinted at the form of Anna weaving through the locker crowd toward her.

"Alyx!" The girl arrived, glorious smile beaming, and tugged along a familiar face behind her. "I'm glad you're here. Did you have a good weekend?"

Alyx replied with a nod, tilting her head, waiting.

"Oh, um. You know Sophie, right? I mean, she said she knows you, so I guess you know each other." A blush bloomed on Annabelle's face as she spoke, her words tumbling out in her haste to speak.

Alyx glanced at Sophie. "Yeah. Hi."

Sophie answered with a smile, "Hi."

"Great. So, I wanted to ask you, I mean, if we're still meeting at the park tonight, that is?" She raised her eyes, waiting expectedly.

Alyx nodded. "Sure."

"Cool. So, if you don't mind, I was telling some friends. Sophie, for one. And I was wondering, I mean hoping really, that you wouldn't mind if I brought along a friend or two with me tonight. For the lessons, I mean?" She waited, wringing her hands in front of her, her body leaning slightly toward Alyx in expectation.

Alyx's eyes widened. "Oh. I don't think I'm really qualified to teach a group..."

"OMG! You are *so* qualified! I told everyone how I saw you fight and take Jared down, and the others, my friends, would like to learn how to do what you did. You're amazing!"

Alyx took an involuntary step backward, the denial on her lips.

"Please? It would mean a lot to us, if we could put an end to some of the... disrespect that some boys show us."

Alyx sighed, her shoulders lifting and falling heavily, as if bricks pushed down on them. "I guess it would be okay if Sophie comes, too."

"That's great! Thanks, Alyx! See you tonight." Anna flounced away, jubilance in every step.

She turned, glaring at Chase. "What just happened?"

"Don't look at me, I have nothing to do with this." Chase shrugged; his eyes gleaming as he held back the laugh. "But it looks like your fan club is growing."

# CHASE

Chase sauntered out of calculus class, arms full of books as he conversed with the boy—he knew his name was Logan from their brief encounters in previous dimensions, but they hadn't been what you'd call friends, and he hadn't been introduced to him yet here—who sat next to him in class.

"Man, I forgot how hard calc is."

The boy looked at him sharply, actually looking over his shoulder as if to say: are you talking to me? Chase wondered if anyone ever engaged with the timid boy. Logan didn't exactly give off an inviting vibe. Everything about him screamed *leave me alone*. His stance, the lack of eye contact, his slumping posture. It was as if his superpower was invisibility. People could see him, but tended to look right through him, anyway. In answer to Chase's question, he grunted.

Chase wondered if he himself should have made more of an effort to befriend Logan back in his home-world. These past few months of jumping dimensions had altered his perspectives on a lot of things. In all honesty, back then he hadn't spared even a passing thought for Logan, and it somehow made him sad that he'd been what some would call shallow and cliche. The popular, outgoing football player who had enough friends—more than enough. Why should he go out of his way to befriend someone who didn't appear to want any kind of attention? His first time through high school, Chase hadn't been a bully in any sense, but thinking back, it was possible his crime had been a total lack of interest in those around him who weren't directly involved in his sphere of friendship. How many times had he walked past this boy and other lost souls as if they were invisible? How many times had he been oblivious to the look of complete dejection he could now see so clearly on Logan's face? Would a simple acknowledgement in the form of a smile in their direction or a friendly "Hello" have made a difference? Could such a small gesture, one that would cost almost no effort at all, change someone's path, give their confidence a much-needed boost? Chase knew he had no control over his past actions, but acknowledged that with this newfound enlightenment came responsibility.

"Hey, you heading to lunch?" Chase blurted in a belated attempt to somehow change the past. Maybe this kid needed a listening ear—or maybe he didn't. But for some reason at this moment, standing there in the hallway with the very uncomfortable-looking Logan while a crowd of students walking past parted around them like water flowing around a river rock, it seemed imperative that he take this lonely boy under his wing.

Logan nodded, if reluctantly.

"Great! Let me put this stuff in my locker, and I'll meet you in there, okay?" Chase said.

Logan's face turned pale as flour, the color draining from his forehead down as if someone had pulled the plug. "I don't think you want to…"

Chase interrupted. "You'd be doing me a huge favor. I'm the new kid, remember? I'd rather not sit alone at lunch, it gives the wrong impression. I'd owe you, man."

"I guess," Logan mumbled, sweat beading his forehead.

Ten minutes later, Chase surveyed the cafeteria, convinced that Logan was not in the room. *Did he ditch school to get out of sitting with me?*

On his third scan of the room, he spotted Logan in the far back corner. Sitting alone in a hunched posture, trying to blend with the pastel yellow wall behind him. The look of surprise that seized his lackluster features as Chase approached told him that Logan hadn't really expected Chase to eat with him. Chase's frown deepened as he realized Logan had probably thought Chase was just messing with him.

"Hey, Logan. Thanks for saving me a seat." Chase flopped into the chair across from Logan at the rectangular table. "Expecting anyone else?"

Logan's eyes widened, and he drew in a quick breath, exhaling on a wheeze. Pulling an inhaler out of his pocket, he took a puff. "Is that what this is about? You're looking for info about Mason?" Blowing out another purposeful breath, he took a second puff of medicated air from his inhaler. "Just leave me alone, alright?" He reached for his lunch tray and rose from his seat.

"Wait, no I..." Chase stammered. "You're friends with Mason?"

"I'm not an idiot, you know. Just go away." Logan's eyes flamed.

"No. No, I don't think you are. Seriously, man. I didn't know you even knew Mason." Chase held out his hand in a 'wait' gesture.

Logan sank back down. "I don't. I mean, I've known him since kindergarten, but we're not really friends. Sometimes he sits with me at lunch, but he doesn't talk, ya know?"

"Is he doing okay?" Chase asked.

"I don't know, I just told you..."

A familiar voice interrupted, the sound grating like metal against metal. "Well, well. Look who we have here sitting at the loser table. Should have known you two geeks would find each other," Jared taunted, his usual posse snickering in response.

Chase immediately pushed his chair back, the sound of the chair legs scraping along the floor wiping the smirk from Jared's face as Chase lurched to his feet and stood nose to nose with him. "Walk away before I take this to the next level, Loser."

Jared stumbled back a step before he caught himself. "Better not repeat that, or you're dead." Jared squinted with contempt. An audience was slowly forming as all around the room people were noticing a possible fight. Drama drew numbers, and this performance was picking up more subscribers by the second.

Chase moved in slowly until he was in Jared's personal space again. His mocking grin was meant to torment, and it succeeded brilliantly as Jared's face turned magenta. "When are you gonna get it? I'm not afraid of you. Bring it, man."

A quick spurt of fear dilated Jared's pupils, but he was saved from responding by the lunch lady, Patricia. "What's going on here, boys?" She placed a hand on both boys' shoulders, and Chase took a step backward.

"Not a thing. We're fine, ma'am."

Jared recovered his smile. "This new kid, he's been bullying me all week." He turned to Patricia, and his performance was award-worthy as he forced his eyes to go wide and innocent. "He's trying to push me around."

Her head whipped back to Chase, her features condemning. "Is that so? Yeah, I heard you were already causing trouble last week. Even on your first day of school, right? Well, we don't tolerate that kind of bullying at Dune Harbor High. I think you need to have a little chat with the guidance counselor. You're new, so I won't send you to the principal again." She turned back to Jared. "Everybody okay?" The group nodded in unison. She started walking, calling back over her shoulder in Chase's direction, "Follow me."

Chase picked up his tray, dumped the remaining food in the trash bin, and followed.

They approached the counselor's office—the same office from his dream—at a steady pace. Patricia motioned for Chase to sit in one of two second-hand, reupholstered chairs. "I'll go in and explain the situation first, then you can go talk to him."

Chase nodded and sat for what seemed like eons. Finally, the metal door swung open, and the form of a man filled the doorway.

Chase, eyes ever widening, rose slowly from his chair. Shock stilled his limbs. He stood frozen in place. Scanning the counselor from head to toe, his brain could barely register what he suspected to be true.

He knew this man. Or, at least, knew of him.

But it was impossible that this man was standing here, flesh and blood, right in front of him. It rendered Chase speechless. A doppelgänger, maybe? Because what he was thinking was impossible.

He rubbed his eyes, then studied the man again. It had to be him, and it yet couldn't be at the same time.

*Impossible.*

# CHAPTER 16
## *CHASE*

The man gestured Chase into his office. Chase willed his frozen muscles to move. Moving with an uncoordinated gait, he entered the office, typical of what you'd find in any high school. Cinder block walls painted white so long ago they had yellowed with age. Institutional metal desk with paint chipping off the sides. Inspirational posters lined the back wall—'Believe in Yourself' hung perfectly spaced next to 'Dream, Believe, Achieve'—and photos of the man's family sat precisely placed on the bookshelf. A desktop computer—probably ten-years-old—sat closed and off to one side of the desk alongside a multi-line phone. Not a paper was out of place, everything aligned and tidy.

The counselor moved to sit in his chair, again gesturing to the cushioned seat opposite his own.

"So, you're new in town?" he asked.

Chase could only nod, words stuck in his throat.

"What's your name, son?" the man inquired.

"Chase," he mumbled, shaking his head in astonishment.

He didn't actually know this man, and yet as a child he'd memorized every line, every inch of his face. The blue eyes had seemed to jump off the photo, the cowlick over his brow that made his hair look unevenly cut.

"I'm Dr. Walker. I understand you've been having some trouble here? Do you want to talk about it?" He steepled his fingers, leaning forward slightly in a show of interest.

"Dad?" Chase breathed the words, swallowing a lump in his throat.

"I'm sorry? Are you okay, Chase?" Dr. Walker cocked his head in question.

"My name is Chase Walker. If you don't mind me asking: What's your first name?"

"Walker?" The man stood slowly, his brow wrinkling as his eyes lit with, not recognition, but knowledge. "Your surname is Walker? And your name is Chase?"

"Yes, just like yours. I think you may be my father." Chase held up his left arm, the watch casting its cobalt blue glow on his skin. If you looked closely enough, you could see the crimson pulse of his blood beating through the hands of the timepiece.

Upon seeing the watch, Dr. Walker deflated like a balloon losing air, flopping back down into his seat. The chair squeaked and groaned; springs stretched beyond what a second-hand office chair should be capable of handling as he precariously slid backward on equally noisy wheels.

"Chase?" he croaked. "Is it really you, Chase?" Tears filled the elder Walker's eyes—eyes a mirror image of Chase's own sky-blue orbs.

"Yes. But how can this be? We thought you were..." Chase felt light-headed as his father reluctantly nodded. "You are my father, right? Nolan Walker?"

"Yes. We have a lot to catch up on." Nolan Walker ran a shaking hand through his dark blond hair. "I didn't realize you were here. Why are you attending school?"

"I'd say we have a lifetime to catch up on. I don't know you. And it seems you abandoned me by choice. I'd never considered..." Chase cleared his throat, pausing to take a deep breath before continuing. "We, Uncle Charlie and I, always assumed you were dead. And recently, when I learned about the twelve parallel worlds and the secret power of the watches, I'd come to the conclusion that the Hunters must have killed you."

"No, though they did their best, and almost succeeded more than once. But that's another story." Nolan Walker was lost for a moment in the past, his eyes taking on a faraway look before re-focusing on Chase. "Let me just look at you." He stared so long, Chase squirmed under the full intensity of his scrutiny. "You're definitely a Walker, alright. And my Dad? Charlie? How's my brother doing these days? I sure miss having my big brother around."

Chase began shaking his head before his father finished talking. "I'm sorry. Grandpa passed away when I was three-years-old. Uncle Charlie raised me. He died a few months back. Right before my eighteenth birthday. Before I was even aware of the watches' existence." His voice broke as he spoke.

"Died?" His father wearily ran both hands up and down over his face. "Both of them? I've missed so much. Charlie was always so full of life. Seems impossible that he's gone." His eyes sharpened. "The Hunters get to him?"

Chase shook his head. "No. His heart did. He had a heart attack."

Nolan sighed. "I knew when I stayed here, I was giving up the people I loved. It was a choice I made. But now..."

Chase slowly rose to his feet. "Hold up. You're saying you chose to stay in this world? So, you are a keeper. I wondered about that."

"Yes." Nolan nodded curtly. "I'll tell you everything. Come to the house tonight, and we can talk about all of it. I pray that even if you don't agree with my choices, you'll at least come to understand my decisions, my past. We only have the time you're here to make up for a lifetime of missed parentage. I'd like to try. I promise, I'll answer any questions you have."

"But why can't you just tell me now? Haven't I waited long enough?"

"Yes. Yes, you have. But you need to get back to class and I have a meeting in ten minutes. Tonight, we'll be uninterrupted." He scribbled something on a notepad, hastily ripped it off, and held it out to Chase. "Here's my address. Can you be there at seven o'clock?"

Chase grasped the paper in his hand, staring into eyes so like his own. "We'll be there."

"We?"

"Alyx and I. She's a keeper of her family's ancestral watch, too. Her home-world is Dimension 4."

"And you're traveling together? Seems you have a lot to catch me up on, too. See you tonight, son." He placed an awkward hand on Chase's forearm before letting his hand drop to his side.

"See ya." Chase turned, looked back over his shoulder at his newly reborn father, and sauntered out of the room to head to his next class.

# CHAPTER 17
## ALYX

As she stood on the field awaiting the arrival of Annabelle and Sophie, Alyx ran over the conversation she'd had with Chase at the end of the day.

*"Your father's alive?" she'd asked, incredulous eyes nearly popping out of her head.*

*Chase, more serious than usual, nodding. "Yes. And he wants us to come to his house tonight at seven o'clock."*

*Alyx wrung her hands. "Are you one hundred percent sure it was him? It could have been an imposter."*

*Chase's answer was immediate. "Not much room for doubt."*

*"Okay. Let me go tell Anna that I can't make it tonight..."*

*He placed his hands on her shoulders. "No. Just meet me there after. You're meeting her at six?"*

*She nodded.*

*"Then you won't be much later. Keep your plans. And besides, Anna would be heartbroken if you skipped out on her." He winked, his dimples flashing.*

*"Ha-ha. You think you're so cute." She snorted.*

*"I know I am." He leaned in, capturing her mouth in a quick kiss. Her heart fluttered and her brain went numb as it always did when Chase touched her this way, no matter how brief the contact.*

*Reluctantly, she leaned back. "You sure?"*

*"Absolutely."*

Alyx nibbled her bottom lip, still unsure if she'd made the right decision. She'd just have to tell the two girls they had only one hour to complete tonight's training session. Leaving Chase to face this reunion with his long-lost father alone was not an option.

Voices reached her from the far side of the park. Maybe a little league practice session, or group of kids eager to swing or slide on the playground equipment, she mused. She heard laughter and feminine voices. A girls' soccer team?

Her mouth dropped open at the sight of a group of at least ten girls walking toward her through the tree-lined trail leading to the park, Anna leading the group. "Alyx! There's Alyx, over there." She pointed and waved. "Alyx, hi!"

Alyx seriously considered running in the other direction. Her foot actually lifted, ready to jump into action in her hastily formed escape plan. *Knew I should've cancelled.*

Then she reminded herself who she was and rounded her shoulders. If she could handle traveling to twelve worlds and take on hunters out for her blood in each one, she could survive a herd of girls. She'd once decapitated her enemy in hand-to-hand combat, and had even survived her own death when Chase turned back time to alter events in her favor. She'd trained since she was a young girl for battle, and was more than proficient in survival skills. Alyx stood taller, her chin jutting out. *I can do this*, she thought, and mostly meant it.

Alyx stood, hands on her hips, legs spread. She nodded to Anna in acknowledgement, scanning the group of ten girls, noting some familiar faces in the bunch before turning back to Annabelle. She cocked her head, raising a brow.

"A few friends?" She asked.

Roses bloomed on Anna's cheeks as her words tripped over each other. "Um. I'm sorry, Alyx. Really, I am. It started with just Sophie, Ellie, and I; I swear it. And then Sophie was talking to Emily about it, and she told Margo. And then of course *she* had to tell Alana because they're best friends and she didn't want her to feel left out and get mad like the last time when she got her nose pierced and Alana only found out when she saw the nose ring at school like everyone else. She was furious about it and didn't talk to her for days. I mean, they *are* best friends, so I kind of get it. You know how it happens." A nervous giggle escaped, followed by a silence broken only by a few whispers. "I hope it's okay."

Alyx blew out the breath she'd been holding, baffled by the entire conversation. She most definitely did *not* know how something like *that* happened. She turned away from Anna, dismissing her.

"I'm Alyx," she addressed the group. Looking around, she noted the manicured nails, designer shoes, and painted faces. Perfectly coiffed hairstyles. She had absolutely nothing in common with these girls, and yet they were here to learn self-defense from her. She sighed, a bemused expression flitting across her face before speaking: "I know some of you from school. I'm not sure I can help all of you, but I'll start with a question so I can gauge exactly what it is each of you wants to gain from this."

Eyes wide, heads nodded simultaneously, different shades of hair bouncing, and Alyx suppressed a grin. They looked like bobble head dolls on the dashboard of an off-road Jeep speeding across an uneven field, spring-held heads bobbing up and down, up and down. She held her humor in check; however, when she noted their serious expressions, determination gleaming from their pupils.

"Let's start with you." Alyx pointed at a tall red-haired girl, a cluster of freckles high on her cheekbones nearly jumping off her ghost-pale face. "Why are you here?"

"I just..." The girl's downcast eyes hid her emotions, but her slumped posture spoke volumes. "I guess I'd like to be able to defend myself."

"From what?" Alyx asked.

"I..." The girl's eyes darted up then away quickly, the glassiness magnified by the pool of unshed tears she struggled to hold back. Fear surrounded this girl like a cloak.

"It's okay. You don't have to tell us why. As long as you're willing to learn and put in the work. What's your name?" Alyx asked.

"I-I'm Em-Emily." Her pale face transformed as blood rushed upward, going from sheet white to rose red in what seemed like a heartbeat.

"Hi, Emily." Alyx turned toward Sophie. "How about you, Sophie? Why are you here?"

An indignant gleam entered Sophie's eyes. "It doesn't matter why I'm here. I just don't want to rely on someone to save me from... from bad people. That's all you need to know."

"Fair enough," Alyx replied. She addressed the group once again. "Does anyone *want* to share why they came here tonight?"

Crickets sang their nightly song, filling the silence. When Alyx was sure no one would answer, a timid voice rose shakily from the back of the group. "I don't want to be helpless, ever again."

Alyx twisted to see a short girl, probably less than five feet tall, her mocha skin and jet-black hair gleamed in the evening sun. Though her words were timid, her stance was anything but.

"Was there a time you were helpless...?" Alyx asked, raising her brows in question.

"I'm Margo."

"Okay, was there a time you were helpless, Margo?"

Her chin jutted out. "Yes." She looked around. "Just like you, and you. And you. Why can't we all just admit we're all here to learn how to defend ourselves from the same person."

Alyx's gaze sharpened. "Wait. The same person? Did someone hurt you?" She gestured; her arm flung wide. "All of you?"

Annabelle cleared her throat. "I think..." She paused. "Alyx, I think you already know who it is. That's why we're all here tonight. You proved you wouldn't let him harass you. When I saw that someone little like you—no offense—could take him down, then I knew we all could."

"*I* took him down?" Alyx clenched her fists, afraid she knew where this was heading.

Annabelle nodded. "Yes. When you broke his nose."

Alyx's eyes flamed, the violet specks sparkling like July fourth sparklers. "Broke his..." Heat filled her cheeks and she clenched her jaw, flexing the muscles, trying to regain control. "Has Jared... taken advantage of all of you?"

Some heads nodded, others refused to answer. But the silence was damning.

Alyx stiffened her stance. Jared would pay.

"Let's get started then. Next time Jared tries anything, he's in for a big surprise."

# CHAPTER 18
## CHASE

On the front porch of his father's house, Chase raised a hand to knock, only to hesitate, arm dropping to his side. He studied the house, hoping to find a clue in helping him understand the man who lived here. Snow-white siding gleamed, lawn neatly manicured, black shutters bordered every window, an inviting set of rocking chairs sat side-by-side on the porch just begging you to relax and enjoy an after-dinner drink while rocking away the cares of the day. Chase could picture his father doing exactly that after a long day of counseling teenagers. Who sat in the other chair? He wondered. He knew exactly nothing about this man who had fathered him.

So many questions raced through his head—questions he wasn't sure he wanted to know the answers to. One thought kept prevailing. *My own father chose to give me up. He didn't want me.*

Nothing else could compete with that hard truth. He'd loved Uncle Charlie—the man who'd raised him from infancy. The only father he'd ever known, though his uncle had never pretended to be his dad. Honest to a fault, Chase had appreciated being the trusted nephew of a man who treasured great honor and virtue. Oh, sure, at times it had been hard to live up to those high expectations, but Charlie had always accepted him for who he was and never asked him to change. All he asked was that his only nephew look at people with eyes wide open so he could always see each situation from all available perspectives. It was only recently he'd discovered that his uncle had held onto the biggest secret of all. Growing up, Chase had zero knowledge of his family's history of being keepers of magical dimension watches until after his uncle's untimely death. He'd discovered the watch in his uncle's belongings after the funeral, and the watch... well, the watch had called to him, for lack of a better explanation. He'd tried to fight the connection. And then he'd met Alyx, and she'd filled in the rest of the blanks, and his decision had been set. He'd accepted the responsibility of becoming the next keeper of the watch in his bloodline.

In all their years together, Charlie had talked about his brother, Nolan, with an air of grief and sadness. A loved one lost but never forgotten. Not long after Chase had been born, Nolan had disappeared, never to be seen or heard from again. Everyone assumed he'd met a tragic fate, though they'd never found his body. Later, after Chase had been brought up-to-date on his family's ancestry, he'd concluded that just as he was now and his uncle had been when he'd been eighteen, his father had been born to be a keeper of the watch, and hadn't survived his year of dimension jumping.

Now, here he was, no real memory of this man who claimed to be his biological father, and carrying this new knowledge that he had been an unwanted child and an inconvenience to a dad who had found it easy to leave a baby behind, foisting him off on the family he had also chosen to leave.

*Why does it matter? It was eighteen years ago, and I had a good childhood.* A little voice whispered inside him.

Nonetheless, it weighed on him like an anchor pulling him under.

He turned, considered for a moment walking away. This was not part of his purpose in being here in Dimension 9. Did it really matter what his father said, or how he explained being absent from his son's life? All that really mattered was that he hadn't cared enough to stay. A parental truancy, in Chase's opinion, that negated anything the man could do or say at this late date.

Decision made; he'd taken one step off the porch before the front door opened. Expecting to see his father standing there, Chase's eyes went round as instead, a blond teenaged boy filled the doorway. Tousled hair the same shade as his own, of equal height if his guess was correct. The eerie sensation of looking at himself in a mirror overcame him. As he stared into eyes the color of warm cocoa, it startled him to realize that minor difference in color—brown versus his own deep blue—was the major contrast between them. Well, on closer inspection, he noticed the other boy's nose was slightly narrower, his hairline a V-shape instead of his own more rounded one, his build lankier. He had a small pock-like scar just under his left eye.

But first impressions rarely lied, and Chase sank onto the concrete porch step facing the street, his gaze on the deep hues of a painted horizon as the sun began its lazy descent. He needed to sit since he didn't know how much longer his legs would support his own weight, as they'd gone numb when realization struck like a hammer blow to the head. It pounded and pounded, as if the nail was driving deeper and deeper into his brain.

*I have a brother.*

The words felt wrong. Everything he thought he knew was suddenly in question. Was nothing what it seemed? His entire existence? His family? Glancing up, he was taken aback by the look of pure hatred scrunching the younger boy's face, his stance stiff, fists clenched at his sides. If the daggers shooting from his eyes had been real—like the uncontrolled power of Cyclops from the X-Men series—Chase would have been incinerated on the spot. Thank goodness that character was nothing but a work of fiction. Chase frowned. *I think.* He thought he understood this boy's anger, though his own thoughts ran more along the lines of self-pitiable melancholy at the moment.

Chase rose, arm outstretched in an invitation to shake. A peace offering. It wasn't the boy's fault. "Hi. I'm Chase."

The teen looked down his nose because he stood in the elevated doorway, and ignored the gesture. If anything, his scowl intensified, and he stubbornly remained silent.

Chase sighed, letting his arm drop. "Look, I'm just here to talk to Dr. Walker, who I assume is your father. Is he here? He was expecting me."

The boy crossed his arms over his chest and gave one curt nod, making no move to invite him in.

"Corey?" a feminine voice called from within. "Corey, is Chase here?"

A low growl escaped between Corey's clenched teeth, and he pushed past the woman, disappearing back into the house.

An apologetic smile pasted on her face, the woman offered what Corey had not. A greeting. "You must be Chase. Come in, come in." She stepped back, gesturing him inside. "We're so glad to finally meet you. I'm Rose. Your Dad's wife. Can I get you something to drink?"

Chase followed, shaking his head. "No thanks. I'm good."

Rose walked to the bottom of a wide staircase, calling out: "Nolan, Chase is here." She turned back, her head of dark curls bobbed as if on a spring. "We'd hoped this day would come. That you'd come here when you were eighteen and you and your father could reconnect one day. I just can't believe that day is finally here." She swiped a tear from the side of her eye and cleared her voice.

How baffling. This woman seemed to know all about him, and he hadn't even known she existed. A thought took his breath for a moment. "Wait? Who are you? Are we...related?"

"By marriage only." She seemed to understand his unspoken question, and sadness flashed in her eyes. "Your father and I will celebrate our eighteenth anniversary next month." She placed a hand on his arm, her eyes darting to the watch.

"Eighteen years?" He croaked. "Are you my...?"

Giving a small squeeze, she continued. "I'm not your mother, Chase. I'm your stepmom."

"How do you know about my family's heritage?"

"Oh, your father and I don't keep secrets from each other. He told me everything. I've known about you all along."

"But..."

"Chase, you came." Nolan Walker hurried down the stairs, hair damp as if he'd just finished showering. "Come, come. Rose prepared a meal for us to celebrate."

"Celebrate what?"

"Why, our reunion, of course. You have no idea how much I've missed being a part of your life, son."

Chase couldn't hold back the snort. "Seems like the best way to do that would've been to stay in my life in the first place."

His father flinched as if struck. "I'm sorry, Chase. I hope someday you can forgive my decision. I want you to know it was a decision I struggled with then, and it remains a struggle to this day. I'd like to share with you why I made the choices I made. I don't expect you to forgive me, but at least you'll know the whys. Maybe at the least we can get to know each other while you're here. But first, let's eat. After dinner, I'll fill in the blanks the best I can. I owe you that." He gestured for Chase to sit, then glanced behind him. "Didn't you say you were bringing someone along..."

"Yes. Alyx." He glanced at the time. "She'll be here soon."

He nodded toward three extra place settings. "Who else is coming?"

His father and Rose glanced at each other before answering. "Oh, that's Corey's seat, that one's for your friend Alyx, and that's Ellie's seat"

Chase's head was spinning. "Ellie?"

"Your sister, Chase." Nolan smiled.

"You're saying I have a brother... *and* a sister?"

Just then, the front door opened, and Ellie—he remembered her from that day on Main Street by the casinos—entered the kitchen. She'd been humming, but stopped at the dining room entrance. "We have company? Thanks for telling me."

Rose's smile was strained. "Come sit, Ellie. I would have been happy to tell you, if I'd known where you were. You didn't answer my texts."

Ellie pulled her phone out of her pocket and glanced at the screen before replacing it. "Oh, yeah." She shrugged, grabbing a pitcher of water and pouring a glass before slumping into her assigned seat. Her eyes swung to Chase.

"So, who are you?" She asked in a bored tone, raising the glass to her lips.

Everyone began talking at once.

# CHAPTER 19
## ALYX

Alyx sped toward the address Chase had given her, glancing at her watch repeatedly. She despised tardiness. One of the girls had kept her behind with defense questions, and she'd been impressed with her tenacity and vigor to learn as much as she could about self-defense. They'd stayed behind, practicing a particular move.

She picked up her pace to a near-jog, looking again at her watch as she rounded a corner and approached the black and white house. She raced up the front steps, rapping three times on the ebony door.

From inside, someone yelled, "Come in!" She didn't wait for a second invitation, immediately turning the knob.

Alyx entered the house cautiously, eyes searching for only one person and not caring about anything—or anyone—else in the room until Chase was in her sight. Right away she saw the stress etched in lines on his forehead, the tension in the stiffness of his body, but felt a smidgeon of relief as she observed his reaction to her as his features relaxed just slightly. With large strides, she reached his side where he sat at the rectangular dining table and placed a comforting hand on his shoulder. He leaned back into her, lying his own hand on top of hers with a sigh. "Alyx." The heat of his hand seeped into her, filling her with his warm presence and immediately uplifting her in a way that nothing else in all the worlds had the power to do. They were like two pieces of a puzzle, whole only when they were together.

"Alyx?" Another voice interrupted the exchange.

Turning, Alyx's eyes widened when she noticed Ellie—whom she'd just grappled with in an attempt to pass on basic self-preservation less than an hour ago—sitting at the opposite end of the table. "Ellie? Why are you here?"

"I live here. What are you doing here? Did you follow me home?" Ellie giggled. "If you were hungry, all you had to do was ask."

Nolan Walker joined the conversation. "You two know each other? Excellent." He clapped his hands together. "Welcome to our home. I'm Dr. Walker, the guidance counselor at DHH. And this is my family. My wife, Rose. Our daughter, Ellie. And our son, Corey, is...indisposed at the moment. I'm sure he'll be down soon." He glanced toward the staircase, his smile faltering.

Ellie slowly stood. She held up her hands. "Hold up, why is he here?" She turned to speak directly to Chase. "I've seen you around town and in the halls at school. What I can't figure out is why you're here now. Not to be rude or anything..." her voice trailed off. "Your name's Chase, right? Are you *the* Chase?"

Before Chase could answer, Rose stepped toward her daughter. "That's what we wanted to tell you. If you would have answered your phone, you'd know the answer to that question." She sighed, placing a hand on her daughter's arm. "This is your brother, Chase."

"Whoa. The legendary Chase, in the flesh." Ellie studied Chase from hair to toes. "I thought you'd be shorter." She shrugged.

Alyx felt as if she were standing in the middle of a movie set, complete with a dramatic script and long-lost family reunion scene. She raised one brow and looked down questioningly at Chase, who remained seated.

"Yup. Apparently, I have a brother...and a sister." Chase croaked.

Alyx didn't try to contain her surprise as she spoke to Ellie: "You knew about Chase?"

"Dad has always told us about our brother, Chase. But I never thought I'd actually get to meet him. I mean, he seemed more like a fictional character than a real person." Ellie shrugged again.

"You talked about me?" Chase asked, staring intently at Nolan. "Told your kids about me?"

"Yes, of course I did. I'm your dad just as much as I'm Corey's dad or Ellie's dad. I loved you, Chase." Nolan's voice cracked. "I've never stopped loving you."

"Then why? Why did you leave me? Couldn't you take me with you?"

"It wasn't possible. I'll have to start at the beginning, so you can fully understand how it all went down. Will you let me tell you?"

Chase gave one curt nod in answer.

Alyx's protective instincts kicked in and she cleared her throat. "Don't you think it's too late for that? I mean, he's grown up fine without you. Why re-live it if people are going to be hurt by the retelling?"

"I've been waiting eighteen long years to see my first-born son again. Last time I saw him, he was an infant dependent on me for everything. I was prepared to raise him alone, even though I was little more than a child myself. But it all changed when I turned eighteen. I have a need for him to fully understand. Maybe, even if you can't forgive me, you'll look at me with fresh eyes. That's all I can ask." He implored Chase.

Rose returned from the kitchen, aluminum foil in hand. "I'll just wrap this to keep it warm while you talk. It'll keep until after." She winked. "Go on."

Ellie protested. "Hey, I'm hungry! Why do I have to wait?" She grabbed a slice of garlic bread off the plate and took a quick bite.

"You'll be fine, El." Rose rolled her eyes.

Nolan nodded, standing. "We can talk in my office. This way."

Chase followed, Alyx close behind. Rose called out, "Alyx, maybe we should let the two of them talk alone first..."

Chase interrupted, "Alyx stays with me." He reached for her hand, their fingers interlocking naturally.

Alyx smiled at him, proud of him for facing this dysfunctional situation head-on as he always did. This couldn't be easy for him. She squeezed his hand and felt his answering squeeze. Two pieces of a puzzle.

Ellie's voice traveled from the other room. "Don't you think we should be part of this conversation? Hey! I was eating that!" She groused.

"No. Let your father talk to Chase. He'll only be here for two more weeks, so they don't have much time to catch up. This is their time."

Alyx's feet faltered. Only two weeks with his father. Sometimes, life was so unfair.

# CHAPTER 20
## *CHASE*

The office comprised a beige love seat, green wingback chair, and an antique wooden desk with a glass-shade lamp next to a closed laptop. A forest painting adorned one wall, a framed map of Dune Harbor on the other. The day's last rays of sunlight filtered through sheer beige curtains, creating a warm glow in the small room.

Chase and Alyx sat side-by-side on the love seat, while Nolan sat across from them in the wingback.

"I'll start with my seventeenth birthday. That's really when it all began, I guess." Nolan sighed, pinching the bridge of his nose. "I'm not proud of who I was then—I was young and selfish. But it helped shape who I am now, so I think you have to take the good with the bad. Guess that's what life's about, I won't sugar-coat it." He crossed his legs. "It was on my seventeenth birthday that my dad told me about the watches. As you can imagine, I thought he'd lost his marbles. I mean, a magical watch that transports you to different worlds? Sounds ridiculous."

"That part I get." Chase said. "Go on."

"So, my dad tells me all about our heritage, and how we as Walkers have a responsibility to our lineage to become this keeper. To leave our life behind, lose a year of our lives, and for what? At least that was my first thought when he told me. I understand it all a bit better now. But then, I was so angry, my thoughts up and down like a see-saw. Was Dad—your grandfather—crazy, or was any of what he said true? I stormed out of the house, looking for trouble. Lashing out against all the things I couldn't control. I didn't want to be a keeper, or whatever my dad said he wanted me to be. I wanted to stay right where I was, graduate in a year as planned, and get out of this town as quickly as possible." He rubbed his temples. "You see, I hated small town life. Everyone knows everyone, and that's never easy. On top of that, as you know we live in a vacation spot with people visiting from all over the country, expecting to be waited on because they're on holiday. I was tired. Tired of being the local boy. Tired of expectations set for me without my consent."

"I struggled with the same when Alyx told me. When the watch called to me." Chase acknowledged. "I've often wondered why Uncle Charlie didn't tell me about it sooner."

"He probably wanted you to have a normal life. That's what my Pop—your Grandpop—said. At least normal until I turned seventeen." Nolan shrugged.

Chase nodded. "Yes. I've had dreams of Uncle Charlie. Dreams where he communicates with me, and that's what he said. He would have told me on my eighteenth birthday."

"Then believe it. Those are more than dreams you're having." Nolan crossed his legs. "So, anyway, that night I went out and got drunk. I had a friend with an older brother and we talked him into getting us the alcohol. We invited some friends to the beach and drank all night. That night, though I only remember through the fog of an inebriated haze, I met a girl. Christa. Oh, we'd met a few times before, but were essentially strangers. She went to school in the neighboring town, and she was only sixteen, going on seventeen. We created you that night. It wasn't a love match. We were both in need of each other that night, and we filled that need for each other, never expecting or even wanting more. We didn't see each other again until two months later when she told me she was pregnant."

He looked down at his hands, fidgeting in his lap, before continuing. "You can imagine it was a shock. At first, I was bitter, thought my life was ruined. I told you I was selfish back then. I railed against one more thing I couldn't control. I was a junior in high school, she was a freshman." His eyes implored Chase to understand. "Despite that, we wanted you. Decided to keep you, do our best by you. Her family was horrified. Mine was furious. At first, anyway. But as you grew inside her..." Nolan's eyes filled. "Something changed. You became less a responsibility and became more real to me. It seemed impossible that Christa and I, in a meaningless night of drunken passion, had created a life. I remember when I first felt you kick inside your mother's womb. Indescribable. I was just a kid, but I loved you. Even before you were born. I still mourned the loss of my youth, all the things I'd miss out on—the selfishness didn't disappear. But still, I also wanted to be your Dad. It didn't matter that your mother and I were little more than strangers, two kids that had slept together one night. You were a part of me. *Are* a part of me."

Nolan cleared his throat. "The night you were born, I was allowed in the delivery room. It was a long delivery. You were breech, and they had to perform an emergency c-section. They quickly escorted me to the waiting room. Things went bad quickly. Apparently, Christa had a rare, pre-existing condition called Brugada Syndrome that I wasn't aware of. I told you we were practically strangers. There was a lot we didn't know about each other. During labor, she had a heart attack. Hard to believe someone so young could have a heart attack. Your mother died in childbirth, Chase. Her family couldn't deal with a baby through their grief, so they didn't fight my rights as your dad to take custody. I brought you home to the townhouse where I lived with my brother Charlie and my dad. That was three months before my eighteenth birthday."

"My mother died the night I was born? I didn't know..."

"I'm sorry, son. Dad, Charlie, and I realized real quick that you were born to be a keeper. Your birthdate matched the magical dates, so how could it be otherwise? I remember feeling sorry for you, that you would have to carry on that burden, same as me."

"It's not so bad." Chase reached for Alyx's hand.

"I can see that. Seems you two have something special going on between you. I'm glad for you. But I'm also glad that because of it, maybe you'll understand a little better why I ultimately made the choice I made."

He got up, walked to the window. "I did the best I could, juggling school and being a dad. I dropped out of sports. We concocted this story that I was interning overseas—the same story we had used for Charlie two years before when he'd been gone for a year, though at the time I didn't know it was a farce—to explain my upcoming absence. I trained in combat, but my goal was to avoid the hunters at all costs." He turned from the window. "I'm no fighter, and we all knew who would win in any kind of confrontation. So, I turned eighteen, and the watch was activated as we all knew it would be. I gave you a kiss and placed it on my wrist, and the coupling began. The last words I said to you before traveling to Dimension 7 on the scheduled date were: See you in a year, big guy. The words were true when I spoke them. I swear it. I intended to come back to you, and you understand there was no way I could take a baby with me to travel the twelve dimensions. The unknown. I wasn't even sure I'd survive it alone. No, you were much safer staying with Dad and Charlie."

"I guess that makes sense." Chase frowned. He couldn't imagine being a dad at seventeen, let alone taking an infant child along with him across dimensional planes.

"So, I jumped. And jumped again. And again. The night I first traveled to this world, Dimension 9, I was in agony. All jumps carry the burden of pain, but this one was particularly painful. When I was starting to get my bearings, the first thing I saw was a girl leaning over me, long dark hair hanging like a curtain around her, eyes like brown sugar. The most beautiful girl in all the worlds. She'd seen the jump. Watched as I materialized in front of her, and even through her fear, she was only concerned with helping me. Unconcerned for herself, only wanting to help others. That's my Rose."

"Rose? You mean your wife, Rose?"

Nolan nodded. "Yes, that was the beginning. I told her everything. I mean, she had *seen* it, so I rationalized it was okay to share our secrets. She marveled at my blood flowing through the watch, and the way it was embedded in my skin, a true part of me until my nineteenth birthday. From that day forward, we were inseparable for the entire month. That kind of love only comes along once in a lifetime. You two know what I'm talking about, I can see it."

Alyx blushed, and Chase smiled. "Yes."

Nolan nodded. "I told Rose all about you. How you cooed and smiled, how your eyes were the exact shade of blue as my own, the hair that was just beginning to curl at your nape. We knew we'd have our romance, and I'd have to leave, but we didn't want to talk about it. I tried to find a way to have you both, but couldn't figure out how. At the end of that month, my heart was ripped from my chest during the transition to a new parallel world. I staggered through the rest of the worlds in a fog, only existing, but knowing I had something to live for at the end. You. I couldn't be with Rose, but I still had you. You're what kept me alive and sane through the rest of the jumps, and right up to the end I was planning to return to you, thinking I'd never see my Rose again. But on the cusp of the very last scheduled jump, the one that would free me from being a keeper forever, my last thought was of Rose, and what she was doing in that moment at home in Dimension 9. I didn't know that my thoughts would take me there instead of home to you in Dimension 6. By thinking of Rose at that moment, I'd made my choice to live out the remainder of my years in Dimension 9 with her. It wasn't a conscious choice I made, Chase. I'm sorry. I'm so sorry it happened the way it did. I had no way of contacting my family at home, no way to cross parallel planes to communicate that I was okay. The watch made the last journey home to Dimension 6 alone, and I was here, with no means of getting to you. I knew my father and brother—you—would live with the pain of never knowing what had become of me. I knew they would likely think I hadn't survived my year of jumping." He gazed out the window, not seeing the curtains and panes of glass, but something from a faraway time and place. "A man should never have to choose between being with his child or the woman he loves. Being a keeper was both my curse and my salvation. You wouldn't exist if I hadn't lashed out that night, fighting my birthright. And I never would have met Rose if I hadn't had the ability to travel to her world. It's a catch-22. Thinking about it too much just brings more pain, and never a more acceptable outcome. But I can't live on only regrets, because I love my Rose and she loves me. I love Corey and Ellie, too. All I can tell you is I'm sorry. I wish I had been there for you. I was there, in spirit. You've never been far from my thoughts. I hope, someday, you can forgive me. If only we had more time."

Chase swiped at a tear that zig-zagged a path down his cheek. He sat frozen for a full minute that ticked agonizingly by. No one spoke. He swiped at another tear, then slowly stood and took one step closer to Nolan. Nolan Walker also stood, staring at his first-born son, waiting.

Finally, Chase broke the silence. "It's not your fault. None of it is your fault. How can I blame you when it wasn't even a conscious choice you made? How can I blame you for falling in love? I've had a good life. I loved Uncle Charlie, and he loved me like a son. Grandpa, too, though he passed away when I was only three-years-old. If it's forgiveness you want, I can give you that much."

The two men embraced, then stepped back to look at each other. "Thank you," Nolan whispered. "Thank you, son."

Chase reached for Alyx, and she melted into his arms. Clearing her throat, she leaned back. "I'm starved. And we need to get back to Bo soon, or he'll tear the hotel room apart."

Nolan, who'd been walking toward the door, stopped. "Bo? Who's Bo?"

Chase smiled. "Oh, no big deal. He's just a chimera hybrid we brought along with us from Dimension 8."

"A...what?" Nolan gasped. "You brought something with you from another world? How can that...?" His eyes widened. "Did you say chimera hybrid?"

"Yep. Seems we have a lot to tell you, too."

Alyx tugged his hand. "Let's tell our story over dinner."

"Deal." The trio emerged from the office; smiles pasted on their faces. Rose looked anxiously toward them, and her entire body visibly relaxed as relief seemed to flood through her. "So, you had a good talk?"

Nolan and Chase looked at each other before answering.

"We're good." Chase said, causing Nolan's eyes to fill again. "Let's eat. After dinner, we'll introduce you to our chimera."

Rose cocked her head. "What's a chimera?"

Chase, Nolan, and Alyx burst into a fit of laughter. "We'll tell you while we eat."

# CHAPTER 21
## *ALYX*

Alyx sat back, stomach full of the best lasagna she'd ever eaten. Rose could cook, she'd give her that.

Nolan pushed back from the table. "Now, I'd like to meet Bo if you don't mind. Where are you staying?"

"At the Happy Home Hotel." Chase was loading his plate with his third helping.

Rose gasped. "A hotel? No. You'll come stay with us for the rest of your time here. You can stay in Nolan's office. We have blow-up camping airbeds you can use. They're actually pretty comfortable."

"Oh." Alyx searched out Chase, meeting his eyes.

Chase spoke to Nolan. "Are you sure? I don't want to cause problems. I mean, Corey may not like it if..."

Nolan held up a hand. "He'll be fine. I'll go talk to him. Please, I'd love for you to stay here."

Ellie snorted. "Corey never gets over anything. But *I* think it's a great idea! Alyx, if you live here, we can walk to school together." She beamed.

"Uh. Okay, I guess," Alyx said, brow wrinkling.

"I'll come along and help you pack." Nolan stood.

Chase shook his head. "We don't need help, thanks. Maybe this is a good time to have that talk with Corey. We'll go get our things and be back within the hour."

Alyx felt his hand on her back, guiding her toward the door.

Rose's face glowed, her smile so bright it seemed to lighten the room. "Excellent. I'll have the beds set up in no time. I'm so happy you're here."

•  •  •

At the hotel, Bo leapt at them, tail swishing, tongue licking. He bounced on his lanky hind legs in a fit of excitement, tiny whimpers of joy escaping as he jumped.

"Think he's happy to see us?" Alyx smiled.

"That's the understatement of the year," Chase answered. "You sure you're okay with this?"

She sighed. "Yes. I mean, I'd rather stay here where we have some privacy—someplace to get away from all the people. But it makes sense, and I want you to spend as much time as you can with Nolan before we have to leave. I'm just worried about Ellie and Corey."

"I don't think you need to worry about Ellie, and hopefully Corey will come around. C'mon. Let's get packed."

When they had everything they owned, at least for this year, packed into their backpacks, they turned to look back over the room, making sure nothing was forgotten. This had been their home since they'd arrived here in this world. They had also stayed in this very hotel during their last jump in Dimension 8. It surprised Alyx to realize she would actually miss the dingy hotel room with its paper-thin walls. Someone had temporarily boarded the hole in the window with cardboard and duct tape, so at least the room was protected from the elements.

She turned. "Let's go."

Chase walked over to her. "Wait. One more thing..." He reached for her, gently guiding her body into his. A perfect fit, every time. Puzzle pieces. She sighed into the kiss, leaning in as it deepened, little tingles dancing throughout her body. Her mind wandered to the younger versions of Rose and Nolan. She was glad for them. Glad that they had found each other, happy to see a love story with a happy ending. But she was sorry for Chase and Nolan and the years they had lost...and the years to come where they couldn't make up for lost time. She wanted to do something, help in some way, but was as powerless as Nolan had been to change the way dimension travel worked.

Chase turned his head, taking the kiss even further. She felt his arms tighten around her, and suddenly she wasn't thinking about Nolan and Rose. It was only Chase. Chase holding her, Chase wanting her. It was always Chase.

# CHAPTER 22
## *CHASE*

As they approached his father's house, Chase saw that Nolan Walker was sitting in the rocker on the porch, illuminated by the lantern-style porch light. He stood when he saw them, indicating he'd been waiting for them.

"I guess I half expected you to disappear." His eyes were misty. "Bo, is it?" he asked, eyes on the pup. He squatted; hand held out.

Bo wagged his tail, glancing up at Chase.

"It's okay, Bo. He's my dad." Chase swallowed past the lump in his throat. He'd once thought he would never have the opportunity to speak those three words. Emotional moment lost on the animal; Bo wagged his entire body as he strained at the leash toward Nolan.

Nolan chuckled. "Cute little guy." He cocked his head, studying the creature. "He had wings, you say?"

"Yes, they were just forming, not fully grown yet. When we jumped here, they just...disappeared." Chase shrugged. "I guess because there's no magic here."

His father's eyes met his. "Oh, make no mistake. Magic is everywhere."

Chase's eyes narrowed. "What do you mean?"

"Magic resides in all the parallel worlds. In some places it's just...more muted than others, I guess you could say." He gestured toward Chase's watch, so much a part of him. "You wouldn't be here if this world was completely free of magic."

"But we don't have the ability to use it here. In Dimension 8, I could perform spells..."

"Yes. Magic is particularly strong there. Here, it's more dormant, for lack of a better description. But believe me, it's there. I once thought I could tap into it to get back to you, but never could figure out a way to do it. And then, when Ellie was born, I didn't know if I could leave, even if I figured it out. Impossible to have to choose between two of your children..." He took a deep breath. "Well, that's all in the past. Let's not use the little time we have together for regrets." Nolan had been scratching Bo, and a near-purring sound rumbled in his chest. Bo rolled so all four legs were in the air, scratching his back on the cement, his body curving this way than that way. "He's a happy little guy, isn't he?"

"Most of the time. But he has suffered significant losses in his young life. He seems to have attached himself to us." Chase smiled down at Bo. "We don't mind. He grows on you. Don't you, boy?" Bo looked up at Chase with adoring eyes, his tail swinging an ecstatic circle in the air.

"I wonder what will happen to him at the end of your travels." Nolan asked.

"I thought he'd just stay with me, I guess." Chase shrugged. "There's no way to get him back to his home-world and, even if I could, he wouldn't have anyone to go back to."

"He'd have his wings again, and magic." Alyx interjected.

Chase looked at her sharply. "But he'd be alone." He hunkered down, and Bo bounded up to place frantic licks all over his chin. "I think if we could ask him, he'd choose to stay with us. Right, big guy?"

"Maybe he wants to live with me in Dimension 4. What do you think about that?" Alyx smirked when Bo jumped into her arms.

Nolan stood slowly. "I hadn't thought." A stricken look slackened his features. "There's been so much going on, so much to process. It hadn't occurred to me that you two may not be together at the end of this. Unless one of you chooses to give up your home, you'll both go back to your separate home-worlds and..." He placed a hand on Chase's shoulder. "I've been focusing on only my own sacrifices, not thinking about what you'll be giving up. It's like Rose and I all over again, only..." Anger contorted his face. "I'm so sorry, son. If I could change things, I would make it so our family never carried this burden."

Chase looked at Alyx, and their eyes communicated their fears. "We haven't really talked much about it..."

Just then, the door opened, and Rose came out, interrupting the melancholy mood. "Oh, my goodness!" She practically flew to where they stood. "What a cute little fella." While she fussed over Bo in a blur of fur and lip-sticked kisses, Chase reached for Alyx's hand, and she clasped his like a lifeline.

Rose came slowly out of her puppy high, went to Chase, and placed a motherly kiss on his cheek. "Chase, I'm so happy that you've given your father a chance. I've seen and shared his pain over losing you in so many ways over the years. I'm sorry for the part I played in making that happen. If Nolan had never fallen in love with me…" Her eyes clouded, even just the thought of not having Nolan in her life was enough to cause her grief. She took a steadying breath. "The guilt has been tremendous, and you've come here and lifted a mountainous burden just by your kind act of forgiveness. I want you to know I'm proud to be your stepmom." A tear trickled down her cheek and she quickly swiped it away. "Now, come. I've made up the office for you. Please let me know if you need anything. Anything at all." She disappeared into the house, and the trio—along with Bo—followed.

Chase and Alex entered the room, which had miraculously transformed into a bedroom in the short time they were gone. Airbeds, one on either end of the room—he noticed she'd split them up for sleeping—were made with matching navy blue and green plaid checkered sheets and pillows. An end table was next to one bed, brass table lamp softly illuminating the space and likely borrowed from one of the other rooms in the house. The computer and various office supplies had disappeared from on top of the desk, which was now pushed back along the back wall of the room to make space for the beds.

"I thought you might need the desk space for homework or something. You can use it for whatever you want." Rose smiled. "I want you to feel at home here, so let us know if there's anything you need. And you don't need to worry that anyone will come in here. We understand a need for privacy. This room is yours while you're here."

Chase nodded. "Thank you."

Alyx seconded the sentiment while Bo sniffed every corner of the room, tail held high in the air but still fluttering in excitement. He flopped onto one of the airbeds, then looked up at the group of people with a canine grin, his tail picking up speed.

"I think Bo likes it here." Alyx laughed, and everyone followed suit.

"Well. We'll let you have some of that privacy now. If you need anything at all…" Rose turned to leave, Nolan following.

"Wait." Chase called out, stopping them in their tracks.

Nolan turned, brow raised.

"Have you talked to Corey about all of this?" Chase asked.

Nolan nodded. "Yes. He'll come around, Chase. He's always known about you, but I think now that you're here, now that you're real to him, he might be a little jealous of the thought of you. I'm sure once he gets to know you a bit…"

"That's just the thing. I don't think we have time for us to get to know each other."

"Well, I'm sure you'll do the best you can in the time you're here. Don't worry about Corey, Chase. He's a good kid. He'll be fine." Nolan winked.

"If you say so." Chase hesitated. Lifted his hand, let it fall to his side. He opened his mouth, then closed it. "I'm not sure I can give you what you need, either. We're strangers." Taking a deep breath, he forged on. "But I want you to know I'm thankful. Thankful to understand what happened all those years ago, and thankful that you're welcoming me into your home as if we haven't lived separate lives up 'til now."

Nolan cleared his throat, nodded as his eyes brimmed with liquid, and gently pulled the door closed, Rose following closely behind.

# CHAPTER 23
## *CHASE*

Breakfast had been awkward, to say the least. Standing naked in full view of a packed classroom while singing a solo of the national anthem would be less unnerving than sharing a meal—if you could call it that—with his little brother.

Corey wasn't as willing to build a relationship with his long-lost big brother as everyone had hoped. His father's prediction that he would 'come around' was looking less and less likely by the minute. He'd marched down the stairs, acting as if he didn't even see Chase, or Alyx for that matter. He grabbed an apple from the wooden bowl centered perfectly in the middle of the table and took a bite. Between chews, he glared at his father and ignored his mother's forced cheeriness as she all but sang 'good morning.'

Ellie had smirked. "Told ya so." She grabbed two apples from the bowl, tossing one to Alyx, who caught it in mid-air without even blinking.

Chase threw an arm around her shoulders, beaming. Always at the ready, his Alyx. *That's my girl*, he thought, just before his sister turned to him. "Morning, big bro." Ellie winked on her way out the door and patted his cheek, calling over her shoulder: "Alyx, you coming?"

Alyx's eyes implored him, but in the end, she'd followed behind Ellie. After they'd gone, silence cloaked the kitchen for a full minute that ticked by as if an hour passed instead of a mere sixty seconds.

Finally, Nolan cleared his throat. "Sorry, Chase. I don't know what's gotten into him. I talked to him last night. I think he's just going through a phase..." He scratched his head, before repeating words that were becoming repetitive. "He'll come around."

Chase shrugged. "Uh, huh." He finished the cereal he'd been eating, rinsed his bowl, and placed it in the dishwasher. "So, what's the story?"

"The story?" Nolan asked.

"Yeah. Like what do we say when people ask us why I'm living with you?"

"Oh. Yes, I guess we need to match our stories." He stood. "I think sticking to the truth, or as close to it as we can, is the best bet."

Chase's mouth dropped open. "So, you think telling them that you're my dad, and you come from another dimension and so do I, and I'm only here until October tenth because I'll be jumping to the next world on that date—is the best bet?"

"No, of course not. We'll tell them you're my son who I just found out about—sorry about that fib—recently, and I invited you to live with me so we could get to know each other better. That much is true. I've always found that the closer to the truth a fib is, the more believable."

"Okay. So, how will you explain my absence when I leave?"

"I'll have plenty of time to think about that after you're gone." Nolan frowned. "By the way, how *did* you enroll in school without the proper credentials, anyway?"

"Well, we may have 'fibbed' a bit." Chase used his father's words. "I was sure we'd be kicked out of school any day now when none of our manuscripts from previous schools can be found. Checking our backgrounds must not be a top priority. I'm amazed we've gotten away with it this long. But now we have the perfect solution. Staying with you should solve that problem."

Nolan nodded. "Don't worry about it. I'll take care of everything on that end. Need a lift to school?" He took his keys off the wall hook.

"Sure." Chase grabbed his backpack on the way to the door.

"You're the only one of my children who is okay with being seen with me at the high school. It's nice."

Chase met his father's eyes. "I figure I only have a short time to be embarrassed by you. We have to make up for lost time."

His Dad barked out a laugh while jovially pounding him on the back. "That we do, Chase. That we do."

• • •

After first period, Chase spotted a hunched figure slinking by. He slammed his locker, rushing to catch up. "Hey, Logan. Wait up."

Logan glanced his way, a slight nod, his only acknowledgment.

"Do you know when Mason is coming back to school?" Chase asked.

"I told you, I'm not really friends with Mason." Logan swiped an arm across his oily forehead.

"I just thought maybe you'd heard something."

Logan's eyes darted left, right, then back down at his shoes. He fidgeted with the strap on his backpack. "I'm surprised you haven't heard. He's back today."

Chase raced off, calling over his shoulder, "Thanks, man. See ya at lunch. Save me a seat, okay?"

Logan's face heated, turning red as a beet, before shuffling off in the opposite direction.

He spotted Mason fumbling with his locker and approached from the side. "Hey, Mason. How are you?" Chase asked.

Mason's head shot up, a blank look on his face. It took a few seconds for recognition to dance across his face, followed by a lightning quick burst of anger. "Leave me alone," he growled, turning to go.

Chase blocked his exit. "Wait. Mason, I just want to make sure you're alright."

"What do you care?" Mason spat.

"I just feel a certain, I don't know, responsibility to you after the bridge."

"Well, don't. You think you're a hero or something? You didn't do me any favors when you stopped me. You shoulda just let me jump." This time, Mason pushed past Chase, who had no choice but to let him go. Glancing at his watch, he got lost for a moment in the cobalt glow, the hexagonal shape of the watch face, the mercury-like silver shine. He didn't think the feeling of awe would ever leave him, even after he'd worn the thing for the entire year. A tingle spread up his limbs just as someone grabbed his hair from behind, yanking his head backward. The fire in his scalp only intensified when the person tightened his grip.

"Well, well. Watcha doin', loser?" Jared's laughter crawled like spiders across his skin.

"Don't you ever get tired of this?" Chase sneered. He doubled over and walked his body backward at the same time, causing his captor to lose his hold on Chase's hair.

"Tired of what?" Jared whined, his anger at losing the upper hand apparent in his tone.

Chase now stood toe-to-toe with Jared. "Pushing people around?" He paused. "Or maybe it's the only way you can get people to pay attention to you. It's sad, really. I feel sorry for you."

Jared's face contorted just before he forcefully shoved Chase back. Chase stumbled backward two awkward steps before righting himself.

Chase's smile taunted. "See, that's exactly what I'm talking about."

Fighting an internal battle, Jared regained his composure, though hatred shone out of his eyes like laser beams. "Heard you had to go to the principal last time. Have a good time there?" The two lackeys standing behind Jared snickered.

"Actually, I got sent to my dad's office. Not so bad, we had a good chat." Chase answered.

"Your Dad?" Jared took the bait.

"Yeah. Dr. Walker. He's my old man. Hadn't you heard?" Chase placed a hand on Jared's shoulder. "I'm going to tell him everything about you. Your days of ruling this school and terrorizing everyone in it are over." He squeezed Jared's shoulder before he could back away, and leaned close to his ear so only he could hear his words. "I'll give you one chance to change your ways. Everyone deserves a second chance, even you. But if I see you bullying anyone, I mean anyone, I'm coming for you." Chase sauntered off, calling over his shoulder, "Have a good day."

Jared sneered, his face a splotchy red, and pushed past his posse to slam into the nearest bathroom. Chase looked up in time to see his half-brother, Corey, standing off to the side. Had he been there the whole time? Chase balked. Was his brother with Jared? No, he must have just been passing by. He was a freshman. Why would a freshman be hanging around with a senior? Chase shook his head. Must have just been passing by and stopped to watch the scene. High school students were like that. The first sign of drama, especially of the physical kind, always drew a crowd.

Corey's animosity shone through his eyes as they made brief eye contact before the boy turned and stomped away.

Chase sighed, pushing his hand through his hair. He didn't want to have a volatile relationship with his only brother in the short time he was here, but wasn't sure what he could do to fix it. He scooped up his backpack from the floor and wandered toward his next class, deep in thought.

Chase didn't think about Jared again until lunchtime, when he caused yet another scene.

# CHAPTER 24
## *ALYX*

Sitting hunched over her desk, head propped up by her hand, Alyx fought her ever-fluttering eyelids to stay awake. The droning voice of her teacher was like white noise, and her eyes fought to close even as she forcefully held them open. Finally, she raised her hand.

"Can I have a bathroom pass?" She asked, even as she balked at having to ask the question. Why can't people just go to the bathroom when they have to? It galled her that she had to have permission for a basic human need. Once the pass was in hand, she rushed from the room. She needed to splash cold water on her face to snap out of the lethargy that seemed to be taking over her body.

Pushing into the restroom, she immediately heard sniffling. Unsure what to do, she continued to the stall next to the one with sneakered feet showing under the stall door. As she finished, the sniffles turned to hiccups, then more sniveling and nose-blowing. Taking a deep breath, Alyx decided talking might help.

"Hello? I couldn't help but notice that you sound pretty upset over there. Is there anything I can do to help you?" Alyx asked.

More blubbering ensued. "No. I-I'm f-fine."

"I don't want to be rude, but it doesn't sound like you're fine. Are you sure I can't help?"

"No. No one can help. My life is over." Alyx had to strain to hear the near-whisper from behind the stall door.

"Your life isn't over. Nothing can be that bad. Why don't you come out, and I'll..." Alyx paused. What would she do? She placed her hand on the outside of the metal door. "I'd like to help you. Somehow. I'm not sure how. If you come out and tell me what's wrong, maybe we can work together to find a solution."

The sound of nose-blowing, long and drawn out, echoed in the small room. Finally, just as Alyx was about to give up, the toilet flushed. The sound of the bolt sliding back as the girl slid it home had Alyx smiling. *Not so bad at this 'friend' thing after all, am I?*

When the door swung out, Alyx's eyes widened. Under the red, blotchy skin, free of makeup that had likely been washed away by the flow of tears down her cheeks, she recognized Margo from her self-defense group. "Margo? Did something happen to you?"

The girl hung her head, her brown hair hiding her face like a veil. Margo glanced up furtively as tears fell out of red-rimmed eyes faster than she could wipe them away. "Oh, Alyx. I-I don't want you t-to see me like this. You must think I'm so w-weak."

"I don't think you're weak. Crying doesn't make someone weak. Looks to me like you made it to school today, despite whatever upset you. That seems pretty brave if you ask me." Alyx lifted her hand, then let it drop, unsure of what to do. She only knew she had to do *something*.

"I'm not brave. If I were, I wouldn't be in this situation," Margo rasped.

"Do you want to talk about it?" Alyx asked. "I'd like to help if…"

Margo shook her head, sending her hair to swinging. "I'm sorry," she whispered as she flew from the room.

Alyx called after her too late, "Wait, I…" She found herself talking to an empty bathroom. When she pushed out the door to follow, Margo was gone. Alyx paced to the right, then back again, hands on her hips, unsure what to do next. Spotting Ellie down the hall, she sped up to catch her. "Ellie," she called out.

Ellie spun around, smiled. "Alyx." She cocked her head. "Everything alright?"

"I'm not sure. Have you seen Margo?"

Ellie shook her head. "No, not since our training last night. Why?"

Alyx hesitated. It felt like she was betraying a confidence, but what else was she supposed to do? The girl was obviously in distress. She couldn't stand by and do nothing.

"I saw her in the bathroom just now, and she seemed really upset about something."

Ellie frowned. "No, I haven't seen her." She shrugged. "Maybe she got a B on the English test. She takes her education very seriously. I don't think she's ever gotten less than an 'A' on anything in her life." Laughing, she gestured. "C'mon. Let's go or we'll be late for class."

Alyx touched Ellie's arm. "No. I don't think that was it. She was distraught. I feel like I should do something to help her, I just don't know what."

Ellie shrugged. "We could talk to Dad about it. He might know what to do. Though I doubt Margo will thank you for it."

Alyx nodded. "Maybe that's what I need to do. I'll think about it, and maybe talk to him later."

"And besides, we'll see Margo tonight at the next training session at the park." Ellie added.

Alyx nodded. "I'd forgotten about that. I'll get a feel for how she's doing tonight, and then we can decide what to do."

# CHAPTER 25
## *CHASE*

Mason was already sitting at the lunch table with Logan, though he sat in the chair furthest from the other boy and didn't offer conversation. In fact, the look on his face suggested a desire to distance himself from those not only sitting at his table, but the entire senior class as well. As the two sat in complete silence, ignoring each other, Chase hunkered down into the seat right next to Mason. "Hey."

Logan grunted, and Mason acted as if he were invisible.

"So, what's up?" Chase asked, munching on shepherd's pie loaded with mixed vegetables. He continued, unfazed, when neither boy acknowledged his question. "Well, I've had an interesting couple of days. First, I found out my dad actually works at this school."

This sparked mild interest from Logan, but Mason studied his dinner roll with great intensity, as if it was the king of breads and had just won first prize in a 'Roll of the Year' contest.

"What, you're not even gonna ask? You mean you're not consumed with curiosity about who my dear ol' dad is?"

Logan made brief eye contact and cocked his head in question, but remained silent. Mason continued on, acting as though he didn't hear a word Chase said.

"Wow, anyone ever tell you two that you're great conversationalists? Okay, okay, quit pulling my leg. I'll tell you. My Dad is Dr. Walker, the guidance counselor."

"Dr. Walker?" Logan finally spoke, unable to remain silent with this new piece of news. "Wait, did you say you just found out?"

Chase nodded. "Yep."

"You mean you didn't know before?" Logan asked.

"Nope."

Logan leaned back in his chair. "Wow."

"You got that right."

"So, how did you find out, then?" Logan asked.

Chase thought fast. "Well, my Mom just told me. I thought my father was dead until yesterday. Guess they were really young and had a one-night fling, and here I am. Friends with benefits."

"Whoa." Logan's eyes went wide. "Sucks."

"Yep."

Mason, though still acting detached from the conversation, tipped his head slightly in their direction as if listening, but clearly not wanting anyone to know it.

"So, I had another confrontation with our friend Jared this morning. What's his deal, anyway?"

Mason visibly flinched at the name. He immediately picked up his lunch tray and fled the table as if the police were on his tail.

"Mason, wait." Chase called after him.

"Just let him go. It has to be weird coming back to school with everyone knowing..." Logan trailed off.

"Knowing what?" Chase asked.

"You know. That he tried to off himself and failed," Logan murmured.

Chase gave one quick nod as he considered his answer. "Yeah, I do know. I was there."

"What?"

"I was there that day on the bridge. I'm the one who stopped him. That's why he hates me."

"Whoa." Logan repeated.

"Yeah. But he shouldn't be embarrassed about it. It was a cry for help, if you ask me. Shouldn't we be trying to help him, instead of treating him like he's the ground zero carrier of a new pandemic? I mean, depression isn't contagious or anything. What are people afraid of?" Chase mused.

Logan hesitated before speaking. "Don't think it's that simple. I mean, it's hard being the loser of your school, you know?"

Chase flinched. He didn't know. But he was trying to understand things from the other side. "I want to understand, but..." his words trailed off. "I'm going to find him." Chase stood, tray in hand, scanning the cafeteria.

Logan said something, and Chase had to strain to hear over the noise of a hundred voices talking at the same time. "What?"

"He likes to go to the library to get away from..."

"Get away from what?"

"Nothing. Just try the library, okay?"

"Thanks, man."

Logan dismissed him, looking down at his tray of food, pushing the remaining shepherd's pie, gravy already beginning the congealing process, around on his plate as if deciding whether it was worth another bite.

Chase left the cafeteria and headed toward the library. It was a nice fall day, and since the fastest path to the library was an outdoor walkway, he pushed out the front door. Tilting his head up toward the sun, he basked for a moment in the radiating warmth that spread slowly from his scalp and moved downward to heat his face. A cacophony of autumnal colors filled his view, and he kicked at the colored leaves at his feet that the landscaping crew would soon need to remove. Taking a deep breath, he breathed the musty scent that accompanied the season, while at the same time yearning for the salty aroma of the beach. Maybe he and Alyx could take the time for a beach day this weekend if the weather held...

Movement off to the side interrupted his reverie, and Chase turned to see a small group of boys standing at the far end of the L-shaped building. He heard taunting voices with occasional laughter interspersed and jogged closer for a better view.

As he approached, the first thing he noticed was his half-brother, Corey, standing at the edge of the circle of maybe six to eight people. Corey's head whipped up, and the newfound brothers looked at each other before Corey looked away. For once, the usual hatred missing from his expression and replaced by...was it embarrassment?

Chase pushed through, gasped when he saw Jared and Mason in the center of the group, Mason on his knees with Jared forcefully shoving something into the other boy's mouth. The thing in Jared's hand came into focus, and a surge of pure fury momentarily blinded Chase. A urinal cake.

When Jared saw Chase, he let go of Mason, who fell to his knees gagging, urinal cake expelled. The shepherd's pie Mason had just eaten erupted out of him, covering the grass and his hands. The putrid smell intermixed with the acidic and overwhelming smell of urine. His face was blotchy with patches of red as tears slid silently down the side of his face. Remaining on all fours like an animal, his head hung in utter defeat.

"Hey!" Chase went on instinct, bulldozing his way toward Jared, intent on one thing: stopping him. He never made it. Hands reached for Chase, grabbing his arms to hold him back. He fought, bucking and kicking, but more hands gripped his arms and even the back of his shirt, and he was powerless to go further. A primitive growl rumbled in his throat.

"What, you thought you'd be his savior? Don't bother, this one's as good as gone." Jared sneered. "But it seems I've got you where I've been dreaming of having you. No way out now, is there, Loser?" He stepped forward, throwing a fist into Chase's face. As Chase rebounded, Jared spewed saliva into his eyes, spittle dotting his cheeks.

Chase growled; the actions meant to cow him, only stoking the fire of his temper. He doubled his efforts to free himself from the grasp of Jared's minions. "What?" he spat, missing his target, who backed up just in time. "You think picking on others makes you special?"

Jared laughed, and his group of 'friends' echoed the sentiment with nervous laughter of their own. Jared reared back and punched Chase in the gut, causing bile to rise his throat.

Chase spat at Jared, then looked around the group, though no one would meet his eyes. "What is wrong with all of you? This is okay with you? That," he jerked his head in Mason's direction, "could be any one of you. Why don't you stand up to this loser?"

For that, he took another blow to the head; the pain making a snarl erupt from deep within. He felt a few hands loosen and took advantage of the moment, bursting forward, the momentum carrying him right into Jared as his fists began flailing.

Chase crashed into Jared, taking them both down. It happened so fast no one had time to react. They tumbled like alligators in a death roll, Chase coming out on top, fists flying, his current state of rage topping the scale, preventing him from halting the blows even when deep down he knew he should.

"Hey!" A familiar voice cracked the wall of fury.

But Chase couldn't seem to make himself stop, seeing Mason's face in his mind's eye as he'd gasped for breath. Chase was intent on his target, and nothing else existed. It wasn't until hands roughly gripped him that he noticed the crowd had dispersed. He looked up through a stream of blood that dripped from his forehead into his right eye, blinking rapidly. The white of his teeth now stained crimson, a feral gleam shining in his eyes as he stared into the face of his would-be adjudicator. Chase blinked as recognition dawned.

"Dad?" He asked, relieved to find his father was the one who'd witnessed the fight. Jared got shakily to his knees. Chase smiled a satisfied grin when he saw the other boy had a bloody nose, blood oozing over his lips and down his chin.

Like an award-winning actor, Jared put on his best performance yet as he groaned, clutching his midsection. "Mr. Walker. Thank God you're here." He panted heavily, another pitiful—and to Chase's ear obviously phony—moan escaped his battered lips. "The new guy came at me from behind. I didn't even see him coming."

Nolan's head jerked to stare at Chase, brow raised in question.

"He's lying. He thinks he can bully everyone in the school and then tell lies so he comes out looking like the victim."

"Chase, he's never had a problem here before, at least not at school..."

"Because everyone in this school is afraid of what he'll do if they tell on him." He spat bloody saliva at Jared's feet. "Except for me. Ask Corey. He was here."

"Corey was..." Nolan's words trailed off, his eyes searching. "Doesn't matter. Both of you come to my office. I'll sign your passes." He gestured with a wave and began walking toward the building. "You'll need to get cleaned up before returning to class." He paused, calling over his shoulder. "Separately."

# CHAPTER 26
## *CHASE*

Chase jerked when he saw his own reflection in the bathroom mirror, barely recognizing himself. His lips were swelled to double the usual size and an egg-shaped lump grew out of his left cheek. He still felt nauseous from the blow to the stomach, though he would never admit it to anyone. He cupped his hands and swished water around his mouth, spitting blood into the sink. The red mucus stained the sink before diluting and funneling down the drain, a macabre crimson slash against the pure white background. Pulling his bottom lip out, he studied the mangled hole from the first punch when his tooth had nearly gone through the skin.

Leaning on the porcelain, he looked at his reflection. Just this morning, he could see the resemblance to his father in the slash of high cheekbones and dimpled cheeks. As he looked now, they weren't recognizable as father and son, except for those nearly identical clear blue eyes. Chase sighed. He had no way of knowing how this meeting would go. Jared, he knew, was good at deceiving people. Would his dad be among the gullible?

Truth was, he and his dad really didn't know each other at all. They were strangers, despite their biological connection. Would it matter? He hoped so, though he feared the worst. This could go either way.

Chase pushed back. No use putting it off any longer. Might as well charge into battle instead of waiting for the war to come to him. He rounded his shoulders with one last glance at his distorted countenance. Giving himself a slight nod, he headed toward the guidance counselor's office across the hall. Dad had sent Jared to the restroom in the other wing to avoid another confrontation, and when he sauntered into his dad's office, Jared was already sitting there, one tissue twisted and sticking out of his nose, the other crumbled in his hand.

*Great. He's already begun the performance without me here to dispute it.*

Chase pulled the chair around to the far side of the desk, as far away as he could get from Jared. "Quit your pathetic act. No one here is buying it." He raised a brow at his dad, a silent challenge.

"Chase," Nolan began. "From what I'm hearing, I think you owe Jared an apology..."

"Yes, sir. If he apologizes, I won't even tell anyone else." Jared took on the persona of a shy-mannered, cowering teen. "I just want him to leave me alone."

"That's bull! This guy goes around terrorizing the entire school, and I owe him an apology?" Anger burst from every pore in his body, and Chase struggled to remain seated.

Nolan Walker held up his hand. "Hold on, son. What I walked up to was you on top of him, pounding on his face. I know what I saw with my own eyes." His tone was that of a father chastising his son.

"Yes. That was after he..."

"Chase, no matter what you think he did, no one deserves to be beaten like that. Violence is never the answer, and in fact, it always escalates the problem. Now, I'm not reporting this to the principal. You won't get written up for it, either of you. But if I see this kind of behavior again, I won't be able to save you from the consequences. Do you understand.?" His eyes bored into his. "Chase?"

"Oh, I understand fine, *Dad*. You know, I gave you the benefit of the doubt. Believed everything you told me about our past. Forgave you on your word alone because, after all this time, I thought I finally had a father. Apparently, I was wrong. *You* think about *that*." Chase stalked from the room without a backward glance.

For the first time, he doubted his decision to return to high school. If they hadn't come here, he would never have learned that his father was alive.

Maybe that would have been best for both of them.

•   •   •

Chase wandered town, Bo in tow, ending up at the beach. He kicked off his shoes and flopped onto the sand, digging his toes into the gritty coolness. The sun was beginning its descent, purples and pinks bled into an orange tinted backdrop. Bo flopped onto his lap and curled his body into Chase, settling in between his legs. He placed a hand on Bo's back and absently scratched. Looking out over the endless expanse of living waters, he calmed for the first time today. He got lost in the ebb and flow. The sea calmed him as it always did, and he could think more clearly, without the rage clouding his judgement.

In an attempt to give the benefit of the doubt, he tried reversing perspective on the situation. After witnessing the tail end of the fight, maybe it was understandable that his father had drawn the inevitable conclusion that Chase was the attacker. And Jared played the martyr so well.

He groaned, pushing his feet deeper into the sand.

*No,* he thought stubbornly.

A dad should have your back no matter what. He hadn't even given Chase a chance to explain before passing his judgment. The guy actually thought he was doing Chase a favor by letting him go with just a warning. Was he waiting for Chase to thank him? Well, he'd be waiting an eternity, then.

He remembered the guileless expression on Jared's face as he sat in his father's office. The wide, innocent message his eyes sent to his father. *Trust me,* they seemed to say. *I would never tell a lie.*

Checking the time, he jumped to his feet, absently brushing sand from his clothing. Bo licked at his leg, his tail waving in a circular motion. He bent down to ruffle the fur on the pup's head, and a smile grudgingly emerged. Bo was in that awkward, lanky stage of growth. His spindly back legs seemed a bit too long for the rest of his body, causing his gait to appear almost clownish. The pup rubbed his body against his leg, looking up with adoring eyes.

"Thanks, big guy. I'm fine." Chase answered the question the creature seemed to ask. "Let's go get Alyx and go home. Guess we don't really have a choice but to go back to the house."

# CHAPTER 27
## *ALYX*

She was distracted as she instructed the girls. After seeing her in the bathroom that morning, Alyx hadn't seen Margo the rest of the day at school. "Is Margo here?" she asked.

Anna had shrugged. "Don't see her."

As they worked on tonight's self-defense move, Alyx had a hard time staying focused. *Where is she?* Despite her concern, she had a job to do.

The girls were split into pairs. "Okay, so for this move, we're going to assume that someone is coming at you. You don't want to let them get close enough to grab you. You'll be using the heel of your palm to strike; the goal is getting away from your attacker. Aim for the nose or throat. Those areas will get you the most reaction, and hopefully the assailant will stumble backward giving you a chance to get away."

"Wait, I thought you were teaching us how to fight, not run." Sophie questioned the intent, hands on her hips.

"Yes. But getting away is number one. We have to assume your attacker will have the advantage of size and strength—assailants usually go for people they perceive as weak, or at least weaker than themselves. Your goal is to get to safety first, not necessarily to take them down. Hand to hand combat is not guaranteed, so you want to use the element of surprise while you have it. Most attackers mistakenly see what they want to see, a helpless female and nothing else, so you fighting back in a confident, trained way will be the surprise. Getting away is always the preferred outcome, if at all possible. This is one way to do it. You're going to use anything you have at your disposal. Keys, purse, elbows, knees, rocks or sticks if they're available, the heel palm strike I'm showing you now. There are no rules in survival. Anything is fair game. I promise you, your attacker won't be playing by any kind of rules."

Wide-eyed, Sophie nodded, and the group joined in.

"Okay, so you'll get in front of your attacker, using your dominant hand, strike upward aiming for the nose or throat, which will cause the head to snap back, hopefully they'll stumble backward giving you that window you need to get away. Let's practice on our partners, not actually thrusting, of course."

The girls went through the motions, Alyx stopping by to adjust trajectory angles or stance. When the hour was almost up, Alyx called the group together. "You guys are doing great. Does anyone have any questions about tonight's move?"

"Yes, what if we do the move and it doesn't work? What if we use the heel palm strike and we still don't get away?"

Alyx nodded. "Good question. I'll work on that as the focus for tomorrow night." She contemplated her next words. "Hey, have any of you seen Margo? I saw her at school today, and she seemed upset about something. I had hoped to talk to her about it tonight. I'm worried about her." She craned her neck, found Alana in the crowd. "Alana, have you seen her?"

Alana, eyes huge, nodded slowly. "Yes. I saw her at school, too. I-I know what's wrong, but I promised not to tell anyone."

"Well, since you know what's wrong, maybe you can somehow tell us how to help her."

Alana shuffled her feet. "I'm not sure how. She asked for space, said she needed some time to figure things out and she didn't want to talk about it."

"Okay. I understand wanting some time, I often feel the same. But let's all keep an eye on her to make sure she's okay, and if we can help in any way, let's try."

A chorus of agreement rippled through the now-subdued crowd. Ellie chuckled, a forced sound that did nothing to ease the tension. "I told Alyx she's probably just upset about a test or something." Her high-pitched, nervous giggle burst forth again, and some of the girl's heads bobbed as if relieved to have an acceptable and not-too-serious answer to the problem.

"Yeah. She does take her grades seriously. That's probably it," Emily chimed in.

Alana continued her extensive study of her own shoes, not participating further in the conversation.

Just then, Chase emerged from the dirt path, and their eyes locked, and Alyx gasped. She jogged to him, studying his mangled face.

"Are you okay?" she asked, her eyes taking in every inch of him.

He nodded in response, unusually quiet. Ellie stood back, observing their interaction solemnly.

"Hunters?" Alyx demanded, her eyes sparkling with plans for revenge.

"No," Chase answered.

Relief mingled with disappointment as she gently reached up to touch his cheek. His flinch had her jerking her hand away.

Bo yipped and was soon surrounded by girls fussing over him. *If only they knew he was a hybrid-chimera from a different world*, Alyx thought.

After everyone dispersed and it was just the two of them, three if you counted the puppy, Alyx cocked her head in question.

"It was Jared. He was attacking Mason, so I stepped in. My Dad broke up the fight, but he only saw the end when I had got the upper hand. Jared put on a good show, and my father believes I was bullying poor, innocent Jared. I don't know if I want to continue living there, Alyx." He looked off in the distance, a faraway look clouding his features. "I don't know if I can forgive him for this." He turned back. "For not even listening to my side. Part of me wishes we never even found him."

Alyx stuck out her hand, waiting for his fingers to entwine with hers. She felt the swelling and gentled her grip. "I'm with you. Whatever you decide, I'm with you, Chase." She sent him a sideways smile. His return smile turned out more like a grimace, and she laughed. "C'mon. Let's go see if we can talk some sense into your dear old dad, and if not, I'm fine with moving back into the hotel."

"Thanks," he said simply.

"For what?" she asked.

"For being there for me, and believing me, no matter what. You're the only one who does."

"Always." She grinned, "I'd kiss you right now, but you look like raw hamburger meat, so..."

Chase stopped, turning her to face him. He leaned slowly forward, placing his battered lips gently on hers. "I'll never turn down a kiss from you. Never."

He leaned his forehead against hers and closed his eyes for a moment, and Alyx marveled that her body could respond to him even as he was fighting back obvious pain and looked the way he did right now. She smiled, closing her eyes as well. She didn't know how long they stood in the field at the local community playground, forehead-to-forehead, just content in each other. Two kids who never should have met, who'd found each other to travel to unknown worlds for less than a year, side by side. Just one year, a drop in the bucket of a lifetime. She didn't know what their future held, but here, right now in this moment, she'd never felt more fulfilled.

Sometimes fate was both a blessing and a curse.

# CHAPTER 28
## *CHASE*

They walked into the Walker house hand-in-hand, heading straight for their office bedroom. Rose emerged from the kitchen, dishtowel in hand.

"Oh, good, you're here. I saved you some dinner. Oh, Chase." Tears filled her eyes. "What can I do? An icepack, maybe?"

"No, thanks."

"Your Dad told me what happened, and he feels…"

"I doubt that. He didn't pause in his judgment to even give me a chance to explain what happened."

"Maybe you should talk to him. You should know, he's upstairs talking to Corey about it now. He wanted to hear what he had to say about the whole thing."

Chase snorted. "Figures. He'll listen to the son he actually has a relationship with."

She splayed her hands in front of her before wrapping her arms protectively around her waist. "Chase, he's really trying."

Chase looked away. "It really doesn't seem like he is." He followed Alyx into the room and shut the door. Leaning back against it, he let the pain—both mental and physical—wash over him as he slumped there, head in hands. He felt Alyx's arms wrap around him and reached for her.

"I'm trying not to sound like a stereotypical belligerent teenager, really I am." He squeezed her closer. "I can't seem to help it. I mean, we have a lot more going on than the usual teenage problems; which I realize should be inconsequential to us because of being keepers. But being back in school, finding my dad…" He shook his head. "I don't know. I just can't control the feelings."

"You're allowed to have these feelings, Chase. Being keepers doesn't make us immune to basic human emotions."

He nodded. "I know. And I don't want to be, but I'm finding I'm even jealous of my resentful little brother who wishes I didn't exist. At least he'll tell Nolan—

Dad—what really happened. But I'm still triggered that my father didn't listen to me, he had to hear it from him."

Alyx remained silent. He stepped back when a gentle knock tapped on the door, followed by his father's voice. "Chase? Can I come in?"

They moved away from the door. "Suit yourself." Chase crossed his arms over his chest. Alyx stood next to him, her stance similar to his own. A united front. A tiny smile tugged at the corners of his mouth before his father pushed the door open and entered.

"May I sit?" Nolan gestured to the chair.

Chase inclined his head, but remained standing.

"I know you're upset, and I'm sorry for that. This is not the way I envisioned our reunion." Nolan sighed. "But Chase, I can't condone this kind of behavior. I know I haven't been there to teach you, to guide you..."

"Unbelievable." Chase took a steadying breath. "You're not even here to ask me what happened, to have a civilized conversation. You're only here to condemn me again." He threw his hands in the air as he paced. "You talked to Corey, right?" At his father's nod, he continued. "Well, didn't he tell you what Jared was doing before I got there?"

A head shake. "I'm sorry, son. Corey told me you started the fight. He told me you came up behind Jared and pushed him, and that Jared was only defending himself when he threw those punches." He gestured toward Chase's face.

An ironic laugh hissed through his teeth. "I knew he hated me, but I didn't understand how deep that hatred ran. He really wants me gone, doesn't he? He can't even handle me being here for the short time I have left in this world."

"No, Chase. Don't say that. He's at that age where everything's a struggle. It pained him to tell me what happened today. You should have seen his face. He's feeling guilty for telling on you. If he didn't have feelings for you, he wouldn't feel guilt for talking out against you. I truly believe he wants you in his life. He just has to get used to the idea that you're here. He'll come around."

Chase's mouth dropped open. "That wasn't guilt for telling on me. It was guilt for lying to you."

"Corey may be a moody teenager, but he's never been a liar. Even as a three-year-old, he couldn't lie to us. He once came to us crying, saying between sobs that he was sorry for breaking that window right there." He pointed, his mind's eye seeing that three-year-old boy. "We never would have known he did it, but he confessed. Lying just isn't in his blood."

"Oh, but it's in mine? That's funny, I thought we had the same blood." Though his hands hung by his sides, he clenched his fists. "So that's how it is? You make excuses for him; he can say or do anything and your motto is: He'll come around.

But with me, you're so ready to convict me on the word of the school bully, and the word of a disgruntled son."

"No, not at all. It's not easy to be where you are now. Believe me, I know it better than anyone. What I think is that your duties as a keeper of the watch have you feeling confused about how to treat your peers. The power the watch brings can go to your head..."

"That's bull and you know it! I can't believe that little shit lied for him. You know, Jared Young puts on a good performance, and all the teachers fall all over him because he's the star football player. It makes me sick. All the students are either afraid they'll be his next target, or afraid that he'll label them losers and no one will have the courage to go against his ruling. I'm the only one who doesn't care about any of that—so he's been after me since day one. But you can't see any of that through your self-righteousness. I don't know why I thought I could trust you. We're nothing more than strangers that happen to share DNA. If you knew me at all, you'd know I'd never be capable of what you're accusing me of. I think we're done here." He searched out Alyx, who had remained quiet throughout the conversation, though her glare spoke volumes.

"Ready when you are," she said.

"Chase, wait. Don't go. At least stay tonight if you insist on leaving. Let me be clear. I don't want you to leave. I'd like for you to stay here until you jump to Dimension 10. But I respect your choice if you no longer feel comfortable living here. Just wait one more night." He stood, headed to the door. "I do want to be your dad, you know. I hope you'll reconsider." Nolan backed out the door, closing it gently behind him.

"We can leave right now if you want. It's your choice." Alyx placed a hand on his arm.

He blew out a breath. "No. I'm beat." He laughed sardonically. "Literally." A hand to his midsection and he couldn't hide the grimace that followed. "Let's get some rest and talk about it in the morning."

That night, they lay together on one air mattress, just drawing comfort from each other's presence.

# CHAPTER 29
## *CHASE*

The town took on a coral hue that tinted the window as the sun began its ascent. Chase pulled the drawstring on his backpack while Bo danced around his feet, occasionally jumping up on hind legs and placing a paw on Chase, tiny tongue happily licking every inch of his bare skin. Chase's amused smile turned quickly to a grimace as the pain of that small action set in. The swelling of his face had gone down, but in its place purple bruising had appeared, making him look like a beat-up eggplant.

Chase looked up at Alyx through a squinted eye. "That's everything. One good thing about not having many possessions is that it's easy to pack up and go."

"True. I'm ready. Let's try for a different hotel. I don't think the Happy Home will take us back after the window incident. Plus, there's Bo to consider."

The smell of eggs and bacon wafted through the slit under the door, and Chase's stomach grumbled. He looked longingly toward the kitchen, shaking his head. "Now that's just a shame." He sighed, the rumbling increasing. "We'll have to stop and pick up something to eat."

Alyx grinned. "Even stress and a thorough beating can't squelch your hunger."

"Let's go." Chase snapped Bo's leash to his collar, heading toward the front door.

"Chase." Nolan hurried down the stairs. "Chase, please reconsider."

Rose peeked out of the kitchen doorway. "You're not leaving, are you? I've made breakfast. At least stay for breakfast, and maybe we can have a talk while you're eating."

"I'm not sure there's anything more to say." Chase set his jaw.

"Chase, I'm sorry I didn't believe you. I feel awful about all of this. I barely slept a wink last night. Can we please put all of this behind us and…?"

He was interrupted by a pounding on the door, followed by a voice screaming, "Walker. Let me in so I can kick your son's ass."

"Who the...?"

"Walker, I'm here to settle a score. That kid beat up on my boy, and he's not getting away with it. Best let me in or I'll break down this door."

A look of astonishment crossed Nolan's face. "Jim? Jim Young, is that you?"

"You know damn well it's me. Now, open up," Jim demanded.

"This just keeps getting better." Chase rolled his eyes. "Guess you better let him in."

Rose cleared her throat. "I don't think that's a good idea..."

"We'll talk it out, it'll be fine." Nolan turned the knob and the door burst open, nearly sweeping him off his feet.

"Where is he?" He pushed past, eyes zeroing in on Chase. "You!" Jim Young barged through the house, grasping Chase by his t-shirt. "At least I see he got some good punches in. Guess I taught him something, after all." He shook Chase and his head snapped back. "My son told me what you did. He may be too nice to press charges, but I'm not deterred by any such feelings of kindness."

Nolan pulled on Jim's arm. "He's just a boy, Jim. Let him go and we can talk about this like rational adults."

Jim suddenly released Chase's shirt, and Chase stumbled backward. Jim rounded on Nolan. "You promised me I'd be out of it. And here we are."

"And I've kept that promise. This has absolutely nothing to do with..."

Jim practically roared. "That's bull and you know it. I told you if you ever said anything to anyone about what we did, you'd have me to answer to."

"And no one has broken that promise." Nolan soothed.

Jim jerked his head in Chase's direction. "Then why is he here, flashing that watch around like it's a new toy? Do you know he came to my house?"

"I knew you knew about the watches! Why didn't you tell me that when we asked you?" Chase interrupted, but the men talked over him as if he were invisible.

"You know damn well he's here by no choice of his own. You also know that he won't be here much longer. Can't we just let bygones be bygones and move on?"

"I'd love to do that. But then my son comes home with his face all mangled, and I ask him: Son, who did this to you? He didn't want to tell me at first, but I got it out of him, just like I always do." He smirked. "And he says he," he paused, pointed at Chase, "attacked him while he was at school. Jared says he was minding his own business, walking along by himself, and your boy accosted him."

Chase, eyes ablaze, growled. "He's a liar."

Nolan placed a hand on Chase's arm. "Chase, don't egg him on. Let me handle this."

Jim fumed. "You think you can handle me? Remember, I can send you to jail along with your son if I choose to tell what I know."

"If you tell what you know, you'll be in jail too, and you well know it. Let's not rehash the past," Nolan replied.

"You're right. Let's talk about right now. What are you going to do about this bully putting hands on my son?" Jim demanded.

Chase stepped forward, his hands gesturing wildly. "Your son is the problem."

Nolan stepped in between his son and Jim, a hand on his chest, as Chase continued. "He torments half the student body, and the other half stands behind him because they're afraid they'll become his next victim. He wasn't alone. When I walked up on him, he was shoving a urinal cake down Mason's throat. There was a crowd there surrounding them, and not one of them made a move to stop what was happening, mostly because they're afraid they'll be the next one eating Jared's piss. I should have known no one would dare tell the truth unless they want to face Jared's wrath. That's when I showed up. He had his goons hold me back so he could beat on me. When I got away from them, I gave him some of his own medicine. That's when you showed up." Chase looked sideways at his father, daring him to challenge his story. His father's eyes widened, but he kept silent.

Jim's face turned a deeper shade of red with each word Chase had spoken. "It's your word against Jared's. No one will believe you."

"I agree. Jared has everyone in this town fooled. Tell him to leave Mason alone, and I won't interfere."

"I'll do no such thing, boy." Jim snorted. "I'm just glad he's not a victim."

Nolan gasped. "You're saying it's okay if he really did what Chase says he did?'

Jim shrugged. "I'm just saying it's never good to play the victim, that's all. Always better to be the one calling the shots."

Chase's voice had an edge as he spoke. "Did you know Mason tried to commit suicide a little over a week ago?"

"And why is that my problem?" Jim sneered.

"I think Jared goaded him into doing it. I think he's been pushing him around for so long that Mason decided the only way free of Jared was death."

"Even if what you say is true, that's on him. No one can force someone to take his own life, and to imply someone else is to blame for his selfish choice to end it all is ridiculous." Jim nearly shouted. "Sounds like the kid needs better parenting with a firm hand, you ask me."

Alyx spoke for the first time. "Sounds to me like that's what *you* need."

"Learn some respect, girl. I won't hesitate to tell you what I think just because of your feminine sensitivities."

A growl erupted from Alyx's throat as she took a step forward, eyes narrowed on Jim Young. "You don't scare me. Would you care if I told you the girls at school are afraid of Jared? That I suspect there's more going on, and that he possibly crossed a line with more than one of them?"

Jim shook his head. "Girls these days give off mixed signals. Wearing next to nothing, batting their lashes. Then, when a boy wants to take them up on their offer, they act all shy. It's just not right. How's a boy supposed to know what a girl wants when they're acting like that?"

"So, you won't take any responsibility for Jared's actions? Or make him take responsibility?"

"For what? I'm just glad he isn't the class patsy." Jim smirked. "Look, I'll let this incident slide this time. But if my son comes home looking like a punching bag again and I find out you had anything to do with it…"

Nolan's voice took on a steel edge. "You'll stay away from Chase, or I'll be digging up secrets you don't want to rise."

"You won't do that, Nolan. You know why I know you won't? Because you won't risk your perfect little family, that's why."

"Don't underestimate me, Jim. You did that once before, and look how that worked out for you. No wonder your family's watch rejected you. You have tainted blood. It's all making sense to me."

Jim's face, already red, turned blotchy and mottled, and he sputtered, his face mere inches from Nolan's. "Maybe you'd like your family to know what *you* did."

His laugh sent a chill racing down Chase's back. Chase took in his father's look of horror as Nolan answered. "No. It's not necessary for them to know. Why are you trying to hurt me and my family, Jim? What happened eighteen years ago was not my fault. I would never have succeeded had you not orchestrated the whole thing."

"That's right. You needed me then, and you need me to keep silent now—like I've been doing all these years. But your family doesn't know the real you, do they, Nolan?"

"They know me better than you'll ever know me." Nolan spat.

"I bet they don't know that you killed a woman, though, do they? Or that we dumped her body along with one other into the ocean late one night. Oops. I guess they do now."

Rose gasped, covering her mouth with a hand, her devastated eyes searching out her husband. Nolan immediately went to her, reaching for her hand.

Jim Young strode to the door, yanking it open. "Stay away from Jared." Speaking directly to Chase, he continued. "Because if you don't, I'll be feeding the sharks one more body. Don't test me." He looked at Nolan. "Either of you."

The door slammed, and everyone began talking at once.

Rose's voice rose above the rest. "What did he mean, you killed a woman? Nolan, what is he talking about?"

Chase stood back, watching his father and Rose grapple for a handhold on the marital ledge they were currently teetering on.

"Rose…" Nolan cupped her face. "I'm actually glad this came up. I'm tired of living with this secret."

She pulled away. "Secret? What secret? I was under the impression that we tell each other everything."

"We do, honey, I swear it. We do. This is the one thing I never told you. No one knows. I didn't want you to look at me the way you're looking at me now. I didn't think I could bear it. I was right. I can't bear it." Nolan's voice broke. "Please. Please, hear me out." He turned to Chase. "Both of you. Will you at least do that for me?"

Though fat tears spilled down Rose's cheeks, she nodded, moving to sit on the couch.

Chase figured if Rose could listen, then so could he. Plus, he was curious, though he suspected the truth. He sauntered over to the love seat and flopped down. Alyx followed, sitting next to him. The warmth of her thigh brushing up against his comforted him, and he placed a hand on her leg.

Nolan visibly gathered his thoughts, then began slowly talking.

# CHAPTER 30
## *NOLAN WALKER*
## *EIGHTEEN YEARS AGO*

*Eighteen-year-old Nolan Walker cowered behind a tree, the shaking in his limbs knocking his knees together, though he desperately tried to remain still. The hunters, Pavo and Ursa O'Ryan, were on his trail. They were after one thing: the watch. He frowned; the lines etched in his forehead accentuated by the shadows surrounding him. Always the watch. He wished he'd never put the thing on his wrist. Wished he wasn't a Walker, born into the legacy of becoming a keeper of this stupid watch during his eighteenth year of life. The whole thing is crazy, he thought. Losing a year of his life to a magical watch. Except...*

*Except without his family's legacy, he would never have met Rose. He couldn't imagine his life without ever being aware of her existence, though he was sure some part of him would have impossibly known her across dimensional planes, somehow. Nolan knew his essence would never have been complete without her influence on his life—even in the little time that they had, her impact on him was as strong as the heart beating in his chest.*

*Rose with the porcelain skin, melted chocolate eyes, and a beatific smile. He couldn't imagine never having met her. And he couldn't imagine leaving her after they'd spent nearly every minute they could together for the past three weeks. Just last night, they had spent the night in a tent in the woods—the same tent he would call home until November eleventh—holding each other, talking about their hopes and dreams, sharing their innermost secrets. They'd held each other, laughing the silly way young lovers do about everything and anything. Life was good. At least temporarily.*

*His thoughts flashed to his infant son back home: Chase. Pain ripped through Nolan's heart. The baby must be growing bigger every day, and he was missing all the beginning stages of his young son's life. Would Chase even remember him when they* were finally reunited? By the time his year was up, he'd have spent more time away from the boy than he had with him. The baby had only been three-months-old when he had left.

Nolan shifted, leaning further around the tree for a better view. *Think I lost them.* After waiting another five minutes with no sign of the pair, Nolan took one deep breath and slowly eased away from the tree trunk. Furtively looking in both directions, he stepped onto the paved walkway and hurried toward home—or at least what he considered his home away from home in this world.

After walking half a block with no pursuit, he slowed his pace, his mind inevitably wandering to Rose. His body tingled at just the thought of her, and a romantic sigh parted his lips as he pictured her eyes that seemed—at least to him—to shine with awe at his every word. She made the cutest little purring sound when he kissed her and it drove him mad. No one else had ever made him feel this way, as if she alone was the center of his universe, and everything revolved around only her and her happiness. His Rose was special, indeed. As he walked along, a bounce lifted his step as he forgot all about his pursuers. They were made to be together, he and Rose, Nolan was sure of it. *If only he could find a way to stay here...*

Suddenly jerked backward by the arm, he gasped as they forced a bag over his head. Survival instinct kicked in, and he struggled blindly, kicking out at his attackers. *A trap, then. He should have known he'd lost them too easily.* Nolan doubled his efforts, but it was like that feeling you get when punching your fist through a wall, hand finally breaking a hole through the plaster in a satisfying moment of victory, only to be followed by a mountain of pain and immediate regret. Despite his feeble struggles, he felt his body rise upward as he was roughly lifted, and he lost his sense of direction as they carted him away as easily as a toddler in the midst of a tantrum. His screams, dulled by the cloth sack, were muffled to the point of incoherency, and after some moments passed, he ceased his struggles altogether. *Might as well save his strength for whatever was to come.*

• • •

A car ride and yet another trek of being carried, and he found himself dumped onto a chair, hands tied behind his back. He heard what sounded like a human groan off to his left; dripping water from a possible leaky faucet to his right. Nolan focused all his energy on his senses: the smell of rust that flared his nostrils even through the bag, the mustiness of the damp air that pasted his clothing to his skin. Another groan had him *jerking in the direction where the sound originated, though he still could see nothing but shadows through the black bag over his head.*

*Footsteps retreated, returned, retreated again. He heard occasional whispered voices, one male and one female, but just couldn't seem to make out the words no matter how hard he strained to hear.*

Think! *Nolan's breath came in gasps, and he concentrated on slowing his intake of oxygen. Panic was taking hold, its icy claws slicing deep into his skin. He fought it back, knowing beyond a doubt that if he gave in to the panic, he was as good as dead.*

*Think about Rose.*

*Just the whisper of her name pushed the terror into the background noise of his brain. Rose. He had to get back to Rose.*

*Nolan began working at the rope tying his wrists, searching for a weakness or opening big enough to slide his hands free. It was no use.*

*His body lurched as they ripped the sack from his head. The immediate shift from dark to light had him slamming his eyes closed as he blinked back tears. Gradually, as his eyes adjusted, he scanned the room. There was another person sitting next to him but separated by about six feet. This must be the source of the moaning, Nolan realized.*

*Ursa, the female watch hunter, ripped the bag from the other boy's head. The boy was not familiar to him, and he briefly wondered why they were here in this situation together. Did he know about the watches? Nolan waited until the boy's eyes acclimated to the light, and they made eye contact. Whoever he was, they were on the same side, at least for now. Allies of circumstance. Maybe that would work to his advantage.*

*The woman spoke, her intense voice sending a chill down his spine.* "Tell me, what is it like to travel the worlds?"

"I don't know what you're talking about..." *Nolan muttered.*

*Ursa paced to stand in front of him, hauled her arm back and let it fly into his face with such force the chair leaned precariously back on two legs before settling back down with a thud. Light exploded in his vision, the pain an unwelcome shock.*

*Ursa sniffed, flexing her hand.* "Let's not waste time playing out this farce. You are wearing the watch; I can see your blood oozing through the watch face. Now, you're going to tell us," *she paused, glancing up when Pavo entered the room,* "everything we want to know, and we'll kill you quickly instead of slowly. Got it?"

*So, death either way. Was he fated to never see Rose again? Never again hold his son in his arms? Nolan tried desperately to communicate with the boy next to him—he guessed he was approximately his own age. Hunched over, he had a mop of unruly brown hair partially covering his hazel eyes, the clearly broken slant of his nose, the* purple bruising circling underneath both eyes. Nolan again wondered why this boy was here.

He was distracted by the approach of the burly, menacing man dressed in black from head to toe, with hair of the same color, giving off a gothic vibe. His broad shoulders stretched the dark, button-down shirt he wore, pulling at the seams as if he might burst out of the cloth at any moment. Nolan knew who he was, but had previously only seen the mountain of a man from a distance. Up close, the hard gaze lacked even an ounce of empathy, and when those midnight black eyes focused completely on Nolan, it resulted in tremors of dread coursing through his body.

Nolan gathered his courage, speaking before the man could. "I know who you are, Pavo. But I don't know him." He inclined his head toward the other chair, causing the throbbing in his cheek to intensify. "Why is he here?"

"I'm asking the questions. Is there a way to transfer the watch's power from one person to another?"

Nolan shook his head. "No. I mean, if there is, I don't know how."

Pavo studied him for a beat before moving to stand in front of the other captive. "And you? Do you know of a way?"

"No. Look, I don't know anything. Watch? Power? I think you have the wrong guy."

Pavo smiled, a vampiric aura surrounding him, and for moment Nolan had the crazy notion that the man's canine teeth took on the triangular shape of those predatory creatures of the night. Nolan closed his eyes. When he peeked again, the horror-like quality of his teeth had dissipated.

"Don't play me for a fool. I know who you are." Pavo's voice was deceptively calm. So much so that Nolan began to relax for the first time. If we have to negotiate, maybe he's the one who will listen, he thought. The woman seemed much more volatile...

Pavo spoke in a deceivingly smooth voice: "You'll tell me now. Or you'll lose a finger. Each time I ask you a question and you refuse to answer, I'll cut off another body part. But, I'm not a monster," Pavo continued conversationally. "I'll let you choose which finger goes first. See, I can be fair." The menacing grin flashed once again. "Now, which one will it be, James?"

"I'm sorry! I'm sorry. That's not necessary. I'll tell you anything you want to know."

"Excellent."

The words tripped over each other in his haste to get them out. "My name is Jim Young. My family has a watch. I have it, but it's at home. When I turn eighteen next *year, well in eleven months to be exact, I'll be a keeper of the watch, same as him." Jim pointed to Nolan.*

*"What?" Nolan practically yelled. "You're a keeper of the watch, too?"*

*"Yes. I've been training to travel the worlds for years. Which world is your home?"*

*"Enough!" Pavo, in one swift move, grasped Jim's hand and, using a bronze cigar-cutter, sliced off Jim's pinky finger as calmly as if he was trimming an asparagus stalk. "This is not some keeper reunion. Jim, we're going to let you go home to retrieve your family's watch and bring it back here. If you tell anyone, this keeper dies." Amid Jim's horrified howls of pain, Pavo gestured toward Nolan.*

*Nolan's eyes widened and he drew in a sharp breath. "No, please."*

*Jim panted, sweat beading on his forehead, the hands still tied behind him leaving a bloody puddle on the floor as it poured from the spot where his finger used to be, the severed nub lying forgotten on the floor. Forgotten by everyone except Jim. "Please. I'll do whatever you want."*

*In that moment, Nolan knew beyond any doubt that Jim was contemplating leaving and never coming back.*

*"Jim. Jim, please do as he says. I'm a father—I-I have a baby back home t-to take care of, I have to get back to him..." Nolan pleaded.*

*"Oh, how touching. You're making me all emotional." Pavo dabbed imaginary tears from his eyes. Jim flinched as Pavo walked behind the chairs and cut the rope binding. He immediately searched his unbound hands, desperate to make sure all remaining fingers were still in place. Pavo calmly handed him a towel to wrap around his mangled hand. "Do you know how long we've been waiting for this opportunity? We have been planning for this longer than you can imagine. I'll be going with you, and I'll wait right outside. If you don't do as I say, your family will pay the price. Your little sister looks like a screamer." A chilling grin lit his face. "I like when they make noise," he whispered.*

*"No!" Jim's face contorted. "Please, leave her out of this. She doesn't even know..."*

*Ursa bent to face level, her voice rising with each word: "Do you think we care what she knows? We didn't ask to become hunters, but weren't given a choice. A long time ago, Pavo and I were cursed to the hell of near-immortality by your kind. By the very person who made you what you are. Elias Walker." Just the name alone caused a bitter expression to settle on her face. "We were cursed with knowledge of the twelve dimensions, but no way of leaving this plane of existence to see them for ourselves. Everyone we once knew is dead and buried, as we should be. Now, we want what is rightfully ours, and you two are our ticket to freedom. Nothing will stand in our way."*

Nolan whispered, "We didn't ask to be keepers, either."

She paced away, dismissing him. "Go," she ordered Pavo, and he pushed Jim, hand cradled in the bloodstained rag, feet tripping over each other as he stumbled through the door and up a rickety staircase that squeaked with each step.

"Now, we wait." Ursa turned her back on Nolan, pacing to an almost-ceiling-high, dirt smudged window to peer outside. Using the sleeve of her sweater to clean an oval-shaped viewing area, she remained focused either on whatever lay just beyond the window, or memories of times past. Nolan didn't care. He was only glad she wasn't paying attention to him.

He inspected the room. It appeared to be some kind of unfinished basement, cement floors with a drain at the center, washer and dryer in the far corner, furnace in the other. Boxes were stacked under the staircase with no label to indicate what was packed away inside. The long-dead body of a creature—probably a mouse judging by the size of it—lay in the far corner of the room, the stench of rot long ago faded from its corpse as decomposition finished its final act leaving behind nothing but a husk of bone and fur. Nolan's nose scrunched, and he turned his face away to continue his inspection, pushing aside compassion for the tiny animal. A yellowing utility sink stood on four wobbly legs next to the washing machine, the faucet dripping at nearly perfectly timed intervals. Nolan focused on the water, silently counting in between each drip.

One, two, three, four, five, six, seven, eight, nine. Drip. One, two, three, four, five, six, seven, eight, nine. Drip-drip.

As he focused on the pattern of falling water, he worked at freeing his hands. There was just enough space within his bonds to wiggle his hands back and forth, and he thought maybe some of the rope was on top of the watch, giving him leeway to work the rope further toward his fingers. The dripping water became a cadence to his struggle to free his hands, and he focused so intensely on the monotonous splash of water that it was like a lifeline.

One-pull, two, three-tug, four, five-stretch, six, seven-slide, eight, nine-push. Drip.

After a while, Ursa ripped her gaze from the window, and Nolan froze. She glared at him, saying nothing, and strode to the stairs, taking them two at a time. He breathed a sigh of relief, doubling his efforts without her presence to hamper his struggles. Now he fought in earnest to free himself until he was panting with effort. His muscles rebelled, cramps gripping his biceps and the chords of his neck as he tore open his wrists in his quest to be free. Not sure what he would do if he actually succeeded, he continued his efforts, deciding to complete one task at a time. He was no fighter, and *he knew it, so he would have to use his wiles when the time came. But he would think of that later. First, he had to get free.*

*It was easy to lose track of time down here, but Nolan knew that sunset had come and gone by the darkness creeping in the small window and casting sinister shadows over the dimly lit room. After what seemed like an eternity had passed, Nolan ceased his movements and hung his head.*

*It was no use. He'd thought he felt the rope give a few minutes ago, but it remained intact, knot a little less firm, but still it held. I can't do this. He wallowed in self-pity for precious moments until one name filled his thoughts.*

*Rose.*

*Snapping his head up, he renewed his struggles. Even if they kill me, she isn't safe, he realized. They may try to silence her. I can't let that happen.*

*His hands returned to the arduous task of twisting and turning under the burning rope, the wetness of oozing blood making the movements slick. Holding his breath, ignoring the searing muscle spasms, he pushed with all his might at his bonds. The moment his hands slid free of the rope, his chair fell sideways and he with it as the momentum landed him on the hard floor, his shoulder taking the impact of the fall. He called out in surprise and just as he fought to his feet, footsteps pounded down the wooden staircase.*

*Standing now, his arms, numb from being bound for so long, tingled and hung limply by his sides. Ursa approached, stalking like a panther on the hunt. That's what she reminded him of as she impatiently swiped a swatch of ebony hair out of her narrowed eyes.*

*"So, you think you're so smart, do you? Just because you escaped your bonds doesn't mean you're free, keeper. Sit down." She righted the chair, gesturing toward it with a jerky motion. "Or I'll make this worse for you."*

*Nolan shook his head, backing away. He had no idea what to do next, but sitting complacently while she tied him up wasn't an option he could live with.*

*"Oh, I'm going to enjoy taking you apart, limb from limb. But first, I'll have that watch. We don't really need you, stupid boy. All we really need is the watch and I'm sure we'll be able to figure out the rest." She charged at him with a low growl, the force of her body slamming into his, knocking him backward, his head bouncing off the cinderblock wall as internal fireworks exploded in his vision. Vaguely, he felt her reaching for his left arm, her fingers grasping the watch in her hand as she pulled. A burst of pain encircled his wrist as the watch, embedded under his skin and intravenously, began to separate from its host.*

*A sudden flash lit the dingy basement, and in horror, Nolan watched as a thin bolt of electricity flashed into her skull, entering through her forehead. She released the watch as her body convulsed, spasms wracking her entire body as she jerked like a marionette at the will of a rambunctious toddler working the strings. Scorched flesh flared his nostrils as a wave of nausea gripped him. After a full minute of seizing and flailing, Ursa's stiff body fell to the floor, smoke twirling upward from the heels of her feet.*

*Nolan placed a hand over his mouth, gagging behind his hand while tentatively pushing at her with his foot. She was dead; he was sure of it. He held his breath in an attempt to hide the smell of scorched flesh, but it was no use. Another wave of nausea gripped him, and he doubled over. She was as dead as the mouse that rotted in the corner of the room. The black crusted circle on her forehead paled in comparison to the bloodshot eyes bugging out of her face, and Nolan gagged again.*

*He felt a wave of shivers grip his body as he stared down at the watch. Where had the electricity come from? It seemed to him as if a lightning bolt had erupted from the watch into Ursa's head. But how could that be? Nolan didn't have time to gather his thoughts before more footsteps sounded on the stairs.*

*Pavo stood in momentary disbelief when he took in the scene before him. He cursed, advancing on Nolan. "What did you do to her?" He nearly screamed.*

*"Nothing. I didn't do anything." He backed up as he spoke, hands held in the air as if he were under arrest. "I don't know what happened. It wasn't me, I swear it."*

*A goose-bump raising laugh burst forth. "Oh? I guess someone else came in here and killed Ursa?" Pavo grasped Nolan by the throat and picked him off his feet.*

*Nolan could feel the muscles in his throat closing as his airway was cut off. He gripped Pavo's hand with both of his, desperately fighting for even a tiny bit of air to enter his burning lungs. His legs kicked, and he knew in that moment he would never see Rose again. Never hold Chase again. In one more burst of energy fueled by love alone, he tore at the hand around his throat. But it was no use. He was no match for Pavo. It was over. The tiny space was quiet but for the desperate choking sounds coming from his own throat. He briefly wondered if they would leave him to rot in the corner alongside the poor, unfortunate mouse.*

*Just as darkness descended on him, closing in on the outer edges of his vision and moving toward the middle until there was nothing left but a pinprick of light in the center, Nolan was released suddenly, his body crumbling to the cement floor, heaving and gasping for precious air. He coughed and retched, on all fours like an animal, and in fact he felt like a wild beast in that moment, just fighting for his right to life on the food chain.*

*"Get up. We gotta get rid of the bodies."*

*Nolan was barely aware of Jim speaking. It was as if he were whispering from down a long tunnel, and he couldn't quite make out the words. His eyes landed on Pavo, a broken broom handle jutting out of his chest, blood pooling underneath his sprawled body, which lay half on top of Ursa's corpse.*

*"Huh?" Even that one attempt to talk hurt his battered throat.*

*"Good job, taking care of the woman. I took care of the big guy. But we gotta figure out what to do with their bodies. I know where we are. If we can get them to my family's boat, maybe we could dump them in the ocean. Think I know just the place."*

*Nolan swallowed painfully. "I don't..."*

*"Look, we're in this together, whether we want to be or not. I'm not happy about it either." As Jim spoke, he pulled an old quilt out of one of the boxes. "We'll wrap them up in blankets, take them out on the boat, and toss their bodies. No one will ever know."*

*"I really don't..."*

*"Stop whining and get up. You don't have a choice. Don't we have some kind of fellow keeper bond or something? We are bound to help each other. If we leave their bodies here, we can get caught. No bodies, no crime. Here, help me roll them up."*

*Nolan, body aching from the pounding drumbeat from his head down to his feet, slowly reached for the blanket.*

# CHAPTER 31
## *CHASE*

When Nolan finished his tale, he sat back, shoulders slumped, rubbing his hands up and down over his face.

Rose cleared her throat, her voice hushed in reverence to the past. "I remember." She closed her eyes but continued speaking, as if she were there now, eighteen years in the past. "I remember going to the tent that night and finding it empty. I was so worried about you." She opened her eyes, filled with unshed tears, and spoke to Nolan as if they were the only two in the room. "And the next day, when I saw you. You said you'd been mugged. That you'd fought off your attackers and got away. I believed you."

"Yes. I'm sorry." Nolan's voice cracked. "So sorry for lying to you. I didn't want to involve you in the dark side of being a keeper. It made me sick, what I'd done. It still makes me sick. I'm no killer, Rose. I still don't understand what happened that night. All I know is something killed Ursa, and then Jim killed Pavo."

Chase cleared his throat. "I think I can help clarify that part."

Both Rose and Nolan turned to him, eyes wide.

"The watch has a sort of, I don't know, self-defense mechanism built into it. I guess to preserve its own existence or something. If anyone threatens to remove the watch from a keeper's wrist, it emits a burst of electric power. We've seen it happen in other worlds we've visited. Several times."

Alyx nodded in confirmation. "Yes. It took down the hunter in Dimension 7 when she went after Chase's watch, and there have been others."

Nolan shook his head. "Impossible. When they kidnapped me, the watch didn't harm them. Ursa even punched me, so I was definitely being threatened before the, ah, lightning incident or whatever you want to call it. Not to mention that it didn't hurt Pavo when he had me in a choke-hold."

"No. It's not defending *you*. It's only when someone directly tries to disconnect the watch from its keeper—its energy source—that the electrical charge emerges. I guess the watch trusts us keepers to take care of ourselves in most cases. It's the severing of the watch-keeper bond that activates the defense."

Nolan gave him a sharp look, his eyes drifting to the watch on Chase's wrist. "I didn't know that." He looked down at Bo, lying at Alyx's feet, and continued. "There's so much I apparently didn't know when I was traveling the twelve dimensions."

"I think that's true of all of us. We learn as we go, and of course, from the journal written by Elias Walker. Our ancestor."

"Yes, I remember the journal. I never found it very useful, I guess, because I thought the whole idea of being a keeper was a burden. Do you still have it? I left it at home when I made my first jump. In hindsight, I probably should have taken it with me."

Chase nodded. "Yes, we're adding notes to it with each jump."

"Good." Nolan sighed. "You're a better keeper than I was, Chase."

"Your story explains why we haven't run into the hunters here," Alyx said.

Rose reached over and placed a hand on top of Nolan's. "I guess I can understand why you didn't want me involved, though the lie still hurts. Is there anything else you haven't told me?"

"No. I swear it." Nolan raised her hand to his lips, gently kissing it. She turned her hand so their fingers entwined, and relief instantly relaxed Nolan's features. "Thank you. I'm not sure I deserve your forgiveness, but thank you for giving it, anyway."

"I love you, Nolan," Rose answered simply.

"I love you, too." The two gazed into each other's eyes for a moment before Nolan turned to Chase.

"Chase, I owe you an apology, too. I'm still not really sure what happened with Jared at school yesterday, but I'm your dad and I should have had your back either way."

Chase's mouth dropped open. "Wait. You still think I'm probably lying, but you think you should have had my back, anyway? Is that what you're saying?"

"Both Corey and Jared said the same thing...it doesn't matter now."

"Oh, of course. That's right. Corey doesn't lie, does he?" Chase rose to his feet. "Everyone around you has to listen to all your explanations, but you won't even consider that I might be the one telling the truth. I'm out of here."

"Wait. There's a bit more you need to know. It's important to your dealings with the Young family, I think." Nolan held up a hand.

"What is it?" Chase, arms crossed, remained standing but paused to listen.

"Since I ended up staying in this world instead of returning home when my time as a keeper was up, I got to know Jim, who was a senior in high school, better. He was arrogant and obnoxious. I think the power of knowing he would become a keeper on his eighteenth birthday went to his head, and he wasn't a nice person to be around. We didn't spend much time together, but on his birthday, October tenth at ten minutes after ten o'clock, I went to be with him as he coupled with his watch."

"I'm sure he was happy to have you there for support," Rose smiled.

"I doubt that." Nolan continued. "The time for connecting with his family's watch came and went, and it never happened. He tried to place it on his wrist, but it wouldn't bond with him. The next day, the watch remained dormant, and every day after that. I guess it rejected him. I don't know. But for whatever reason, Jim Young never became a keeper of the watch, even though he was born on one of the chosen dates and with the right bloodline. It," Nolan struggled to find the right words. "It...did something to him. He became even more unbearable, bitter, more volatile than he'd been before. After that, we didn't spend much time together, and in fact, he seemed to somehow blame me for his insufficiencies. I have heard rumors that he's been a very strict parent to Jared, and a very demanding husband to his wife, Sadie."

"The watch rejected him?" Chase asked, eyes wide. "I didn't know that could happen."

"I guess the watch deemed him unworthy." Alyx, hands on hips, interjected.

"What do you mean a strict father and demanding husband?" Chase asked.

"I'm not sure what I mean. I've just heard rumors, that's all. I try to stay away from Jim and his family the best I can in this small town."

"So, you turn your head if you hear bad things, or if the son is following in his father's footsteps?" Chase shook his head. "Just so he'll keep his mouth shut about you killing the hunter?"

Nolan looked down at his clasped hands. "I told you, I'm not a fighter. I just want to live my life in peace with my family. Is that too much to ask?"

"No. I guess it isn't." He snapped Bo's leash on his collar. "Let's go, Alyx."

"Right behind you," she answered, moving toward the door.

"Wait, Chase. Will you come back?" Nolan asked.

"I don't know. Right now, I just need some time."

"I understand. But please know that you always have a place here. This is your home as much as it's ours. I do hope, I pray, that you'll reconsider. We have so little time together." Nolan's eyes implored.

"I'll think about it. But right now, we need to go to school."

"What about Bo?" Rose asked. "You can leave him here. I enjoy having him here. Really. It's the most logical thing to do. He knows us and will be most comfortable staying here while you're at school."

Chase squatted in front of Bo. "What do you want to do, Bo-Bo? Do you want to stay?"

The pup jumped up, his tongue darting out in frantic little kisses all over Chase's chin, then turned to run to Rose, jumping at her legs. Rose bent to scratch behind his ears, looking at Chase expectantly.

Chase blew out a breath. "I guess it makes the most sense. Thanks."

"Chase?" Rose called out as he went through the door. He paused, looking back over his shoulder. "They say dogs are the best judges of character."

He nodded before shutting the door behind him.

# CHAPTER 32
## *ALYX*

Replaying this morning's confrontation in her mind, Alyx carried her lunch tray to a round table in the center of the cafeteria, sliding it onto the table with a *scrape* as she sat down. There was an uncommon hush in the room, unusual during the lunch hour. Gone was the normal cacophony of overlapping conversations interspersed with the clanking of silverware. Eyes narrowing, Alyx scanned the room. By the expressions she saw on some student's faces, she could tell something had happened, but couldn't guess what might have caused this melancholic atmosphere that now hovered in the air like a tangible entity. She turned to Ellie to ask what was going on, but Chase's sister was involved in a frantic and hushed conversation with Alana, her eyes round as the apple on her tray, hands gesturing wildly. A feeling of foreboding squeezed the air out of Alyx's lungs as she waited for enlightenment with dread in her heart.

Finally, Ellie saw Alyx. She reached out, grasping her arm in a vise grip. "Have you heard?" Her eyes were brimming with tears, two fat crystalline drops just waiting to spill over.

Alyx frowned. "Heard what?"

"It's Margo." A giant tear broke free, gliding down her cheek. As if on cue, another tear fell, followed by another. Her breath hitched as she spoke. "She's dead."

"What?" Alyx practically yelled. She slowly rose from her metal chair, gripping the edge of the table. "No, she can't be. What are you talking about?" She looked from one tortured face to the other and shook her head in denial.

"It's t-true. We just found out. She wasn't in gym class this morning—that's the only class we have together—and I got a bad feeling. I mean, after she didn't come to the park last night, and you said she was upset and all, I started to worry. So, in my next class, I told Alana she wasn't in class, you know, like I said. Alana texted her, and Margo's mom answered the text with a callback. She's a wreck, obviously, and she wanted to know why Margo killed herself last night. She asked if I knew if she was upset about something."

"Killed herself?" Alyx gasped. "Last night?" A pain gripped her middle, and she wrapped her arms protectively around herself. "But I just saw her yesterday."

Alana nodded. A fresh wave of tears raced down both cheeks simultaneously.

Alyx felt her own eyes fill and blinked back the salty liquid. "I should have..." Alyx trailed off. "I knew how upset she was, and I did nothing." A vise squeezed her heart, each breath tightening until she felt as if she were smothering. Her breathing was as labored as if she'd just finished running a long-distance race. "While we were at the park practicing self-defense, we left Margo on her own to face whatever was upsetting her."

Ellie placed a hand on her back. "You didn't know how bad it must have been for her, Alyx. None of us did."

Alana's shoulders shook, a look of devastation etched on her face. "But *I* did. I knew what upset her, and I decided to give her space when she said she needed time to herself. It's my fault." She hunched over the table, covering her face with both hands. "Oh, my God. She's dead, and it's all my fault. She's my best friend, and she's gone."

Ellie put her arm around Alana's trembling shoulders. "Shh. It's no one's fault. We didn't know how bad it was. If we had, we would have...I don't know. We would have done something."

"I can't stay here. I have to go," Alana, face splotched and puffy, pushed away from the table, stumbling once and then righting herself.

"Wait. Alana, wait." Alyx stood. "You shouldn't be alone right now. Let's get a pass and go to Dr. Walker's office. Maybe you'll feel better if..."

"Feel better? Did you really just say I'll feel better? My best friend is dead, and I just stood by and let it happen. Nothing is ever going to make it better. Nothing will ever be better again." Fresh tears formed, overflowing from her eyes like a dam bursting.

"No, I didn't mean..." Alyx took a deep breath. "I'm sorry. I'm not great at this. I just meant I'm worried about you. Please, come with me."

Ellie hugged Alana. "I think you should talk to my dad. Maybe we all should. Maybe he can help."

Alyx nodded. "Ellie, can you walk her there? I need to talk to Chase, and we'll meet you."

Ellie nodded, guiding Alana toward the door. Alyx watched until the girls were out of sight, and went in search of Chase.

• • •

That evening, Alyx, Chase, Nolan, and Rose sat in silence. The time for talk was past as the reality of the day began to set in for each of them in different ways. Ellie had long ago excused herself to go upstairs without eating a bite, and Corey had gone to a friend's house. The four that remained sat numbly around the dining room table, food in serving bowls on top of frilly pot holders to protect the wooden surface of the table from the food's heat no longer necessary as the meal had cooled long ago. Roast beef, gravy, potatoes, broccoli casserole. Dinner rolls. Even so, no one made a move to eat as much as a bite of it.

The silence in the small room seemed to bounce off the walls in a silent siren scream, and Alyx wanted to either press her hands over her ears and cry, or curse the heavens. A numb feeling of hopelessness cloaked her body like a shroud, and she kept picturing Margo's face the last time she'd seen her only yesterday in the girl's restroom at school.

How could she have taken her own life? How could anyone? Alyx questioned it for the hundredth time. It all seemed so unreal, as if she would go to school and see Margo there tomorrow, and it all would have been a terrible, unbelievable dream.

If only she had done something to prevent this from happening. Going over a dozen scenarios in her head, she cursed herself for not trying even one of them. She could have cancelled the self-defense session, or better yet, not let her leave the bathroom without finding a way to comfort the girl. Though they had been little more than acquaintances, now that Margo was gone, Alyx felt a loss. Maybe it was the loss of a classmate when she'd never had friends in the past, or maybe it was the sense of responsibility she now felt toward the girl, but she knew she would feel the pain of this loss long after she left this realm and moved on to the next.

If only I could turn back time and...

Alyx gasped. "Chase! That's it!" She jumped up, staring down at her watch.

"Huh?" Chase asked, confusion clear in his expression. "What?"

"The watch! We can turn back time, like you did in Dimension 7. When you saved me from the hunters and brought me back after I died." Alyx clasped her hands, a look of utter determination on her face. "Show me what you did."

Though she had no memory of it, Chase had told her all about how the hunter had murdered her right in front of him, and how helpless he'd felt. She thought she understood that feeling now. He'd used the watch's power to turn back time to right after they'd arrived in that world and had recruited reinforcements to change history and save her life. She remembered how he'd told her he'd seen her die, and she hadn't believed him at first. But when she saw the torment on his face as he'd talked about her death, she had known he spoke the truth.

Chase stood, nodding once. "It's worth a try." He focused entirely on his watch, framed by a pulsing indigo light that seemed to have a life of its own. "A small knob appeared on the side of the watch. After it did, all I had to do was turn the knob to travel back in time within the confines of the current dimension. We could go back to two days ago and prevent her from taking her own life. Do you see a knob on yours?"

"No. But we have to do this, Chase. I'm not giving up until we do."

"Alyx, I..." Chase paused. "If the knob isn't there, I don't think we can..."

"Yes, we can! Don't say that, Chase. If we can't turn back time, then we can't save her! We have to. We have to do this." Her eyes were wild.

Nolan cleared his throat. "Alyx, I don't think it works that way. If you've already used the knob to turn back time, then you can't do it again. Each enhanced watch power you uncover in a world is a onetime deal. Once you use it, you can't use it again."

"No. I said don't say that!" Her hands fidgeted in front of her. "There has to be a way."

"I'm sorry, Alyx. You just have to accept that she's really gone, and there's nothing we can do to change it."

She felt the flame of hope sputter and die, and the loss felt somehow worse than before after having seen a glimpse of a more desirable alternate reality, only to have it ripped away again. Sinking back down into the chair, she felt Chase's hand groping for hers and held onto it like a lifeline.

# CHAPTER 33
## THE TOWN OF DUNE HARBOR

A cloud of despair hung over the school community. They could feel it in the air, hear it in the continuous sounds of sniffling in the hallway, see in so many tormented eyes. The school had become a mortuary populated by the living who'd been left behind to deal with the anguish of a darker reality than they'd known previously. It opened their eyes to the realities of life and death as they had never wanted them to be, but now that the truth glared darkly in their minds, there was no going back to the prior innocence that was now forever out of reach.

As is the way when a person is taken from the Earth unexpectedly, especially at such a young age, the survivors in the wake of such a tragedy continue to suffer long after the last scoop of dirt is smoothed over the rutted gravesite.

Even those who didn't know Margo personally, and had only hovered like drones on the outskirts of her world, were shaken to the core. How could this happen, right here in Dune Harbor? How could the people of this small, close-knit community have been blind to the signs? And most importantly: With the proper help, could she have worked through whatever issue had seemed so final to Margo in those last minutes of her life? These are the tormenting questions which would remain exactly that for eternity: questions. Without answers, resolution would never come.

A candlelight memorial was scheduled to honor the life of a young girl who was suddenly gone, ripped from their lives without warning. They set a new suicide hotline up in town as people fought to try to control, and somehow prevent, this very real and saddening trend in so many teenage lives. Social resources in the form of pamphlets with headings that read *Help Is Available, Dealing With Grief,* and *Seeing the Signs,* were placed on tables scattered in various hallways throughout the school, available to students and faculty in need of the false assurance that everything would be alright. Though these recent additions were put in place too late to help Margo, there was now an urgent desire to prevent this tragedy from repeating itself.

And of course, the rumors spread as easily as an airborne pandemic in the community's quest to lay blame. Empathy turned quickly to conjectures about the cause of Margo's depression. Her family was criticized by those who were of the belief that something horrendous must be going on at home since Margo had chosen to take her own life rather than talk to them about it. Was it neglect? Abuse? Maybe untold family secrets she just couldn't bear to live with?

As far as anyone knew, Margo hadn't left a suicide note. That brought up baser suspicions. Maybe she hadn't taken her own life after all. Maybe murder, instead of death by her own hand, had been the culprit. In the creative minds and the silent judgement of onlookers, all manner of alternate options were available for speculation.

Until, little by little, the details surrounding Margo's suicide slowly emerged. Details that helped explain why a young girl might be desperate for some kind of resolution to what she deemed an unsolvable problem. In reality, she'd had choices. A variety of options available to her to solve this predicament that had befallen young girls for centuries. But in such a state of depression—the kind that would have someone taking their own life—those choices often become clouded by a darkness so deep there seemed to be no way back to the light, at least in the mind of the severely depressed.

And so, when the town discovered her secret, an almost collective gasp traveled like falling dominos throughout the community of Dune Harbor. Because now it was common knowledge that on the fateful night when she'd committed the act of suicide, the night she'd driven her cherry red Ford Fusion into the family's garage and sat in the running car breathing deadly fumes until she slept forever, she hadn't been the only casualty in her ultimate decision to end it all.

Ironic that the secret she'd so desperately tried to hide in her final act of life was suddenly public gossip. But the autopsy report didn't lie, and so the news spread. Now, everyone knew that on the night Margo Gallagher had died, she had selfishly and knowingly taken the life of another.

Her last breath had also been a death sentence for the life she carried within her womb.

Margo, on the day before she died, had discovered that she was pregnant. The new information took prior speculation in the town's gossip mills to the next level. Everyone wanted to know only one thing: who was the father of the child?

# CHAPTER 34
## *CHASE*

Chase approached Mason's house, a beautifully built, roomy, two-story stone house with a slate roof and perfectly manicured landscaping bordering a well-tended brick walkway. Victorian-style shutters adorned the windows with a recent coat of coral paint. Located in a gated community on the upper crest, this was a far-cry from the house Mason and his family had lived in back in Chase's home-world. He wasn't sure what kind of reception he would receive, but knew he had to try to help his long-time friend—even if only one of them in this parallel universe knew of their lifelong bond.

If Margo's sudden death had taught him anything, it was that you couldn't wait until tomorrow or the next day to help someone teetering on the edge of abandoning their own self-worth. Later might be too late, and Mason hadn't been in school today. Not to mention that the sight of Mason dangling off the bridge on the day they'd arrived in this world kept replaying in his memory. Margo's was not the first suicide attempt in the town of Dune Harbor since his arrival to this dimension. The only difference was that Mason hadn't succeeded, but Margo had.

Chase banged on the door with a huge brass doorknocker, polished to a shine, so his own distorted reflection stared back at him. It took a full two minutes that seemed more like two hours before the door was finally pulled inward. Mason's mom, Jean, beautiful smile in place until recognition set in, nearly growled with instantaneous fury when she made the connection.

"You! What are you doing here?" she demanded.

"Hi, ma'am. I'm here to check on Mason. He wasn't in school today."

"What do you mean, he wasn't in school today? I saw him leave the house this morning, on his way."

"Well, he must have been on the way somewhere else, because he never made it to school. I'm worried about him," Chase said.

"You? Worried about Mason, after what you did to him? Get off my property before I call the police." Jean pointed to emphasize her words.

Chase stood his ground. "I can't do that, ma'am. I'm sorry, but I need to know that Mason is okay before I leave here."

"Why wouldn't he be okay?" she asked sharply. "If you're here to bully him..."

"Look, you and I both know that he's not okay. That day on the bridge? Regardless of whether you want to admit it, he was trying to commit suicide by jumping off that bridge. If I hadn't grabbed him, he would have succeeded. So, I guess when he didn't come to school today, after what happened to Margo, I just wanted to make sure he wasn't thinking about ending his life again."

"I can take care of my son, thank you. Mason's fine, and he's nothing like the girl that...did that. Now, I've asked you to leave."

He cocked his head. "Do you know where Mason is?"

"Of course, I do. And it's none of your business." She pulled her cell phone out of her pocket. "I'm dialing."

Chase backed down the steps. "Just, please. Look for signs of depression. Look up the 'tells' so you'll know what to look for. Don't let Mason be another statistic because the people around him are in denial." When he reached the end of the flagstone walkway, he turned to look back at the house, and his brows raised at Jean Moore, still standing there. "You should know that a boy at school is giving him a hard time, too." She didn't acknowledge his words as she moved further into the house, quickly closing the door on his probing eyes.

•   •   •

# ALYX

Sitting cross-legged in a circle, the girls sat stiffly on the soft grass at their normal after-school meeting place, shoulders hunched and occasionally shaking with the force of their emotions.

"I remember, this one time, I was failing Algebra 1, and Margo tutored me after school. She volunteered to help in the tutoring department. Did you know that?" Ellie asked.

A few heads bobbed among the sniffles.

Sophie spoke softly: "When we were in elementary school, we were best friends. I-I..." She paused to cover her face with her hands. "I'm sorry that we grew apart. Maybe if..." Sobs wracked her body.

Alyx shook her head. "No. We can't blame ourselves, or each other, for Margo's choice. I went down that road when I first heard. The questions bombarded me: Why didn't I *do* something more? What if I would have cancelled our self-defense class to go look for her? Would I have found her in time? Or what if I had reported it to a teacher when I saw her crying in the bathroom? Would they have intervened before she decided that taking her own life was the only option left? You have no idea how much I wish we could have prevented this from happening, believe me. And I know it would be easy to take the blame onto ourselves, internalize it. Who knows, maybe we all *could* have done something had we known how deep her depression was, but we'll never know that now. Ultimately, she made this decision. No one made it for her. Yes, we could have seen the signs, and in fact, we did see them. But she could have gone looking for help, too. And it sucks. But there it is. We can't blame ourselves for all the what ifs or could haves. Tonight is about honoring Margo's memory. Remembering all the good things about her, not casting blame on ourselves or others. Anyone else want to share?"

"Last year, remember when she came to school after she got her nose pierced? She smiled so big when I told her it was beautiful. She had such a pretty smile. I'd do anything to see her smile one last time." Emily sniffed, holding a tissue to her nose.

Alana wailed. "I was so angry with her for not telling me about the stupid nose ring. Why did that make me so mad? I can't even remember why that would infuriate me. It was stupid. So stupid. She was my best friend, and I didn't know she was so low that she would..." Her shoulders shook uncontrollably, causing another round of crying around the circle. "I listened to her when she said she needed to be alone. Why did I listen? I didn't know she wanted to be alone so she could..."

"Shh. It's not your fault, Alana. You were trying to be a good friend by respecting her wishes."

Alana jerkily shook her head. "But it is. It is my fault. She told me she was pregnant, and told me not to tell. I thought I was being a loyal friend, but really I was her executioner."

"No, no. You were being a good friend, right up till the end."

Alana hiccupped, crying so hard that her words were slurred. "I knew when she went with him. I knew, and I let it happen."

"Went with him? Who?"

"She wouldn't want me to tell. Margo wouldn't... she would want to protect him, even in death. But he isn't worth it. He got her pregnant and told her it wasn't his, even though he was the only one she was with. He threatened her life, and the lives of her family if she told anyone it was his."

"Who? Who did this?"

Alana stood up slowly, a look of pure hatred in her eyes. "We have to take him down. For Margo."

"Revenge won't bring her back."

"No. No, nothing can do that. Even though that's all I want. To be able to look across the park and see her walking toward us, ready for another session of defense class. But that's never going to happen again. Do you know he's the reason she wanted to learn self-defense? After that first time, well, she told me she didn't enjoy it. He was...rough." She looked around, a determined gleam in her eye. "It wasn't rape. She consented because she thought she had to, you know, keep the golden child happy. No, it wasn't rape, but it was no love match, either. And when she told him she was going to have his baby, he laughed at her. Laughed. Can you believe that?" She sneered. "Do you want to know who got Margo pregnant? I bet every one of you could guess, couldn't you?"

No one answered, the air as thick as a down blanket, waiting for her to continue.

"It was Jared Young."

# CHAPTER 35
## *ALYX*

Margo's locker had become a shrine of handwritten notes, candles, balloons, and stuffed animals. In a show of solidarity and support, people needed to *do* something to offer comfort in a tangible way.

Alyx thought it had the opposite effect. Every time she walked down the hall on the way to class or lunch, she was hit again with a wave of loss and helplessness. She guessed the act of leaving an object behind in Margo's honor was more for the giver than for any other purpose.

Chase hurried to her, flinching as he glanced at the shrine on his way past. "Mason isn't here again today."

"Oh no. You don't think..."

"I don't know what to think. I haven't seen him since Jared was attacking him on the school lawn. I just hope he hasn't..." Chase hung his head.

Alyx reached for his hand, giving it a gentle squeeze, just as a commotion broke out behind them.

At the other end of the hall, Jared stood in front of Margo's locker, just as Alana rounded a corner. "Get away from there!" She rushed over. "She wouldn't want you here."

"I can stand here if I want. What do you care?" Jared sneered.

Alana's hands fisted at her sides. "What do I care? You didn't stand by her when she was alive, so you don't get to pretend to mourn her."

He grabbed her arm, jerking Alana toward him, whispering in her ear in fierce undertones. Alana's face went pale and just as Alyx was lunging toward the pair, Alana threw her elbow into his nose. He howled, clutching his nose as blood spurted from both nostrils, his face already bruised from his fight with Chase just a few days before.

Alyx pulled Alana away while tremors racked the girl's body. Since they were in the math wing, the geometry teacher Mr. Griggs burst from his classroom down the hall and hurried to them, eyes wide, hand held out in front of him as if that alone would stop the commotion.

"What's going on here? Jared, is that you? You okay?" Mr. Griggs studied Jared's battered face.

"I w-was just stopping by Margo's locker, and *she* attacked me. I mean, I barely knew Margo, but I thought it would be nice to at least pay my respects."

Alana shrieked, lunging for Jared, but Alyx continued to hold her back. "Alana..."

"No! He doesn't get to get away with this! You pressured her into sleeping with you and..."

Jared forgot himself for a moment, letting his sneer show. "She got what she asked for."

"Jared. That's enough." Mr. Grigg's stern voice broke through. "Let's get you to the nurse's office so she can take a look at your nose." He turned to the crowd that had gathered. "Everyone, get to class. Nothing more to see here."

As the crowd dispersed, Alana threw her arms around Alyx. "Oh Alyx. It's so unfair." The girl sobbed into Alyx's shirt.

Alyx awkwardly patted her back. "I know. None of this is fair, but I'm proud of you for handling the situation. You used what you knew, didn't let him get the upper hand. Can't ask for more than that."

Alana stood back, swiping the sleeve of her shirt across her nose. "It did feel good, giving him what he deserves." Though she didn't quite smile, her eyes dilated with a satisfied gleam.

"What was he saying to you?" Chase asked.

Alana's face went beet red. "He-he said that I-I better not tell anyone about him and Margo or else people would be making a shrine in front of my locker, too."

Alyx looked at Chase. His voice sharp, he said: "Let's go see my dad."

"Oh, I don't think I should involve teachers..."

Chase interrupted. "Alana, please. This has to stop. We can't let Jared get away with this game of chess he's playing with people's emotions. If we don't stop him now, who will it be next?" As if magnetically drawn there, all three looked to Margo's locker memorial. They stood there, gazing at all that was left of a girl's life.

Finally, Alana nodded. "Okay. I'll go. But only if Alyx comes."

"You got it. I wouldn't want to be anywhere else," Alyx said.

Nolan Walker sat somberly behind his desk, occasionally asking a question, but for the most part, just listening. He blinked his eyes rapidly several times throughout the tale-telling, as if something was lodged in there he couldn't get out.

"I can't believe I've been blind to all this. I'm calling Jared in for a chat as soon as you leave," Nolan spoke with a growl.

Chase leaned forward, placing his hands on the desk. "You know he's going to lie about everything, Dad."

Nolan only nodded. "I won't be fooled again. Alana, would you like a pass to go home for the day? You don't have to..."

"No, thank you, Dr. Walker. I don't want to hide from that bully anymore. None of us should," Alana said. "Besides, if I go home, I'll just think about.... No. I'll stay here."

Nolan nodded. "Let me know if you change your mind, or just need to talk more. I'm right here if you need anything at all. Alana, I don't want you to hurt yourself or otherwise try to..."

"You don't have to worry about me. I'm not going to...do what Margo did. I see what's left behind when someone chooses to end it."

Nolan nodded, then looked at Chase. "Chase, will you stay behind? I need to talk to you about something personal."

Chase sat down in one of the student chairs and waited for Alana to leave the room. Alyx flopped down next to him. "I'll stay, too. I'd like to hear what you have to say."

Nolan's eyes searched Chase's. "She stays if I stay," Chase said.

Again, Nolan nodded. "I thought you'd say that." Nolan melted into his chair. "I owe you yet another apology, Chase."

"What for?"

"Corey came to me this morning. He admitted to lying, and he corroborated your story, that Jared was the aggressor, and you were trying to stick up for Mason. If it's any consolation, he feels awful about it."

Chase snorted. "Of course, if Corey tells you it must be true."

"I know. I know how hard this must be for you, Chase. I should have listened to you before. It's just that old habits die hard, you know? I've been a part of Corey's life since he was born, been a part of all of his ups and downs. It's hard for a father to let go of the automatic defense mechanism of being a father. I haven't been there for you that way because we were apart, and now that you're here, I have failed in that basic parental duty. The duty of defending my children, which includes you. I'm sorry for it, though I'm powerless to change what has already been. But what I can change is how I proceed moving forward."

"I get it. Nothing about this is easy. Even though it's hard to accept, I do understand."

Alyx cleared her throat. "What will you do about Jared?"

"I'll be watching him very closely," Nolan Walker said, his eyes narrowing.

"He's very sneaky. He's not dumb enough to do any of his bullying in front of you or any other teacher," Alyx interjected.

"And what about Jim Young?" Chase asked.

Nolan shrugged. "I've spent my life worrying about what Jim Young will say. It's time to do what's right."

"And Dad?"

"Yes?"

"I'm worried about Mason. When we arrived, he was trying to jump off the Gull Street Bridge. Now, Jared attacked him right here at school, and it's probably not the first time. He hasn't been in school for two days since that happened. I'm afraid he'll do what Margo did, or worse, that he already has. Can you help?"

"I'll call his parents and have a chat right now. If there's anything I can do to prevent this from happening again, you have my word I'll do it. And Chase?"

Chase cocked his head, listening.

"Don't do anything stupid, okay? I know you want to end this, and I do, too. But there's a right way to go about it, and a wrong way. I don't want you to risk yourself. You too, Alyx. Promise me you two won't go off on your own without telling me."

"I don't know if we can make that promise, Dad. What if something happens in the moment and you aren't there for consultation? You of all people should understand that events aren't always within our control."

"I understand that. Just promise you'll contact me first if you can, son."

Chase nodded. "That we can do. You have my promise, Dad."

Nolan Walker's eyes filled with tears.

"Thank you for that. After everything that's happened. Thank you."

# CHAPTER 36
## *CHASE*

That night, while eating a pizza Chase had picked up on his way home, Rose held back tears. "I can't believe any of this is happening." She'd been holding a slice for the past five minutes but hadn't taken a bite. "What is going on? Things like this don't happen in Dune Harbor." She put the pizza back down onto the paper plate in front of her, uneaten.

Nolan reached for his wife's hand. "Unfortunately, things like this can happen anywhere."

"I wish we could do something. I feel so helpless..." Rose dabbed at her eyes with a napkin.

"We're doing everything we can. I spoke to Jared and Jim this afternoon about his bullying behavior toward the other students at school. For all the good that will do. It seemed as if Jim was listening, though. Maybe he'll hold Jared accountable for his actions for the first time in his life."

"I hope so."

"And, if Mason doesn't come home tonight, search parties will go out first thing in the morning to look for him."

"I want to be part of that," Chase said.

"Me, too," Alyx responded.

"Yes, you both can have the day off...oh, there's my phone." He looked at the screen.

Chase and Alyx stared at each other, waiting to find out the identity of the caller, fearing the worst.

"The school has closed for tomorrow's search. That way, anyone in the community who wants to be involved can go. Including Mason's classmates and friends."

"Hopefully, he'll turn up before then," Rose whispered.

. . .

The next day, Mason was still missing. Nolan had spoken to both David and Jean Moore, and neither had any idea where Mason was. The town had shifted from a dark cloud of mourning to a storm of determination in finding—and possibly saving—one of their own. Hope shone down like a lighthouse beacon, providing the community a unifying ray of light to cling to. A dead girl was something they were powerless to change, but saving a living boy, well, that was something they could do with their time that might be more productive and would surely be more satisfying.

Search parties were assembled and sent out. Both local law enforcement and volunteers from all over the community set out in search of one troubled teen in the hopes that he would be recovered before he did something drastic. No one talked about what would happen if they found a body instead of a living being— there couldn't be two deaths in less than a week. There just couldn't be.

The townspeople held their breath and searched in silence. The students involved didn't want to discuss their own relationships—or lack thereof—with Mason. Since he was a loner, and shunned by Jared and his crew as a loser, few of them had paid him any mind. Guilt ran rampant amongst the search parties, as it had after they'd learned about Margo's fate. Why didn't we pay more attention? What could we have done to help a struggling boy, besides ignore him or remain silent as Jared bullied him?

The search continued throughout the day: the school grounds, football field, Mason's neighborhood, the beaches, the bordering forest land. School was closed to give everyone an opportunity to take part, and the turnout was impressive. The 'Save Mason' project was well underway, but no one from school had seen him since the day of the fight with Jared—if you could call one-sided bullying a fight.

With each place searched over and over, Chase was losing hope of finding Mason alive. After all, with the exception of his home-world, in all the other worlds they'd visited, Mason was either already dead before he arrived, or he had died while he was there. It seemed Mason, in most worlds where his other-selves existed, was doomed to certain death no matter what Chase did to try to prevent that from happening. He briefly wondered how his best friend, the version of Mason he had grown up with in his own home-world of Dimension 6, was faring without Chase there to protect him. He realized that was exactly what he'd done since the two had met in second grade. Mason had thrived under the shield of popularity and protection being Chase's friend had provided. Without that friendship, Mason's other-selves had become a much different person than the one he'd known so well. It was jolting to realize just how important one person can be to another, and how much someone's influence—or lack thereof—can so powerfully affect another's life and alter their path.

Chase walked on, eyes on alert for any sign of Mason. He was with a group of boys, including his new friend Logan, Annabelle's older brother Brian, and some other boys from school. They were searching the woods bordering town. An occasional bird call broke the silence in an otherwise somber group and the scent of pine enveloped them as they strode further into the wooded area. So far, nothing had turned up. Chase wondered briefly how Alyx's search was going. He was sure they'd have heard if any of the search parties had turned anything up since the Dune Harbor Police in charge of the hunt were constantly communicating on portable transmitters. Holding his arm up to shield the flashes of sun as he walked through the trees, he stubbed his toe on a tree root and grunted in pain. Despite the discomfort, he kicked out at the root, then paced, frustration punctuating each step.

"Where is he? I can't believe we haven't found him yet," Chase blurted.

Brian, Annabelle's brother who sometimes followed Jared in this world but had been a good friend to Chase back in his home-world—and in the other worlds they'd visited—had been shocked to his senses in light of the recent loss of Margo and the disappearance of Mason. He'd spoken to Chase's dad about his associations with Jared, and was among a growing number of students who were speaking out against the school bully. Brian had confessed that Jared had once tried to throw Mason off the bridge when they'd been in middle school, and how he suspected Jared had encouraged the boy to swallow a bunch of pills to end it all. Though he himself had not witnessed it, he still felt responsible for doing nothing to stop it after he'd learned about what Jared had done. Brian begged to be a part of the search, having known Mason all his life. Lines of guilt marred Brian's face as he tried to make amends for his part in Jared's harassment.

"I hope he's okay," Brian murmured. "Jared was really tough on him. Even in elementary school, he just didn't let up on the poor kid. Of all the people Jared has harassed over the years, his obsession with Mason has been relentless. I don't know why I ever hung out with Jared."

"I think what matters most is that you're changing that now. Lots of people bowed down to Jared for lots of different reasons. You can't blame yourself, but what you can do is what you're doing. Change it. Talking to my dad was a start. Breaking with Jared was another. Joining the search is a step in the right direction."

"I hope Margo has opened other people's eyes. I never liked Jared, but I did what he said because I didn't want to be the focus of his attention like Mason was, so instead of standing up to him, I let him make me a follower. It's a twisted kind of peer pressure, I guess. I hate myself for not doing something...but I'm only one person."

"People don't realize how powerful their words are. If only everyone would stand up to the tyrants of the world, then things like this just wouldn't ever happen. Most don't realize that a bully draws power from those who follow him," Chase said. "Take away their followers, they become impotent."

Brian looked off into the distance. "I know. It all seems so easy, but until you're faced with the situation, it's hard for people to understand the power someone like Jared can have over you. I'm not proud of it, or of what it's made me become: An enabler."

"But now that your eyes are open, you'll be free to make your own choices from now on." Chase patted Brian on the back. "Everyone's just doing the best they can to survive, I think."

"From now on, I'm going to try to do a better job of it," Brian mumbled.

"That's all anyone can do. Come on, let's search over here." Chase moved to the left, away from the other searchers. He'd taken three steps when someone shouted. Chase turned as if in slow motion in the direction of the voice. His feet, now solid as bricks, refused to move for a full minute's time. A weight sat heavy on his chest, and he found it difficult to breathe.

He didn't want to hear what the voices in the distance were shouting, and could imagine well enough what they might be saying. *They found his body*; he thought morosely. Shaking his head in denial, his feet started moving toward the sounds of shouting. *How many times can I lose my best friend? Is it my fate to witness Mason's death in every world I visit?* Chase didn't know if his heart could survive it.

As they approached, Chase started breathing again as words became clearer.

"Jared Young has been taken to the hospital."

Chase frowned. "Don't you mean Mason Moore?"

Bray, a familiar and welcome face, commented. "No, unfortunately, we still don't have any news about Mason. Jared has been beaten badly. He's on his way to the hospital now. It doesn't look good."

"What?" Chase whispered. He looked away. Though he disliked Jared as much as any person could dislike another human being, he didn't get any joy from this announcement. And then his head whipped up, eyes huge in his pale face. "Who beat him?"

Bray shrugged. "No way of knowing yet."

"Mason couldn't have done it. Could he?" Chase asked.

"Anything is possible, I guess," Bray answered. "If you have any knowledge about who could have done this, you better speak up about it now."

"It's just that...I don't know, really I don't. I know Jared gave Mason a really hard time, and now Mason is missing. He may think he has a score to settle or something. And I also know that my dad, Dr. Walker, the guidance counselor at school," he clarified in case they didn't know who his father was, "Dad called Jared and his dad into his office at school to talk to them about Jared's bullying, and Jim Young said he'd handle Jared."

"Jim?" Bray frowned, sorrow in his eyes. "I'll talk to Officer Murphy about that. Maybe he can make a run out to their house and check on things."

Chase nodded.

"In the meantime, let's continue doing what we came here to do. Search for Mason."

# CHAPTER 37
## *ALYX*

Alyx walked with Ellie on one side, Annabelle on the other. Sophie, Alana, and Emily followed behind. Tears came and went throughout their search, spirits sinking as the day raced closer to night with no word on Mason's whereabouts. She wondered what was happening with Chase's group, wishing she could lay her head on his shoulder and feel his hand on her hair right now. He was the only one who could ease her sudden storm of emotions. Only Chase could, if not make things better, than at least calm her ever fluctuating mood.

It wasn't fair to put that on him, making him responsible for her feelings of inadequacy in this situation as well as his own, and she felt a twinge of guilt at even having thought it. She'd felt more emotions in these first months of her eighteenth year than she had in her entire life preceding this, and wasn't sure how to handle it. It was as if she'd lived her first seventeen years in a bubble, and hadn't really been present in the real-life world until she'd strapped the watch on her wrist. She sighed, wishing yet again that Chase was here with her right now.

Alyx snapped her attention back to the present. They were searching the school grounds and sports fields, under bleachers, behind the snack bar. Anywhere they could think to look, just in case Mason was hiding out. If they could only find him before he did anything drastic...

Her thoughts mirrored that of a hundred searchers that were doing the same thing she was at this very moment, she knew.

If only the watch would give them the power to see where Mason was. Alyx sighed. If only they still had magic in this world, she could portal to the places they thought he might be much faster than this search was going...

But they didn't have magic here, at least not like in Dimension 8. Nolan Walker had said that all worlds contained some modicum of magic, since the watches themselves were powered by a spark of magic. But Alyx didn't know how that could help in their current situation.

Moving to search underneath the bleachers, she ducked down and hunched her back to avoid hitting her head on the lowest seats. Grass grew sporadically in the patchy dirt where the sun's rays shone through between the seats, and she found the space deserted and began moving on when something caught her eye at the end of the bleacher section she was searching. As she approached, Ellie, who was right next to her, gasped. She reached out to gently touch the letters written across the underside of the seat. Alana ran to her side, and began sobbing, the sound low and ululant like the baying of wolves mourning the loss of a pack member. Her shoulders shook as if in a sudden seizure, but it was the force of her sorrow that took her, not convulsions.

On the bleacher, written in black marker, were words scrawled in an unsteady hand.

*I'm sorry. I wish I could be a stronger person—Margo Gallagher.*

Alyx moved to stand close to Alana, who was swamped on all sides by Ellie, Annabelle, Sophie, and Emily, each with their arms around the girl, every one of them crying. Unsure what to do, Alyx reached a hand out and then let it drop helplessly to her side. Ellie's tear-streaked face popped up, and she reached out and grasped Alyx, pulling her into the huddle of mourning.

They stood that way for a long time, grieving and comforting each other. Alyx felt the moisture streaking her own face, and let the tears flow freely as she held on to her friends.

• • •

When they emerged from the bleachers, matching red blotchy faces and bloodshot eyes finally wrung dry, a commotion coming from the football field drew their attention.

Mason's parents, Jean and David Moore, had arrived with a news van and a local news crew. They emerged with flashing lights, cameras, and microphones at the ready. Not wanting to appear on television, the girls moved off to stand behind the cameras. The Moores stood stiffly, Jean adjusting the collar on her lavender button-down shirt, David fidgeting with his navy blue tie. The camera man set up with the outline of the school strategically set as the backdrop, and counted down silently holding up fingers. *Five, four, three, two, one...*

"I'm here with David and Jean Moore, whose son Mason has been missing since Tuesday afternoon when he was last seen at school. What do you want to say to your son's abductor?"

Mr. Moore, currently running for town mayor, responded. "Please. Bring our son home. Mason's a good boy, doesn't get into any trouble at all. We'll pay you a ransom, if that's what you're after. Just bring our son home."

Jean Moore stood at her husband's side, swiping a lone tear from her face. "Mason, if you're out there, we love you, and we'll do anything we can to bring you home." Her voice shook with emotion.

David Moore continued: "We won't even press charges. I believe my son's kidnapping is a political stunt." He turned to look at the newscaster. "As you know, I'm running for political office here in the great town of Dune Harbor, and there are those in my opposing party who would stop at nothing to remain in office here." Now he turned, talking directly to the camera. "Bring Mason back, there's no need to involve our families in this fight. I can make sure the law goes light on you if you choose to do the right thing. Bring Mason home safely. That's all we ask."

The reporter, who had been standing back to let the Moores air their plea, now moved into the light, microphone bearing the Channel Fifteen news emblem held up to her perfectly painted face framed by elaborately coiffed hair the color of autumn leaves. "David Moore, what do you say to the townsfolk who have spread the gossip that Mason was a troubled boy who may try to harm himself in some way? That he wasn't kidnapped at all?"

"That's the most ridiculous thing I've ever heard. Mason would never hurt himself or anyone else. He's the most well-rounded, confident boy I know. This false news is insulting to my family and everyone in this town. Some people will do anything to try to thwart my run for mayor, even stooping to involving my son in their political rhetoric. I'll not stand by and let my son's name become a smear campaign in my bid for public office."

Just as quickly as they'd appeared, they loaded up and drove off. Alyx, Annabelle, Emily, Alana, Sophie, and Ellie stood still as stone statues, their mouths hanging open in disbelief.

"Abducted?" squeaked Ellie.

Alana's brows wrinkled over troubled eyes. "False news?"

"Mason? Confident?" Emily whispered.

Alyx blew out a breath. "What just happened?"

# CHAPTER 38
## *CHASE*

Chase scratched the back of his neck, working the knot that had formed in his shoulder. His head pounded as the sun set in a burst of pastels, creating a picturesque scene pretty enough to put on a postcard; irony at its best. If weather mirrored emotions, rain and charcoal clouds with occasional claps of thunder would be a better backdrop to the activities of the day.

Officer Murphy, who had been leading their particular search party's efforts, had driven off in his police cruiser an hour ago, leaving Bray in charge.

Chase turned to look at Brian and Logan. "Something's nagging at me. I just wish I knew what it was."

"We've been at this all day." Brian looked at the sky. "Don't think we have much daylight left. Might have to call it off for the day."

Chase blew out a breath. "I don't want to stop until we find Mason."

"I know. None of us do. But we won't have much of a choice. Can't go traipsing through the woods in the pitch darkness," Brian said.

"Won't help if we all get lost," Logan, who had been silent for most of the day, interjected quietly.

Chase's shoulders slumped. "I know. It's just that..."

Logan shrugged, spreading his hands helplessly in front of him. "Maybe he left town."

Chase sighed. "It's possible, I guess. Just doesn't feel right. I don't know why, but I feel like I'm missing something. Do you think Mason went to Jared's house and attacked him?"

"Doesn't seem like something Mason would do, but you never know. Maybe he reached a breaking point. I mean, I guess we know that for sure, anyway. But we all assumed that Mason was intent on hurting himself. It's possible he also wants revenge on the person who has taunted him for the past ten years of his life first."

Logan, usually so quiet and soft-spoken, tripped over his words in obvious distress, his cheeks visibly heating. "I understand a little about how he's feeling."

Chase placed a hand on Logan's shoulder. "No one should ever be made to feel inferior, and that's Jared's specialty."

"I think we're wasting our time out here. If he was at Jared's house, then I'm sure the police already have him in custody," Brian murmured.

Chase nodded. "I think they're letting us search so we all feel like we're helping instead of sitting at home waiting for news."

Just then, the high-pitched shriek of a whistle broke the silence of dusk—the signal to meet back at their starting point. It was time to call the search off for the day.

Chase clenched his fists. Something still nagged at the corners of his mind. There was something he was missing. He knew it. Going back to his dad's house to sit and wait with his new family seemed less than desirable, but what else could he do? He shook his head, a frown turning his mouth down.

Could Mason really have gone after Jared? The Mason he knew wouldn't have it in him. But Chase reminded himself, the Mason in this world was not the same Mason he knew. Maybe the events in this world had turned him into someone else entirely. He and Alyx both knew that a person's other-self could be the polar opposite of the person they'd known in previous realities. Resolving to talk about it with Alyx tonight, he straightened his shoulders.

"Okay. Let's go. Hopefully, the police will find him tonight, or maybe he'll even go home." Chase frowned as they plodded to the parked cars, trying but not convincing himself of his own words. He was more tired from a day of searching than he had been on his last jump when he'd fought a giant chimera and lived to talk about it.

Somehow, this situation seemed much worse.

$\bullet \quad \bullet \quad \bullet$

# ALYX

Alyx trudged up the steps to the Walker's front porch, going over the events of the day in her mind. It had turned out to be an overall frustrating and emotional day, and it seemed as if the remaining bits of energy she had left in her body were draining away with each step she took. Her eyes drooped and her feet dragged as she reached for the doorknob, only to have the door swing inward before she touched it.

*Magic?*

Just the thought of reclaiming her magical abilities from Dimension 8 was enough to cause a surge of excitement that instantly perked her up. She stared at her hand for a brief moment before she realized Chase was standing in the doorway. He must have seen her coming and opened the door to let her in. Stepping outside, he reached for her. "Alyx." He lay his head on her hair and sighed, breathing in her scent.

Alyx leaned into him, her arms returning the hug. They stood that way for a minute or two, each drawing strength from the other. Finally, she stepped back, though stayed close enough that she still had to tilt her head at an angle to see him.

"Any luck today?" she asked, though judging by his actions, thought she already knew the answer.

He shook his head. "We searched all day, through the woods on the south side of town, and there was no sign that anyone had been there. When we were almost finished for the day, Officer Murphy—Carson—was called away. Apparently, someone beat up Jared enough to send him to the hospital."

"Who would..." Alyx's eyes widened. "You don't think Mason did it, do you?"

"That seemed to be the consensus. I just don't see it." Chase shook his head.

"I keep telling you..."

"I know, I know. It's not the same Mason. Still..."

"Do you want to go to the hospital?" she asked.

"No. I don't think they'd tell us anything, anyway. Let's just wait to hear. Dad was going to check on things, so when he gets back, he can fill us in on what's happening. As a trusted member of the community, they'll talk more to him, anyway."

She stifled a yawn. "Good, because I'm beat."

"Me too."

"Any food in there?"

"Leftover pizza."

"Perfect."

As Alyx heated a slice in the microwave, Chase sank into the chair, elbows on the table, chin in hand. He looked so exhausted she thought if his hand wasn't holding up his head, it would fall onto the table. His eyes were troubled.

"What is it? Something you haven't told me?"

"No. Not really. I just have this feeling that I'm missing something important. Like I could help Mason if only I could remember this vital piece of information." Chase shrugged. "It's probably nothing more than wishful thinking."

"Well, let's stop thinking about it and maybe it will come to you."

"I'll try."

"Want a slice?" Alyx asked.

Chase shook his head. "No thanks. I already ate some when I came home."

"What? Chase Walker refusing food? Are you sick?" Alyx teased, walking over to lay the back of her hand gently on his forehead. "No fever."

Chase smiled, the first time all day that he let himself relax. "Oh, aren't you the funny one?" He stood. "Now that I think about it, I could eat another slice." Chase laughed as he took a slice of pepperoni pizza from the refrigerator. Alyx stood eating at the counter, and she felt his arms slip around her from behind. As always, she felt that rush of adrenaline any time he touched her. She turned, tilting her head up so their lips were just a breath apart. "How about a pizza kiss?"

His answer was to lay his lips on top of hers. Leaning up on her toes, she wrapped her arms around him, pulling him closer until their bodies fit together like utensils in a silverware case. She twisted her head for a better angle, and the kiss deepened. Chase moaned into her mouth, and a slight smile turned the corners of her mouth upward. She loved the feminine power that could turn someone like Chase Walker into jelly, almost like magic. It was both exciting and humbling at the same time, and she threw herself into the kiss. His hands ran up and down her back, pulling her in, and she reveled in the feel of him.

"Ahem." Rose, face a deep red, stood on the stairs. "I-uh. I was coming down to see if there was any news…"

Talk of the search was like an ice-cold bucket of water, not to mention the addition of an audience to their display of affection, and Alyx sprang away from Chase, her body still remembering the feel of him even as they parted. Her tender lips tingled in homage to Chase's glorious onslaught on her senses, and Alyx teased her lower lip with her teeth, missing the feel of him. With great effort, she tore her gaze from Chase, her eyes focusing on Rose as embarrassment flooded Alyx's cheeks with color.

Chase recovered first. "No news yet. Hear anything from Dad at the hospital?"

"No," Rose answered, descending the rest of the way down the staircase. "Nolan told me about you two saving Mason on the bridge when you arrived. I'm proud of you. Both of you." Rose smiled and, though it was strained, her smile had a way of lifting the spirits of whoever was on the receiving end.

"Oh. Well, it was the same thing anyone would do." Alyx stammered, recovering her voice.

Rose shook her head. "You're wrong. Some people wouldn't have intervened. It's easier for some to remain on the outskirts and not get involved—even go out of their way to stay neutral. Mason, whatever choices he's made since that day, is living a longer life than he would have if you two hadn't intervened. You held his lifeline in your hands that day on the bridge. That's no small thing."

"Well, I don't know about that, but..." Chase paused, his eyes going wide. Alyx looked at him on the outskirts of the conversation as the dreaminess still lingered and thought she could get lost in the misty blue sea of his eyes. She jerked out of her reverie when his tone changed. "Wait. The Gull Street Bridge! That's it! I think that may be the key."

"Key?" Rose cocked her head.

Chase paced, his words tumbling out. "Yes. Brian mentioned that Jared had tried to throw Mason off the bridge back in middle school, and that's where Mason went to attempt suicide the day we arrived. The Gull Street Bridge is, I don't know, symbolic somehow, at least Mason thinks it is. Has anyone searched the area near there?"

The last vestiges of wistfulness melted away, and Alyx stiffened. "The bridge? You think Mason is at the bridge right now?" She asked.

Chase nodded. "It's worth a shot. He may have waited for the night, thinking no one would see him. We've searched everywhere else. Why not the bridge? It's as good a place as any, and I just can't shake this feeling he may be there." He turned to Rose. "Do you have any flashlights?"

Rose nodded, racing to the kitchen. "In here." Pulling two flashlights out of the far cabinet, she handed one to Chase. "I'm coming with you." She held up the car keys and the three of them—Bo in tow—raced to the door, a sudden sense of urgency nipping at their heels.

# CHAPTER 39
## *CHASE*

Ignoring the posted speed limit signs, Rose floored the gas pedal as she raced the familiar streets toward the far side of town and the Gull Street Bridge. Chase held his arm out to steady Alyx, Bo in her lap, around a particularly sharp turn. Rose, obeying traffic stops when accompanied by other cars on the road but ignoring them when they were alone, made record time as she screeched to a stop in the middle of the bridge and threw on the handbrake. Three doors flung open simultaneously; Rose, Chase, Alyx, and Bo lurched from the vehicle as it remained running, high beams cutting through the thickness of night and illuminating the faded canary-yellow paint of the double lanes. At first inspection, the area appeared to be deserted.

The metal bridge, painted silver but rusting in circular patches in the corners and along the eaves of the girder, stretched on for a mile. Though cars usually filled the lanes above while perpendicular traffic sped by underneath the arch-shaped underpass, the area was relatively desolate at this time of night, shrouding the bridge and surrounding area in an eerie stillness that seemed to envelop them in their own tiny bubble of solitude.

Splitting up, the three of them each took off in different directions. The north side of the bridge was illuminated as far as the car's headlights allowed before dropping off into total blackness. Alyx, Bo at her heels, took off in that direction. Rose and Chase, flashlight beams crisscrossing from one side to the other, took off toward the south side.

Chase cupped his hands, calling out repeatedly: "Mason! Mason, are you here?"

A barely audible voice answered from behind. Chase spun around where he stood in the center, holding his hands up in front of him. "Mason? What are you doing up there? Come on down and we can talk about it."

Mason was on top of the steel girder in a squatting position, clasping the top ledge with his fingers to steady himself. "Go away. Think you're my guardian angel or something?" As he spoke, Mason rose shakily to his feet, barely balancing on the balance beam-like rail, nothing but air surrounding him. "You're a little late."

"No, man. I just want to help you. You don't want to do this…"

A mocking laughter filled the air, and gooseflesh rose along Chase's arms and legs. Mason's eyes beseeched him. "People are always telling me what I 'want' to do. This time, it's my choice. That's what you don't get, I *do* want to do this. It would be better for everyone if I just disappear. Go away."

"I can't do that, man. *We* can't do that." Chase took a small step closer to Mason, but froze when Mason became agitated and wobbled before regaining his precarious balance on the ledge.

Mason's voice was so low, Chase had to lean forward to hear him, as if he were speaking only to himself. "You don't get it. There's nothing for me here. I'm ready. Unless you want to be here to witness my brain splattered on the highway, you need to go. Just leave and pretend you never saw me here. You can act surprised tomorrow when you hear I'm gone. No one cares whether I live or die. Believe me, everything will be better when I'm gone."

"I care. Your parents care. All those people who searched for you today care, too. You're not alone. There's always another way. Always a solution. What seems bad today can be resolved tomorrow. But if you jump, you won't get that chance. Is it Jared? Did he push you to this? If you do this, he'll be getting what he wants. Don't give him that power. He doesn't control you. Show him you're better than that. Better than him."

"You think you know? You don't." A sob shook his voice. "You know nothing about it."

"You're right. I don't know what pushed you to this point, so low that you think there's no other way besides death. But what I do know is…"

Mason's voice rose. "Shut up! Just shut up!" He wobbled precariously, his arms flying out to regain balance. "There's nothing you can do or say to stop me. Even if you do stop me now, I'll just find another way, another place. It's my time." As if in slow motion, though in reality only seconds ticked by, Mason turned.

"No!" Chase felt the scream rip from deep within his soul and ran. Even as his feet moved, he knew. Knew that, this time, there was no physical way for him to reach Mason in time. Knew beyond any doubt that there was absolutely no way he could prevent what was about to happen right before his very eyes.

Even as he heard pounding feet running by his side, heard Alyx and Rose screaming for Mason to stop, heard Bo whining, even as in his peripheral vision he saw them take off toward Mason just as he himself did, deep in his heart he knew it was futile. This awareness did nothing to stop him from trying. Knowing it was hopeless neither halted his steps nor stilled his voice. It did not stop the pup or the trio on the bridge from trying, with all of their combined strength, fortitude, and determination, to stop what they knew was about to happen. Even as they ran, even as their throats burned with the force of their screams, their psyches shied from the reality—the sheer horror—of the gruesome scene they were about to witness.

Nothing they did now would affect the outcome of this event. Even knowing all of that, they reached the railing with a tiny ray of hope still clinging to their hearts.

But, as they had known they would be all along, they were too late.

Mason whispered, "Tell my mom and dad I'm sorry." And then he closed his eyes and stepped off the outer edge of the girder into the dark space just beyond the bridge.

# CHAPTER 40
## *CHASE*

Chase heard someone scream as if through a long tunnel, unsure if he was hearing his own anguished voice or the voice of another. Mason's life flashed before Chase's eyes, the life of his forever best friend. He pictured the two of them in second grade sitting next to each other in the school cafeteria, trading sandwiches or bartering chips for pickles; laughing at an inside joke only the two of them thought was funny; as teenagers on the beach playing volleyball, trying desperately to impress teenage girls sporting bikinis and showing off their newly acquired vacation suntan; he pictured them at home playing video games, Uncle Charlie cheering them on; he pictured both of them walking down the long aisle to receive their diplomas, throwing each other's caps in the air when they were declared graduates of Dune Harbor High. He thought of all of Mason's other-selves he'd encountered in previous dimensions, who were lost to him forever, and wished with all his heart that he could save this one—this version of Mason here and now even though in the mind of *this* Mason Moore, they were nothing more than strangers in the same graduating class. Tears welled along with the memories, threatening to fall as they blurred his vision. As if in slow motion, Chase reached out, arms outstretched as he saw Mason's foot in thin air as he made that final leap, as if he wasn't too far away to grab onto him, as if he could prevent this imminent tragedy that would forever affect the lives of so many.

A flash reflected off the watch in the moonlight, his pupils drawn in that split second to look away from Mason and toward the shine. He gasped when he saw what it was. He'd seen it before, back in Dimension 7, though it had been conspicuously absent since then.

It was the knob. It appeared now, just as it had on his very first jump. One minute the outer rim of the watch was smooth as the wax on an apple's skin, the next a small round knob stuck out on the right side near the four o'clock mark.

He'd seen this dial only once before, but it had helped him then. Oh, how it had helped him. A small shudder gripped his body as, in a flash, he relived Alyx's death in that world, even as he continued to move toward the lonely boy who'd stepped off the ledge. The first time Chase had used it, he had been able to turn back time to save Alyx from death. A gruesome death that had already happened right before his horrified eyes. Through his ability to turn back the clock—reverse the passage of time itself—he'd been able to change the past, save Alyx, and re-write the future within the confines of that world. Could he use it that way now? If he turned the knob now as he had then, would they go back to their arrival time here in this world, changing the fate of both Mason and Margo?

No, his dad had said once you used the watch's 'power' in each world, you couldn't use it again. So, he acknowledged, turning back time probably wasn't an option here. And yet, there it was. The knob. It must do something, or else it wouldn't be there, he reasoned in that split second of time. Whatever transpired after he turned the knob had to be better than what he knew would happen without it—it *had* to be. There was no choice, not really. Reaching out with his right hand, he clasped the small protruding knob and twisted, even as Mason's other foot left the bridge into the nothingness beyond.

•　　•　　•

The surrounding air grew stagnant and so still even breathing became difficult, as if the oxygen surrounding them had solidified into jelly. Chase held his breath for a minute until he couldn't any longer and gasped, drawing the thick air into lungs that filled with the awkwardly heavy substance, like breathing at an extremely high elevation. He coughed as his lungs adjusted to the change. Air became nearly visible, though he could see through it with an unnatural clarity. Chase waved a hand through the air, and the translucent particles of congealed water vapor seemed to part as his hand sliced through it. He blinked, disbelief halting him in place.

A coldness descended on the bridge, accompanied by a blue mist that seemed to spread out from the watch directly in front of him. To the right of him, he saw Alyx shudder and rub her bare arms against the sudden chill. To his left, Rose expelled a breath, condensation visible in a cloud of cooling vapors that floated from her mouth, much the same way it did on a cold winter's day. Even as that registered, Chase felt gooseflesh travel across his exposed flesh. All of this seemed inconsequential compared to the scene in front of him engulfed in a cobalt cloud.

Chase took another step closer, the tips of his sneakers bumping the metal girder as he reached a hand out toward Mason. Mason, who had seconds ago stepped off the ledge of the bridge. Mason, who should rightfully be dead or at least severely injured on the highway down below. Mason, who was surrounded by that misty, blue aura.

Mason was definitely not dead. But was he alive, then?

Chase breathed out another puff of cold steam and leaned out over the railing. "Mason?" his whispered word mirrored his incredulity. He blinked again, trying to make sense out of what he was seeing.

"What happened?" Alyx croaked. Bo, pressed against her side, shook from head to tail.

"It's the watch. It's doing something to Mason." He turned, wide eyes looking into hers. "The knob appeared again, and I turned it…"

"Oh." Alyx paused, head cocked. "Is the knob still there now?"

Chase glanced down. "No. It's gone. But my watch stopped. The second hand isn't moving."

Alyx glanced at her own watch, the violet glow shining through the mist. "Mine, too. As if time has halted. Oh-my-gosh—you stopped time, Chase."

"What should we do now? How will we undo what's been done?" Chase asked.

"Well, I think the first thing we need to do is get him down." Alyx nodded toward Mason.

"Right." Chase glanced at his friend, dangling in the emptiness. "We need to figure out how to do that."

"Yes. And since we don't know how long this will last, I think we better hurry," Alyx answered.

A hand on his arm stilled Chase, and he turned to see Rose, face pale as baby powder, staring at Mason. "How did…" Her whispered words trailed off, leaving her thought unfinished.

"It's some kind of magic, Rose. It's okay. It's the watch." Chase soothed.

"I-Is he alive?" Rose asked.

"I think so. Let's get him back up here and we can check for a pulse," Chase said.

The three of them looked at Mason with equal expressions of skepticism, the depth of their disbelief momentarily stalling their actions, for what they were looking at was beyond anything they had ever seen before. Mason, who moments ago had been conversing with them while standing on the ledge of the bridge, was literally frozen in place. Not only were his limbs stuck in mid-flail as they'd been when he'd taken that last final step into nothingness, but the expression on his face remained contorted in a sort of peaceful fear, his eyelids squeezed shut causing deeply creased wrinkles on his motionless, scrunched face which brought to mind a wax museum display figure. He hung there impossibly, still as a tree trunk, not a muscle moving—not even a twitch—on his entire body.

The impossibility was magnified tenfold due to the fact that he hung that way *in the air*. There was neither anything under him to stop his fall, nor was there anything above him to offer a handhold in the unlikely event that Mason should suddenly regain his mobility and decide he'd changed his mind, after all, and no longer wished to plummet to his death below. Yet there he stayed, frozen in place like an insect pinned to a wall, limbs forever frozen in that last position just before death. Only there was no pin, no wall that Chase could see; only the void. No scientific reason existed to explain how a body could be suspended in nothing but air the way Mason was now. The eerie stillness only served to intensify the utter inertness of the air surrounding his body as he hung impossibly unsuspended in space.

Chase leaned over the rail, reaching so far he was balancing on his abdomen with his feet off the ground. If he stretched, he could just swipe the tip of Mason's outstretched hand with his fingers. "I can't reach him." He stood, looking around. "We'll need something to pull him closer."

Rose turned. "I may have something in the car." She turned, jogging to the vehicle. Climbing into the driver's seat, she popped the trunk, then got out to hurry to the back. Bending so that the top half of her body disappeared into the trunk space, she rooted around. After a few moments of rummaging, she raced back to where they stood. "How about this?" she asked. In her hand, she held a rusted crowbar. "Nolan had it in the compartment with the spare."

"Perfect! You're the best, Rose!" Chase clasped the crowbar in one hand and leaned toward Mason once again. He held the tool out as far as he could, nearly hooking it around Mason's closest arm several times. Each time he tried to pull back to draw Mason's prone body closer, his hand would shift just enough so the slight curve of the hook lost its purchase on him and his hand slipped out. "It's not working. Any ideas?" Chase asked, handing the crowbar back to Rose.

"Maybe if I get on top of the rail..." Alyx began.

"No. No way." Chase vehemently shook his head.

"Hear me out," Alyx said.

"No. There's no way I'm letting you stand on the ledge of a bridge."

A defiant gleam entered Alyx's eyes. "Letting me? We'll finish *that* discussion later, believe me. But right now, we have to get Mason down before this magic wears off and he plummets to his death. If I climb to the other side of the railing, you can hold on to me, and I'll be able to reach closer to Mason and hook his clothing. Then, you can help me over and we can pull Mason along."

Chase scrubbed his hands over his face and sighed. "I don't like you going over there, Alyx."

"Tough. I'm going to do it with or without your help, so you might as well suck it up and help me. Give me a boost, will you?" Alyx put her knee on top of the railing, reaching out for assistance.

"Fine. But if you fall, I'll never forgive you."

She blew him a kiss. "You won't let me fall. I trust you, Chase."

With a little grumbling, he heaved her up until she was sitting on the railing with her legs dangling over the outer edge. She eased over the ledge until her feet were on the other side of the bridge, with the railing at her back, while Chase wrapped his arms around her torso from behind with all that he had. "Hurry, Alyx. You have fifteen seconds and I'm pulling you back."

Alyx took the crowbar from Rose and leaned forward and down. Mason's body hung at an angle slightly below them. The spell had taken effect after he'd already stepped off the bridge, but just before gravity had been magically halted—even as the passage of time had been. Straining forward as Chase steadied her, she reached out in an attempt to grab hold of Mason's hair in order to yank him upward. She leaned further until Chase supported all her weight, but still couldn't get close enough to get the crowbar under his armpit.

"If only I could..." Alyx's words trailed off as there was a sudden flurry of movement coming from the bridge behind her. "Chase, what's happening?"

"Bo? It's Bo! Good boy, Bo-Bo!" Chase barked out a laugh as Bo, wings that had been missing since their arrival here in this world, unfurled in a glorious display of autumnal feathers as he awkwardly took off and flew in a choppy circle around both Mason's prone body and Alyx who still stood with her back to the railing, parting the blue mist as his wings flapped. Glowing blue droplets clung to the animal's fur and surrounded his wings, illuminating the miraculous creature with an unearthly aura. Unbeknownst to them in his non-magical disguise, the pup's wings had grown in the weeks since they'd left his world, though they would surely continue to grow and fill out until he reached maturity, they were still a sight to behold in all of their feathered, coppery-gray glory. Bo threw his head back and howled in delight, a canine grin blooming on his foxlike features, and his fluffy tail wagged through the air in time with his flapping wings. Bo dipped in close enough to give Alyx a quick lick on her forehead that had her giggling before he clumsily zig-zagged away. This was the pup's first flight, and he was so full of a combination of obvious pride and adorable clumsiness that Chase couldn't help but grin.

"Bo, you're flying! It must be the magic—when the magic touched him, he reverted to his true form!" Alyx mused.

"Hurry Bo, that's right. Get behind Mason and see if you can push him toward us. Good boy!" Chase called out.

The chimera pup in all his natural splendor flew with awkward jerks and dips around Mason. He backed up, put his head down, and rammed into Mason's shoulder with the top of his head. Unfortunately, the action caused Mason's body to move further away so that he was even more out of reach than before.

"It's okay, Bo. Try again. Go lower this time," Chase urged. "Push upward."

Bo flew in a wide, uncoordinated circle, then repeated the bump on Mason's back as he angled up from below. Though Mason's body remained in the exact position, he moved slightly toward them. Bo repeated the action several times, backing up and nudging with his head. With each contact, Mason's body moved inch by tedious inch. Just enough for Alyx to clasp onto the back of his cotton t-shirt. As she was hooking one side of the crowbar into the fabric, the air began warming around them, and the pressure on their lungs eased.

"Alyx, hurry! I think the spell is wearing off!" Even as Chase breathed the words, Mason's arms began moving, if only slightly, and the weight on the crowbar became more intense as gravity reinstated itself in slow degrees. With each second that ticked by on the clock, science was winning the battle over magic.

Chase pulled Alyx so hard, while at the same time she pulled Mason closer with the tool and grabbed him around his middle. She felt Chase heave her up and over the rail, nearly falling in a heap onto the blacktop below. Immediately turning, they combined their efforts, awkwardly pulling Mason until he hovered over the railing once again where, as magic dissipated like fog, he fell with a *thud* onto the bridge's blacktop below—a much shorter fall than he originally intended. Mason was starting to come to, and Chase squatted next to his friend.

"Chase! Bo needs help! Hurry, I can see through his wings. I think they're disappearing!" Alyx screamed the words even as she began climbing back up onto the railing. "Grab hold, Bo needs our help."

Chase supported her as he had done before, but Bo was out of reach, floating erratically down toward the highway below as his wings fluttered in and out of focus, flashing between solidity and transparency like a flickering bulb. After one last spark, Bo's wings disappeared completely. Without the wings to glide him through the air, he plummeted willy-nilly toward the highway below. Alyx looked up in horror as headlights approached, heading straight for the place where Bo was seconds away from landing.

# CHAPTER 41
## ALYX

Alyx ran to the car, Chase by her side, and flung herself into the driver's seat. "He's okay, he's okay, he's okay," she chanted, praying that if she said it enough times, the sheer force of the words alone would will it to be true.

"Rose, stay with Mason," Chase called over his shoulder as he dove into the passenger seat and Alyx took off. The drive across the bridge seemed to take an eternity, even with Alyx flooring the gas. When they reached the exit, Alyx continued through the toll booth without stopping, banking to the left. They had to drive around a loop to merge into the lane that would take them under the bridge.

"Where is he, Chase? I don't see him," the catch in her voice gave away the panic threatening to rise to the surface. "He was falling pretty fast, and a car was heading that way. What if..."

"Don't go there. He's okay." Chase squinted, searching desperately in the darkness beyond the headlights. "Keep driving and I'll keep a lookout. He flew halfway down before his wings disappeared. He's gonna be fine, he's a tough little guy."

"I don't know, Chase. He's our responsibility, and all he was doing was helping us save Mason. He doesn't deserve..."

"He's okay, Alyx. Think positive thoughts, alright?" Chase reached over, giving her shoulder a gentle squeeze.

"I'm trying. I'm just so worried about him. Where is he?" She reached the approximate mid-point of the bridge, directly below where they had been. Alyx put the car in park and they both leaped from the vehicle.

"Bo! Here, Bo!"

"Bo-Bo! We're here for you. Tell us where you are," Alyx shouted.

A tiny whimper off to the distant left had them both whipping around.

"Bo?" Alyx moved toward the sound.

*Yip-yip.*

Though his voice was weak, it was music to her ears. She dashed toward the pup, still not visible in the darkness of night, the moon's rays not reaching far enough under the bridge to offer help. A low, gruff voice—one she didn't recognize—halted her steps.

"He's okay. I caught him before he landed on the blacktop." He paused. "So, you're discovering how to use the watch's power without my help." As the man spoke, his words gained volume, indicating his continued approach. "You've truly connected with your watch, then. Possibly more than any other before you."

Alyx felt Chase's hand on her forearm, stopping her from going any further.

"Who *are* you?" Chase demanded.

"We've met before, boy, and we're likely to meet again before your year of jumping ends." The cryptic words caused a chill to race up Alyx's back. She immediately reached for her favorite weapon, a blade disc that was usually attached to a holster on her thigh, and realized she didn't have it with her. She had forgone her weapons in an attempt to fit in without drawing unnecessary attention to herself in this world. Now she cursed the choice to leave her blade discs behind. She wouldn't be making that mistake again.

"Pavo?" she asked, desperately trying to see through the dark.

A bitter laugh echoed off the walls of the underpass. "You think I'm the hunter? No, you've no cause for concern. I'm the opposite of a hunter, though their very existence can be laid at my feet, and for that I'm truly sorry. It was an unintentional folly that was out of my control, like so many other things in my life." The man stepped from the deep shadows, and Alyx fervently wished for the flashlight they'd left on the bridge above them. She could just make out his outline, and the swath of white hair that wildly framed his face.

"Wait. Who are you...?" she asked.

"I know who he is." Chase spoke at last. "At least, I think I do."

"I'm sure that you've figured it out by now. But it doesn't matter who I am, when you get down to it. My existence has become inconsequential. It's all up to you, now."

"We've seen you in other worlds, so you clearly know about the dimensions and watches, though I've noticed you don't wear a watch yourself. You helped me turn back time in Dimension 7, and you've been watching us throughout our journey through the parallel worlds."

The man inclined his head. "From a distance, yes. I have tried to leave you to your own devices, but sometimes it's impossible not to intervene. I see you are learning. Finally."

Alyx interrupted. "Have you seen an animal? A puppy? He fell, and we're..."

"You mean the hybrid? Yes, he's right there. I told you, I caught him." The old man pointed to his right. "He'll be okay. The magic took more of a toll than the fall."

Alyx ran in that direction, not caring about anything else now that the man didn't pose an immediate threat to them. He could be the President of the United States and he wouldn't hold as much importance to her as an almost surely injured Bo did. Another *yip*, and Alyx rushed toward his mewling. When she reached him, she squatted by his side, running her hands over his entire body to feel for injuries since she couldn't see him clearly. Gently, she pushed her hands underneath his body, and lifted him so she could cradle him against her. Tears filled her eyes when she felt his happy little tongue rub against her neck, and she sank to the ground, clutching the pup to her chest as relief turned her limbs to jelly. He was okay.

Chase lay a hand on her shoulder, and she sighed, leaning into him and taking a moment to revel in the fact that, by some miracle, both Bo and Mason were alive. He ran his hand over Bo's body almost reverently, as Alyx had. "He's okay?"

She nodded. "Seems to be." Chase sank down next to her, and they took a minute to just be. The events of the day were beginning to take their toll, and this was just the beginning. After a few blissfully silent minutes, Chase spoke: "C'mon. We need to go get Rose and Mason."

Slowly and with stiff limbs, Alyx rose, Bo in tow, and stifled a yawn as she flopped into the car.

Chase turned to speak to the man he thought was a distant relation. "Elias? Elias Walker, are you there?"

Squinting through the black, Chase searched for the man, seeking verification of his identity and possible answers, but the man had vanished into the night.

Chase shook his head before following Alyx to the car, wondering when he and the mysterious stranger who he strongly suspected was his great-great—he didn't know how many greats—grandfather would meet again, if ever.

• • •

Alyx and Chase arrived back on the bridge to Mason sitting on the blacktop, body hunched, head hanging down. Occasionally, his shoulders shook.

Rose squatted next to him, a reassuring hand on his back. "It's okay, Mason," she said, her words meant to soothe.

"I jumped. I stepped off the bridge, right? I remember that much; I'm sure I did. So, why am I still here?" Mason whispered.

"I can't explain it, Mason. You'll just have to trust me that you've earned another chance. I guess you could say it's a miracle. I want to help you get the help you need to recuperate," Rose promised.

"I don't need help," Mason mumbled.

"Yes, you most certainly do need help, Mason Moore, and I'll not hear another word about it. I've already called your parents, and an ambulance is on its way any minute. Your parents will meet you at the hospital." As if on cue, a siren broke the silence of the night, gaining volume as it neared the Gull Street Bridge.

"No, I..." Mason attempted to argue, but gave up when he saw the determined gleam in Rose Walker's narrowed eyes. Bo, who had wiggled free, limped over to lick Mason's hand. He ran a hand over the animal's fur. "I could have sworn I saw..." Taking a jagged breath, he shook his head. "No. It must have been a dream."

"We'll follow the ambulance and meet you there, too," Chase said.

Mason jerked his head up. "Why do you care?" he moaned.

"Because, you matter, Mason. No matter what Jared told you, you matter more than you know. To the people of this town. To your family. You matter to me. You don't realize your value; how many lives would be affected by your loss. I can't explain it, but I feel like I've known you my whole life. I'd like to be your friend, if you'll let me. I mean, for reasons that are out of my control, I'll be leaving the area soon. I won't have a choice. But I need to make sure you're okay before I go."

Mason looked away without responding, though his eyes filled with moisture, and he cleared his throat.

"Mason, can you answer one thing? Did you go see Jared earlier today?" Chase asked.

Mason shook his head. "No. Why would I?"

"Just asking. He was badly beaten, and some think maybe it was you. It would be understandable if you went for him after all he's done to you."

Mason's face went pale. "It wasn't me. I didn't do it."

Chase nodded.

Just then, the ambulance turned onto the bridge, the red lights illuminating the curve of the beams with a rotating spotlight. Within minutes, they loaded Mason into the back, and Alyx watched Chase closely as they pulled away, his relief palpable. She reached for his hand, giving it a squeeze. That one touch conveyed her thoughts more clearly than words could as she felt the return pressure of his answering grasp.

# CHAPTER 42
## *CHASE*

Chase sat on the floor in front of the recliner, leaning back against Alyx's legs as she sat in the chair. Nolan, Rose, and Ellie sat on the couch, and Corey leaned back against the wall, his posture stiff as he intentionally put space between himself and the rest of the family. The television's volume on its loudest setting, and all of them completely focused on the screen as the local news anchor read the night's stories.

*"Dune Harbor is in a state of shock this week, in the aftermath of the suicide of Margo Gallagher one week ago. We've learned that another teen, identified as Mason Moore, son of David Moore, candidate for mayor and long-time resident of Dune Harbor, also attempted to take his own life late last night. Mason has been admitted to Dune Harbor Community Hospital and his current condition is stable. He'll be held in the psychiatric ward until he is deemed safe to return home. Yesterday, we reported him missing. Many town community members planned and executed a search party for the boy, which was largely unsuccessful throughout the day. Late last evening, he was found in the midst of a suicide attempt. We'll keep you up to date on the details as we receive them."* First, Margo's senior picture flashed across the screen, which segued briefly to a picture of Mason followed by a picture of David Moore, mouth open as he stood behind a podium to deliver his speech announcing his candidacy for mayor a few months back.

*"Early reports suggested that Mason Moore may have been the victim of a kidnapping, which we covered in an exclusive interview late yesterday afternoon with David and Jean Moore, but our network has investigated and disproven those reports. It appears as if the boy ran away on his own intending to commit suicide, and that no other parties were involved. David Moore has withdrawn his bid for the mayorship of the town, leaving no current challenger to Mayor Christopher Harris, our current mayor. More on that later."*

Bo limped over, having sprained his left hind leg in his fall, and eased into Chase's lap, his wrapped leg sticking straight up in the air. His lanky, adolescent body hung off both sides of Chase's legs and onto the floor, but the pup didn't seem to notice his own changing size. Chase lay a hand on the pup as he watched the broadcast, absently scratching the animal behind the ears.

*"In other news, we've learned that yet another teen, identified as Jared Young from Dune Harbor High, has also been admitted to the hospital and has been moved to the Intensive Care Unit. He'd been beaten severely, and has multiple broken bones and contusions, as well as some internal injuries. Mason Moore will be questioned as a person of interest, even as Jared's father, Jim Young, is wanted for questioning."* On the screen, the reporter, whose stiff, auburn hair didn't move as she shook her head, stared imploringly at the camera. *"These events in our close-knit community have raised a lot of questions of late. Clearly, something needs to be done to prevent the kinds of events we've seen recently in our fine town from continuing to happen. Here at DHN, we'd like to do anything we can to aid this cry for help in the coming weeks. In an effort to contribute, we are opening a suicide hotline, open to teens; or anyone else who is feeling depressed and just needs a listening ear. The number is at the bottom of your screen. Please write the number down and spread the word. It's also available on our website, along with resources for parents of teens experiencing depression that will remain on our site."* The phone number and a picture of the website filled the screen. When the newscaster appeared, she looked solemnly into the camera. *"If you or someone you know is feeling like there is no way out, please call. Even on the darkest days, there is always a sunrise on the horizon. Thanks for tuning in."*

Nolan pressed a button on the remote and the screen went black. He ran his hands over his face. "This is all my fault. If I had done something about Jim long ago, maybe he'd have been different. If he had been different, maybe Jared would be, too. This entire chain of events is because of me."

Rose placed a hand on his back and rubbed in a circle. "No. None of this is your fault. What could you have done differently? You can't control the actions of another man, just as you can't take responsibility for his choices or his actions."

Nolan shook his head. "But I knew. I knew he wasn't right, and I did nothing."

"There was nothing you *could* do. Jim alone is responsible," Rose soothed.

Nolan shook his head, tears welling in his eyes. "I could have."

Rose threw her hands into the air, her voice taking on an edge. "Tell me. What do you think you could have done to prevent Jim from going down this path?"

"I could have chosen to go home at the end of my year of jumping, instead of remaining here with you. Maybe somewhere deep inside me, I knew that if I thought of you, I'd come back to you. Some part of me chose to stay here, and in that one act I caused all of this by returning here instead of going to my home-world, whether or not intentional. Maybe my staying here negatively altered the course of time by the mere aberrance of my presence."

A tear streaked down Rose's cheek. After a moment of silence, she said: "I don't believe that. Look at our children. They wouldn't exist if you hadn't stayed. Their existence in the world can be nothing but a blessing. You were meant to stay here all along, Nolan Walker. I believe that with all my heart."

The tears Nolan had been holding back fell free, and he sobbed as he held onto Rose and she collapsed into his arms. "You're right. The world would be a darker place without Ellie and Corey."

Nolan looked over Rose's shoulder, catching Chase's eyes. They stared at each other with troubled eyes, understanding the unspoken words as only they could.

Chase's own eyes filled as understanding dawned.

Though they came from different worlds—literally—Chase had always assumed he and Alyx would find a way to stay together once they turned nineteen. One of them would leave their home-world forever in the ultimate sacrifice of love. He'd thought his dad's life here in this world proved that theory.

But now, he knew. Knew the cost of being a keeper and finding his soul-mate on this journey. Everything came into crystal clear focus, though his heart constricted at the knowledge. For with that knowledge came the agony of impending loss.

It was clear to him now that he and Alyx would never be able to stay together at the end of this year of jumping dimensions. Too much was at stake for too many people. The pain of that upcoming sacrifice tore through his chest like a rifle blast, and he reached for her. The smile that lit her face told him that her thoughts weren't following the same path as his own. She remained blessedly ignorant of their looming separation. Chase forced a return smile that didn't reach his eyes. There would be plenty of time for explanations later. All that mattered was right here, right now.

Their time was not up yet, and he vowed to cherish every moment of their remaining months together until they had to part ways, never to see each other again.

# CHAPTER 43
## *ALYX*

"I think I'll go back and finish out the week." Alyx blushed as Chase's mouth dropped open.

"Wait. You're saying you *want* to go back to school?" Chase asked, his brows raised in twin arches. He'd just given her the out she needed to stop attending Dune Harbor High. After all, they'd be leaving this world in less than a week.

"Well, it's not that I want to, it's just that I think we should since..." her words trailed off in the face of Chase's mirth.

His shoulders shook as his booming laughter cut her off. "I never thought I'd see the day," he blurted between guffaws. "When Alyx Eris, badass dimension traveler, master of alien weaponry, professor of tactical self-preservation skills, practically *begs* to go back to high school."

"What? It's not a big deal, really. And it's not school, necessarily. It's just that I feel a certain responsibility to..." Alyx's face heated as she searched for words that didn't come.

Chase threw an arm over her shoulder, offering an olive branch. "I understand completely, Alyx. No need to explain. You have friends now, and you don't want to let them down. Makes perfect sense to me." He winked.

Impossibly, her cheeks mottled pale white, flushed with darker shades of patchy scarlet. She nodded and gulped back a wave of emotion threatening to burst forth. The girl from Dimension 4, that fearless keeper ready for any crisis thrown her way, had somehow morphed into a quintessential teenaged girl in the span of just a few months. Before her eighteenth birthday, if her former-self could have looked into the future to see who she was now, she would have gawked at what she would have most assuredly perceived as a pathetic, self-serving, ignorant, and shallow excuse for a human being. That girl had needed neither friendship nor companionship. She hadn't needed reassurances of any kind and had been sure she'd known what her future would hold. Never did any of her plans involve a partner, a pet, or friends. Socializing had been for the weak and needy, mere distractions to what really mattered, or so she'd reasoned. The old Alyx Eris had needed no one but herself. Even her family had held back typical parental affection in an attempt to instill in her the importance of the survival and preparedness she required for this year of jumping. She had to wonder what they would think of her now.

Present day Alyx had changed in ways both subtle and obvious. Oh, she could still knock out an opponent. That would never change. She imagined her eighty-year-old self, white hair pulled back, body aged but still toned, taking down a young, energetic mugger with a well-placed elbow jab, and a small smile tugged at the corners of her mouth. But now, she had something she'd never known she wanted: friends. Chase. Ellie, Anabelle, Sophie, Bo. Margo. Mason. She'd even formed a special bond with Rose. Alyx was learning that they were all a part of her now, and would be long after she left this place. They would travel with her always, deep inside her heart. She knew now that in life, every person she encountered played a part in shaping her own future into something different from what it would have been without their presence in her life; something better. Even those who set out to harm had a role to play and a lesson to impart in the game of life.

Alyx tilted her head and said a quick prayer of thanks. She wouldn't change a thing. Everything that had happened until now had helped to shape her personality and bring her to this here-and-now version of herself, and she was content in her becoming, though she was sure she still had a lot of blossoming yet to come.

"Earth to Alyx. Hello Alyx? Whoa, thought I lost you for a minute. You okay?" Chase asked, his eyes searching deep into her very soul.

"Yes. Yes, I am. Let's go to our room to study for the Calculus test." She made a grab for her backpack on the dining table.

Chase laughed again. "Who are you, and what have you done with my Alyx?"

She punched him in the arm, holding nothing back, and smirked when he rubbed the sore spot.

"There she is." He smiled, his eyes shining into hers, and she knew she could spend forever lost in those sapphire depths. This was home.

In her dreamy state, it took her a moment to shift gears when the front door burst open with a *bang* as it bounced off the wall; the sun outlining a menacing silhouette blocking the exit. That hesitation cost her as belatedly, she fell into battle pose and reached for the blade discs but once again found nothing but empty holsters. The old Alyx would never have been without her weapons, though now it had happened twice in as many days. She desperately opened her backpack in search of a weapon but found only textbooks, folders, and notebooks; realized that her artillery was stashed away in the room down the hall as she heard Nolan's scream as he shoved them aside. No time for firepower, then.

A large person, most likely male judging by his brawn, with details obscured by the light illuminating his form with a sort of back light that hid his features. When the intruder advanced, Alyx blinked her vision into focus and immediately recognized Jim Young just as he raised his arm. In the time it took for Alyx to gasp, the Walker's living room became a battleground. The muzzle of the weapon flashed in discharge, the light temporarily blinding them, followed by a sickening *thud* that seemed to shake the wood floor. Her mind was slow to catch up, not realizing at first what the sound meant. She shook her head in denial as she stared down in horror. It was the sickening, unrestrained sound of a body hitting the ground with no resistance and nothing to cushion the fall. Alyx's eyes widened as she stared at the inert form of the person that had been upright just seconds before, but now lay unmoving on the floor, distorted crimson silhouette setting the macabre scene as the bloody outline spread. She shook her head, one quick shake, in denial of what had just happened. It took her another agonizing moment to force her mind to shift gears before springing into action. Letting instinct take over, she lunged.

# CHAPTER 44
## *CHASE*

"Dad!" Chase screamed, crouching down next to his father, who lay completely unmoving on the floor. He had dropped with the force of a cannon ball careening on a downward trajectory. One second, Nolan Walker stood upright, and the next he lay sprawled on the wooden floor, a growing crimson stain underneath his left side that bore a macabre resemblance to an image from Rorschach's psychological inkblot test in its symmetry.

"No, no, no," Chase chanted. "Please, no."

As if from a distance, Rose's ear-piercing scream registered as he put pressure on the seeping hole in his father's side. Chase called out to her, demonstrating how to staunch the flow of ruby red blood—a skill he was sure she knew though the knowledge was currently frozen in panic—that poured steadily out of Nolan's torn flesh and oozed into the gaps between the hardwood tiles. Blood seeped through his fingers and for a moment he was transfixed by the sight—this, the blood of his father, a man who had been little more than a guy in a picture he'd been told stories about as a child but now was as essential as breathing air to him. He couldn't lose him now. Tremors shook his arms, but he managed to keep his hand steady to push down on the wound. Rose snapped out of her haze and raced to the kitchen.

Chase's focus shifted as a second shot rang out, seeming to shake the foundation of the house, and he was gripped with dread as he saw Alyx grappling with Jim Young for control of the gun, a hole in the ceiling that had appeared when she'd charged him, redirecting the bullet. If not for her, Jim surely would have finished the job of murdering his father, the man's hatred so apparent on his contorted face.

Jim shouted, spittle flying in every direction, even as he wrestled with Alyx. "All of this is your fault, Nolan! You and your family of ingrates. You couldn't just be happy with having this ability to travel to other worlds. No, you had to stay here and take the ability away from the rest of us. Even those of us who were chosen to share the power. Why did you take that from me, Nolan? Why?"

Using her elbow, Alyx angled the hit upward toward his Adam's apple just as she'd taught the girls in her self-defense class to do. The gun thumped to the floor as Jim reached for his throat.

Chase was torn between saving his father and helping Alyx. Rose appeared holding a dish towel in her trembling hands, and she took over pressing it to Nolan's wound. As soon as he was sure Nolan was being tended to, Chase leaped into the fray, pounding his fist with two solid jabs into the large man's nose. Jim staggered back, still clutching his crushed windpipe as blood spurted from his mangled nose, over his upper lip, and onto his front teeth like a feral animal just after a recent kill. Bo appeared, biting deep into Jim's calf muscle, as the man made a futile attempt to shake him off. He turned to go back through the doorway only to be stopped short by Officer Carson Murphy, whose presence now blocked the exit.

"Stop right there, Jim. You're coming with me to the station. Shoulda known better than to let you go after questioning. Good thing I thought to follow you and heard the gunshots. Won't happen again. This time, you'll be in a cell. Don't move, or you'll force me to use this." He nodded to the handgun currently pointed at Jim's chest. "I'd rather have you rot in prison than take a bullet. I've been talking to your son, Jim. I don't like what I'm hearing. Add to that attempted murder? You're going away for a long time."

Jim's face contorted into a sneer. "Lawyer."

"Sure. Right after I read you your rights." The flashing lights of an ambulance suddenly illuminated the house. Carson called over his shoulder. "Stand back until we have him secured."

Alyx and Chase helped Officer Murphy along with two other officers as they loaded Jim Young into the back of the police cruiser. Bo barked through the entire process, forgetting about his injured leg as he stood rigid and tall, in full-on guard-dog mode. Once the car door closed securely, the EMTs rushed into the house. Within minutes Nolan Walker was loaded into the back and whisked away to the hospital amid the shrieking of a receding siren as the ambulance raced away, eerily interspersed with the heightened sounds of grief that inevitably accompanied the falling of helpless tears by the people left behind to wait.

•　　•　　•

The bright lights and the smell of a combination of disinfectants mixed with the subtle stench of sickness invaded his senses as Chase walked the long, sterile halls of the hospital toward the waiting room. Memories of another time, the same hospital but in another place, flashed through his mind, and he wondered if he would say goodbye to his father here just as he had to Uncle Charlie. Was this the price of being a keeper, then? Or maybe it was a curse reserved only for members of his own family?

He shook his head, pushing back the memories, trying to replace them with optimistic thoughts of hope. Hope that his father would survive. Chase began to pray. Prayed as he had never before. His father was a gentle soul who never should have had to bear this responsibility. He'd found happiness, at least for a time. As Chase entered the stark waiting room, he continued his litany.

*Please Lord, let him live. I need to know he's okay before I leave here. He's innocent in all this. He didn't ask for this life, but still he's turned it into something positive. A father, husband, role-model. Please, be with him, be with all of us to show us what to do.*

He felt a hand on his shoulder and looked up into Rose's tear-streaked face as he grasped her hand. Her words nearly stopped his heart. "He's going to make it, Chase."

"What?" Chase could scarcely believe his ears, so sure had he been of impending doom that he blinked to let the words sink in. Relief caused his limbs to tremble, making his knees go weak and his eyes burn. "Are you sure?"

A fresh wave of tears filled Rose's eyes. "The doc was just here. It's a long, complicated surgery, but the bullet went straight through and he thinks they can stop the bleeding. They need blood, and I'm not a match. Can you go see if you can donate? They want all family members to give if they can."

Chase nodded. "Where?"

Rose pointed down the hall. He scanned the room before turning to go. Ellie sat, head leaning back in the chair, eyes closed.

Alyx, who'd been sitting in a cream-colored metal chair, rose as if to follow, but Corey stood at the same time. "I'll walk with you," he said. "I've just come from there; I'll show you where to go." He got up, gesturing Chase to follow.

Alyx met Chase's eyes. At his slight nod, she sank back down into the chair, though her eyes spoke to him. He knew she would prefer to be with him, but still she silently agreed to give Corey time to say whatever it was he needed to say. The brothers walked together, side-by-side, down the sterile corridor in silence for a full minute before Corey rallied the courage to speak. His cheeks pinkened, and he cleared his throat.

"I wanted to talk to you alone," Corey began, staring straight ahead as they walked. "And tell you I'm sorry. For everything. I was wrong to go along with Jared, and it was also wrong to blame you for everything. Guess I was mad because Dad talked about you all the time. All my life, I've heard stories about my big brother Chase, who could do no wrong. You seemed like a figment of Dad's imagination until you showed up at our door."

"I'm sure none of that was easy for you," Chase replied carefully.

"No, but I didn't stop to think about what it must have been like for *you*, growing up without him in your life."

"It was okay. I had Uncle Charlie." Chase stood straighter, shoving his hands into his pockets as they ambled along.

Corey nodded. "Still. I know it's too late for us to be friends, but I'd like for us to at least be on good terms before you go."

"I'd like that, too. I wish I could stay longer, but I won't have a choice. Do you really think he'll be okay?"

Corey's body visibly relaxed, his stance losing its rigidity. "He will be." A determined and confident gleam lit his eyes.

They turned into the lab, where Chase rolled up his sleeve. This was something he could do. As he donated blood for his father, his brother stood to the side, leaning against the wall. There was an awkwardness between them that couldn't be avoided. Not much they could do about that at this point, with the clock ticking on his time remaining in this world. They'd mended their relationship as much as possible, and Chase was happy they'd done that much. He'd never had a brother before. At least, not one he knew about.

With blood drawn, Chase sat sipping orange juice from a paper cup. He crumbled the cup and tossed it into the trash, and they returned to the waiting room in silence. He dropped into the empty chair next to Alyx, and she immediately reached for his hand.

Six hours later, the weary doctor came to talk to the family, surgical mask hanging around his neck, blue surgical gown and hair cover still in place. "He's out of surgery, which went surprisingly well. He had lost a lot of blood, but since both his sons are a match, we were able to give him the transfusion he needed. After recovery, we'll keep him in the ICU until he's proven to be stable, and then he'll be moved to another floor. I'm not going to sugarcoat this: it won't be an easy recovery. He's going to need all of your support over the next months. It won't be quick, but after six months, maybe a year, he should make a near-full recovery, with your help."

Chase leaned forward in his chair, elbows on his knees, as he covered his face with his hands. Relief warred with regret. A knot formed at the base of his neck; the tightness spread quickly to his shoulders. His temples throbbed, and he massaged in circular patterns to ease the pain. He wouldn't be here to help in that recovery. Most likely, he wouldn't even have the opportunity to see his father go back home from the hospital. Chase would have to be satisfied knowing that at least his father was going to survive this. He glanced at the date on the calendar hanging from a bulletin board. October fifth. Five days. He had five days left here in this world. Five days left with his father, stepmother, brother, and sister. Five short days with the family he had only known for only a short time, but somehow, miraculously, they had become a part of him. Now that he knew them, he would mourn the loss of their presence in his life for the rest of his days.

# CHAPTER 45
## *ALYX*

Alyx stood staring up at the school building from the bottom of the steps. She shook her head, and a small smile turned up the corners of her mouth. So much had happened here in the short weeks since she'd arrived in this world. She'd learned so much; changed in so many ways.

While Chase had decided not to leave his father's side and stayed back at the hospital with his family, she had chosen to return to school one last time. The irony was not lost on her, but she felt as if her friends—yes, she had friends now—needed her. It was the least she could do since she'd soon be leaving them forever. Regret tugged at her soul, a sigh lifting her shoulders.

She thought about her mother, her father. Her brothers. What would they say about this new Alyx? She was sure she knew, because not too long ago she would have agreed with them. Pathetic, silly, weak-minded. *Friends are distractions you don't need,* they'd say, *can't trust anyone but yourself.* In her mind, she could hear the disappointment in her mother's voice. A sadness gripped her heart. After this year of jumping, she was doomed to disappoint her family with this new version of herself. If only she could explain to them, make them see that there was more to living than training for one year of her life. In the course of a lifetime, three hundred sixty-five days was like the prologue in a book. While true, it sets the stage for the story to come, in the end, it is the compilation of chapters and growth within those succeeding pages that comprise a tale worthy of finishing. She wished she'd had the chance to impart this newfound wisdom to Margo before she had made that final decision to end it all. As bad as things must have seemed to her at that lowest point of her short time here on Earth, if she had only given herself a bit more time and the chance to realize that this was only a miniscule sampling of her story. Would that she could have seen that coming out on the far side of despair would have only molded her character with a stronger ink. One moment in time, one decision to end it all, and that chance had been erased from her tale as quickly as one stroke of an author's pen. Only this was real life, not a fictional story.

"Alyx!"

Turning, Alyx saw Annabelle hurrying to her side. "Anna. Hi."

"I'm so glad you're here. How's Dr. Walker?" Annabelle asked.

"He's doing well. He was awake and talking when I left. The family is with him. But I wanted to come back for my last day of high school. I mean, I worked so hard on that Literature report, there's no way I wasn't handing it in."

Anna laughed, and the sound immediately lifted Alyx's spirits.

"Come on. I don't know anyone else who would go to school if they didn't have to." Anna shook her head and linked their arms as they headed up the steps together.

"I guess I missed out on all of this at home, being home-schooled and all." She cleared her throat. "I'm gonna miss you. All of you." It surprised Alyx how easily the words had come.

Anna halted, mid-way up the stairs. "Oh, Alyx. I'm going to miss you too! Are you sure there isn't some way you could stay? I mean, talk to your parents and tell them..."

Alyx shook her head in one jerky motion, finding it hard to swallow past the lump in her throat. "No. There's nothing I could say that would change us leaving on October tenth. It has to be that way. I'm sorry."

A single tear leaked from the corner of Anna's eye, zig-zagging down to her chin. She didn't bother to swipe it away. Giving Alyx's arm, still linked with hers, a gentle squeeze of comradery, Annabelle sighed. "Well, if that's true, then let's make the most of it. Come on." They marched into the school building together.

Alyx paused, her breath hitching upon entry.

The sterile hallway, devoid of decoration, was somehow comforting to her. The familiar scuffed linoleum floors and drab gray walls would always be connected to her time here, and a barrage of emotions clogged her throat when she realized she would not walk this path again after today. She wondered briefly what kind of world they would be cast into on their fast-approaching next jump date, then pushed those thoughts aside as she approached Margo's locker shrine, still intact. She bowed her head, sending up a mental prayer for her lost friend. Alyx hoped she was at peace. That was all she could do for the girl who had fallen so deep into despair she'd chosen to end her life long before her time. She bent to pick up a teddy bear that had fallen face down on the floor and gently replaced it on top of the pile.

"Goodbye, Margo," Alyx whispered. "I won't forget."

Standing, she headed off to homeroom to attend the last day she would ever spend in high school.

# CHAPTER 46
## *CHASE*

His father was ornery as a trapped bear. Rose adjusted the lumpy hospital pillows behind him. "You don't have to fuss over me. I'm fine," Nolan growled.

"I know I don't have to. I want to." She sighed. "I need to, Nolan. When I think about how close I came to losing you, I..."

Nolan grumbled, but leaned forward, allowing her to complete her task. Easing back against the newly adjusted pillows, he looked around the room, his eyes landing on the wall-mounted television playing game show reruns. Chase sat in the corner by the window, drawing comfort from the fact that he was simply spending time with his father. He figured that if he was well enough to grouse; it was a good sign. Trying to avoid raising his dad's ire, he was content in his silence.

Rose did not feel the same. "You're getting some color back in your face, Nolan, and your eyes seem clear. How is the wound feeling? Do you need anything?"

"When can I go home?" Nolan grumbled in answer. "What I *need* is to leave this place and go home."

Rose soothed, patting his back as she spoke in a calming tone. "The doctors are working hard to see that you get home. But you have some recuperating to do before..."

He grasped her arm, his voice dropping to almost a whisper. "I need to be home when Chase leaves. I can't say goodbye to him from a hospital bed."

Rose paused to look him in the eye and nodded. "Yes. So, then, we'll make that your goal. You have to be well enough to go home before the deadline."

He nodded, his eyes brimming with tears he would not allow to fall. He glanced in his son's direction; his face furrowed with longing.

Slowly, Chase rose from his chair and approached the bed. "Dad. I wish I didn't have to leave you..."

"I know, son. But we both know you don't have a choice in the matter. Neither of us do." He looked away, staring out the window. "We never did."

"We can't go down that path, Dad. It won't do us any good now. I'm just thankful that I had the chance to meet you." He met Rose's eyes and a small smile curved his lips. "And the rest of my family."

Rose rushed around the bed and clutched his hand, tears falling in earnest now. "Oh Chase, I feel the same. I've always known about you. You didn't have the same luxury of knowing we even existed." Her breath hitched. "I'm so glad to know the *real* you, and not just an idea of a person. I wish we had more time, but since we don't, let's all make the most of the three days you have left here."

Chase cleared his throat. He turned away to gather his emotions, then straightened his shoulders and nodded. "Okay. Let's focus on getting Dad home, then. Your doctors said you needed to get up and walk around. Let's start with that."

Nolan grumbled a bit, but pushed himself awkwardly up. He reached for Chase's hand.

Rose clutched a hand to her heart as she watched father and son meander through the halls of the hospital. When they turned, she noticed their profiles were nearly identical. There was no doubt of Chase's parentage. Once they turned the corner and moved out of sight, she collapsed on the bed as sobs wracked her body. She couldn't help the thoughts swirling in her mind. They'd missed a lifetime of father-son bonding, and it was all because of her. Though the guilt hunched her body and made breathing difficult, she acknowledged that even if she had the power to do so, she would not change a thing. The selfishness of her admission caused another round of sobs, which shook her body to the core.

# CHAPTER 47
## *MASON*

Mason Moore leaned back on the flat hospital-issued pillow and closed his eyes, pulling the threadbare blanket up to ward off the chill. His parents had just left, and he didn't think he could take the sight of his mother's eyes filled with tears, worry lines marring her forehead another minute. She tried so hard to be upbeat and positive, but he could tell it was forced by the high pitch of her voice and the trembling of her hands. He was thankful that they had come, but was just as thankful when they walked out the door after an awkward hug, followed by a pat on the back.

While his Mom was heartbroken that her baby had almost died by his own hand, his dad was wallowing in guilt. He just kept apologizing, swearing he hadn't meant to put his political career before his family as he paced the tiny room. Vowing to leave his aspirations of life as a lawmaker behind. At least, being on the psychiatric floor, he didn't have to suffer sharing a room with a complete stranger. There were few benefits of being deemed mentally unstable, but that one thing was a blessing.

Truth was, Mason didn't know how to respond to his parents in his current state of mind. He thought back on Chase's words that night on the bridge: *You matter, Mason. No matter what Jared told you; you matter more than you know. To the people of this town. To your family. You matter to me. You don't realize your value; how many lives would be affected by your loss.* He knew that yesterday, and the day before, and even the day before that, Chase had tried to visit him here, but on this floor, only family members were allowed in, so he had been turned away. Chase had even dropped off a long letter that had been delivered by a nurse to his room. The envelope remained sealed, but he could tell by the thickness it was several pages long. It lay on the side table next to his bed, waiting to be read.

Mason's eyelids fluttered open, and he glanced around the room, filled to the brim with flowers and cards from people he knew, and from complete strangers, too. His thoughts were conflicted. In his daily group sessions, they said that was normal, but he wasn't so sure. Sometimes, it seemed he had no control over his own thoughts, and it scared him.

One moment, he was soothed by the power of Chase's words. *You matter*. And taking in the happy garden of blooming flowers and well-wishes scattered all over his hospital room, he could almost believe it. His eyes landed on one card in particular. It depicted a snapshot of a dog lying in bed with his foot in a sling, and handwritten inside in a flowery script: *I'm here for you, Mason. Whatever it takes, anything you need, I'm here. I won't forget. With Love, Rose Walker*. Apparently, he had two moms now. He didn't smile, but closed his eyes again and the pressure on his heart eased, if only slightly.

Then, in the next moment, his mood could shift back to the darkness. He wondered why anyone bothered, how long they would care, if they even did at all. Why did people think sending random flowers could have any kind of effect whatsoever on a person's health and mental state? It was almost as if they sent them more for themselves, to make themselves feel better, than for the person who received them. No one really cared about him. They never had.

Mason sighed. He acknowledged he had a long road ahead, if recovery was even possible for a suicidal person like himself. He didn't know. Sometimes the darkness overwhelmed him, and he didn't know if that would ever change. What he did know was that for the first time in a long time, he felt a tiny spark of hope. *It only takes a spark to build a blaze,* his counselor, Derek, had said. Maybe it was true. He placed his fingers on his wrist and felt the steady *thrum-thrum-thrum* of his own strong pulse beating there. Evidence that his heart was still beating, despite his best efforts to bring it to a halt. Instead of being repulsed by it, he found himself soothed by the flow of blood through his body.

It was a start.

He reached for the letter that Chase had left him days ago, ripped open the seal, and pulled out several pages of handwritten script.

*Dear Mason, I know you have lots of time on your hands, so I wanted to share a story with you to help you pass the time and let you know I'm thinking about you. It's just a fictional story I wrote, but maybe it will help you understand a few things. It's about two boys who met in second grade and became best friends, a magical watch, and twelve parallel worlds. And Mason, even though you don't remember me, and even though I can't stay here, I'll always be your friend. Enjoy the story. As you read it, remember; you matter to me. Your friend, Chase.*

Mason, though he wanted to shrug it off because Chase Walker was clearly loco, began reading the words. Once he started, he couldn't put the pages down until he finished, his hands trembling as he read the blocky script. His heart pounded at some parts, and his eyes filled with tears at others. When it was over, he once again leaned back against the pillow. It all seemed so real. Almost as if he himself had lived through all of it. Mason felt a pull of a memory, but blew out a breath and a nervous chuckle escaped his lips. He shrugged off the feeling. The boy could write. Maybe he would become a famous author someday, thinking up a story like that, drawing the reader in as if they were living the story as it was told.

But still, he couldn't shake the feeling of déjà vu that came with the tale...

# CHAPTER 48
## *CHASE*

*Jump Time: October 10th, 7:36 am*

The sun was rising on his last day in this world. In three hours, he would leave his family behind. So many emotions swirled inside of him, he thought they might burst out of him like a Fourth of July firecracker. He remembered a long-ago summer day when he and his Uncle Charlie had set off store-bought fireworks in the backyard. There was one that spewed sparks in a cascade of mixed colors into the sky and seemed to go on and on as if it would never end. If he examined his feelings right now, he felt as if they would discharge from his core in much the same way.

If he was honest with himself, he wished he and Alyx could stay here forever. Get to know his family. Have a normal life. If only. He sighed, running his hands through his already scruffy hair. No sense in wishing for what could never be. Added to that, it wouldn't be fair to ask Alyx to leave her own family for him.

And besides, Chase had one last thing to do before he left this dimension. He'd put it off until the last possible moment, but knew it was something he had to do. Dragging his feet as he walked down the hospital corridor, he slowly approached Jared's room. When he reached room number two hundred-six, he lightly rapped on the door before entering.

Jared lay on the bed, face barely recognizable with all the swelling and bruising. *How could a father do this to his child?* The boy's neck was ringed in purple bruises, in an almost perfect silhouette of a handprint, leaving nothing to the imagination. One eye swelled completely shut, but Chase could see the other blackened eye tracking his progress into the room. He thought he saw contempt there, but shrugged it off. He felt nothing but sadness for this battered shell of a person who had somehow survived this horrendously brutal beating.

"Hey, Jared."

Though Chase could see what it cost him physically, Jared turned his head the other way, dismissing him.

"I'm sorry about what happened," Chase said.

Jared snorted in response.

"Really, man. I am sorry. Sorry you've had to live with an abusive father. It sucks, and no kid should ever have to go through what you've gone through. It's not fair, and I'm sorry for it. But I have to say something to you before I have to leave this place. Being abused does not give you the right to abuse others. You know how it feels when Jim attacks you? Well, that's how others feel when *you* push *them* around. Be better than that, Jared. I hear you're going to make a full recovery, and I'm glad. This is your chance to change. You can choose to make this a turning point in your life. You're not your step-father, Jared, and you don't have to act like him. Rise above it." Chase placed a business card on the table next to Jared's bed. "Here's a card. It's for a counselor my dad recommended. After you're better, you should call and talk to him. You never know, it might help. And I don't know. I think maybe all your actions up 'til now may just be a cry for help."

Jared continued to ignore him, keeping his head turned to the window. Chase stood there for several more minutes in silence. He sighed. "I wish you the best of luck, and I hope you get the help you need."

Chase turned and left the room, heading back to his father's floor. Relief flooded him with each step, and as he strode the hospital corridor, he felt somehow lighter. With that dreaded task complete, he was free to focus on the impending jump. He absently pushed the button and stood to wait for the elevator, his thoughts splitting off in a myriad of directions. Nolan was getting released this morning at eight o'clock, just in time for Chase's departure to the next world. They should have plenty of time to get home so he could jump from his father's house, surrounded by his new family. It would be hard to say goodbye to all of them...

Chase was so preoccupied, he barely glanced at the other person inside the elevator until the doors were closing and it was too late to disembark. Recognition crashed like a tidal wave, and he took one involuntary step backward, denial warring with disbelief. "How...?"

The last thing he saw was Jim Young's beefy fist swinging toward his face before blackness claimed him.

# CHAPTER 49
## ALYX

*Jump Time: October 10th, 10:00 am*

Alyx glanced at her watch for the tenth time in less than two minutes. *Where are they?* She'd asked herself the same question repeatedly over that last hour. Nolan had been released from the hospital this morning, and the family had gone to bring him home. He was supposed to be here for the jump, no problem. They all were. Alyx had decided to give them some family time and had opted to stay at the house with Bo to prepare for the jump. That was hours ago.

She rushed to the front window, lifting the curtain to peer out at the deserted street. Letting the curtain fall, she resumed her pacing.

Her violet-colored backpack was packed and firmly in place; blade discs secured in her favored thigh holsters, Bo was groomed and ready to go. She glanced down, and he wagged his tail. *Yip.*

"I know, I know. He'll be here. But he's cutting it very close." Resuming the pacing, she once again peeked out the window, then glanced again at her watch. "It's ten o'clock. Only ten minutes until jump time..."

Bo mewled, catching some of her nervous vibes. He tilted his head, placing his paw on her leg. His whimper distracted her, and she scooped him into her arms. "It'll be okay. He's bringing his dad home from the hospital with his family. Probably just saying his goodbyes. He'll be here." A frown line wrinkled her forehead. Ten-oh-two. *How could he cut it this close?* Then another worry weaseled its way into her brain and a coldness took over her body. *Something's happened. Chase, where are you?*

With Bo still in her arms, she marched out the front door, grabbing Rose's car keys from the hook on her way by, then froze in mid-step on the stairs down from the porch. Ten-oh-three. *I can't be driving at jump time; I could cause an accident.*

A growl erupted from deep within her. *What should I do?*

Ten-oh-five. *Five minutes.*

Racing back inside, still carrying Bo, she grabbed Chase's backpack from the couch where he'd left it packed and ready to go, and threw it on top of her own backpack on her back. The combined weight bore down on her shoulders, but she had no time to worry about that. Whatever they were wearing or touching when they jumped went with them to the next realm, so all she had to do was take it with her. *Wherever he is, he'll jump to the next world at ten minutes after ten o'clock. I'll bring his backpack with me, and we'll find each other. It's as simple as that. We'll just have to find each other when we get there. No problem, right? There's nothing in the rules that says we have to jump from the same place. The power of the watch just comes to us when it's time. It'll take him, no matter where he is. Not a big deal. We can do this.*

Her wild eyes scanned the room, and she looked one last time out the window. He wasn't going to make it. Already she could feel the electricity filling the house. The spark of power as the fine hairs on her arms stood on end. Static electricity pulsed through the house as if the inert structure was alive. Bo snuggled closer to her body; his head curled around her neck.

"It's okay, Bo-Bo. No problem. We're gonna do this together, you and I. Just stay with me. I have to be holding you, so you'll come along. No worries. Chase will meet us there. We'll see him when we arrive in Dimension 10. Just a few more minutes, and we'll all be together. I promise."

Tiny tremors shook Bo's body as he tried to bury himself even closer against Alyx. She ran her hand soothingly over his soft fur, glad for his presence. Suddenly, the now familiar mercury colored blob appeared above her head, and she sat on the floor of the living room, closed her eyes, and gave in to the power.

As the hand of the clock moved one more notch, the liquid substance grew in size, pulsing, throbbing with its need to claim her. Though all windows were closed and secure, wind blew through the house, and from somewhere to her left the sound of shattering glass as a ceramic lamp crashed to the floor.

Even as she turned toward the sound, the substance snatched her from the living room of the Walker residence in Dimension 9, and catapulted her into the next world, the unknown, ready or not. She and Bo entered Dimension 10 in a whirlwind of pain.

Alone.

To Be Continued...

# FROM THE AUTHOR

Thank you for reading the third book in the Keeper of the Watch Series. This one was tough for me. An emotional *write*, if you will. The words on these pages poured out of me like blood from a wound, and I can only hope that even a portion of the honesty and depth of my feelings will be transferred from the page to my readers. Added to the serious nature of the topics of teen bullying and suicide covered in the storyline, while in the midst of writing this novel, the world experienced a national pandemic and everything that went along with it. Hospitals at capacity, work lay-offs, shutdowns—no need to continue the list as you all lived it with me. My family also lost our beloved Bernese Mountain Dog, Koda, and everyone that knows me knows my dogs are true members of my family. My creative side took a hiatus, and this novel took me longer to write than many of my books. In the end, it is something I am proud to share with you, my faithful readers. I hope it sends not only a message of awareness that bad things can happen, but also a message of hope that things will get better, even on your darkest days.

If you are able to leave a review for this book—or any of my other books—I would appreciate it more than you know! Simple word of mouth accompanied by reviews are what get authors noticed.

Thanks in advance for your continued support!

All my love,
Kristen

# SPECIAL THANKS TO

- My wonderful family, for all of your love and support in my writing—and everything I do. You are my rock. Every one of you. I love you all!
- Glenn, my Mom, and my long-time friend Nancy B., whose insights extend to all my books. I can't thank you enough for volunteering your time and expertise to pre-reading my writing. Thank you!
- My readers, for all your support
- Laura Danielle Photography
- Black Rose Writing
- Suicide and bully prevention support groups who offer encouragement and hope to those who feel they are lost

"In your eyes, I see the fight of someone with nothing to lose.
Changing laws not set in stone, 'cause I see a lot left in you.
Thought it'd be better in a world so cold.
But I'm here to tell you what I've been told:
Life ain't that bad, look what you have.
When the highs aren't so high, just do what you can.
A world you can change, and a life you choose.
'Cause somewhere out there, somebody wishes they were you."

Dave Bassett, Rick DeJesus
(Sung by Adelita's Way)

# BOOKS BY KRISTEN L. JACKSON

*Young Adult Novels*
## KEEPER OF THE WATCH SERIES

*Prequel Novella—Dimension Keeper*

*Book One—Keeper of the Watch, Dimension 7*

*Book Two—Magic Harbor*

*Book Three—And Time Stopped*

*Fiction Novel*
## BENEATH THE WAVES

*Children's Picture Book*
## JOCELYN'S BOX OF SOCKS

# ABOUT THE AUTHOR

Kristen L. Jackson has been a teacher for over twenty-five years, and lives in Reading, Pennsylvania with her husband and four large-breed dogs. She is the proud mom of two sons, who live nearby and visit often. Books inspire her. From children's picture books to adult literature in all genres, she has loved reading all her life. Becoming a published author is her dream come true, and she loves to share her stories with readers of all ages—the reason she writes in multiple genres and age-groups. Kristen loves the three D's: dogs, dolphins, and daisies. She enjoys writing, reading, and spending time with her family and dogs at their cabin in the Pocono Mountains, her favorite place to escape to and write!

*www.kristenljackson.com*
*Contact: kristenjacksonauthor@yahoo.com*

*Find Kristen on Social Media:*
*Facebook @kristenjacksonauthor*
*Twitter @KLJacksonAuthor*
*Instagram @krisjack504*

# NOTE FROM THE AUTHOR

Word-of-mouth is crucial for any author to succeed. If you enjoyed *And Time Stopped*, please leave a review online—anywhere you are able. Even if it's just a sentence or two. It would make all the difference and would be very much appreciated.

Thanks!
Kristen L. Jackson

We hope you enjoyed reading this title from:

BLACK ROSE
writing™

www.blackrosewriting.com

Subscribe to our mailing list – *The Rosevine* – and receive **FREE** books, daily deals, and stay current with news about upcoming releases and our hottest authors.
Scan the QR code below to sign up.

Already a subscriber? Please accept a sincere thank you for being a fan of Black Rose Writing authors.

View other Black Rose Writing titles at
www.blackrosewriting.com/books and use promo code
**PRINT** to receive a **20% discount** when purchasing.

www.ingramcontent.com/pod-product-compliance
Lightning Source LLC
Chambersburg PA
CBHW010735100726
47899CB00009B/3068

* 9 7 8 1 6 8 4 3 3 9 5 8 7 *